Dedicated to David,
I am so proud to be your husband.

'' If I know what love is, it is because of you."
— Hermann Hesse

A PETROL BOMB OF LOVE
BY PATRICK E. MONE

Table of Contents

Chapter 1: Bonfire Night 9
Chapter 2: Transgression 23
Chapter 3: Timebomb 37
Chapter 4: Machine Gun 54
Chapter 5: The Tufty Club 71
Chapter 6: Observation Point 83
Chapter 7: VCP 91
Chapter 8: Thanks for Being A Prick, Alan 108
Chapter 9: Car Freak 115
Chapter 10: Black Mountain 123
Chapter 11: Bad Pie 147
Chapter 12: Escaping The City 157
Chapter 13: The Spark 177
Chapter 14: One Mighty Explanation 187
Chapter 15: Irrational Behaviour 195
Chapter 16: Community Event 208
Chapter 17: Then What? 225
Chapter 18: Mural 238
Chapter 19: Interface 248
Chapter 20: Pick-up 271
Chapter 21: Roadworks Smell 281
Chapter 22: No Hard Feelings 290
Chapter 23: Aftermath 300
Chapter 24: Reflections 319
Chapter 25: Lots of Love, Will 332

@PATRICKEMONE

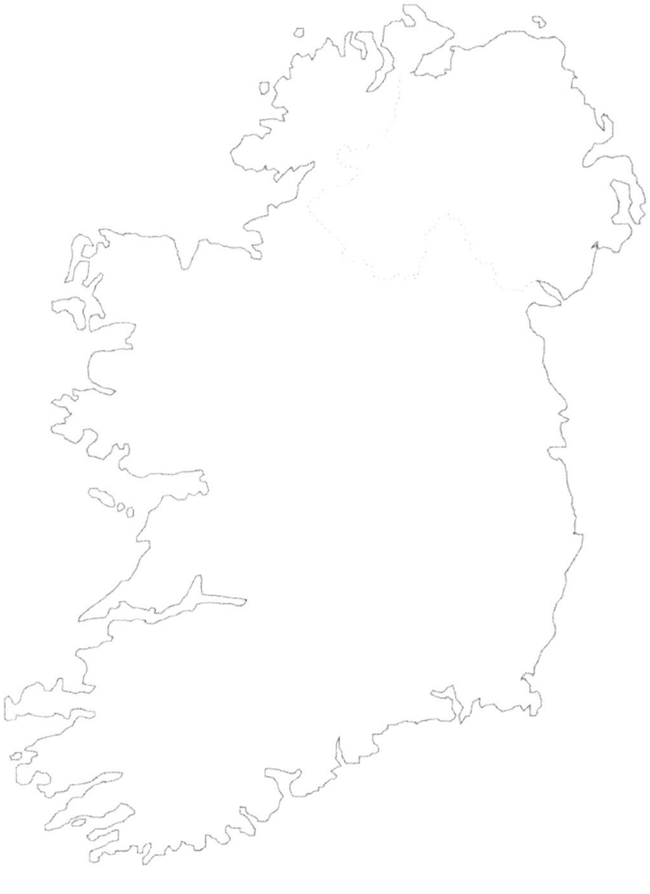

PART 1.

Chapter 1: Bonfire Night

Friday 11th July

It was well after dark, but small children in summer shorts and t-shirts scrambled over the two-storey-high stack of furniture. The pile had grown from a base of old, tatty sofas pushed together, with chairs and tyres piled on top of them. Harassed mothers tried to get the kids off again before the whole thing came tumbling down again, while the rest of the milling crowd ignored them.

Union jacks hung from every lamp post, the orange lights shining through the coloured fabric – a patriotic stamp on the carnival scene of music and happy chat and drinking below. Above it all was the steady thud and drone of a British army helicopter keeping a watchful eye on proceedings, a constant background presence for anyone who needed the reassurance, or the warning.

Up at the top of the pile, a couple of lads were fixing the pièce de résistance – a large Irish tricolour, a banner of green and white and orange. Will Johnston proudly studied the wooden pile as he slid his arm around his girlfriend's waist. A gentle breeze stirred the muggy evening city air and he automatically brushed back the blond forelock that escaped the grip of the Dax Wax and dropped into his eye.

"It'll be a fine fire, so it will!" He didn't take his eyes off the stack. "What do you think?"

Wendy put her arm around him in turn, under his jacket, hand flat against his smooth and muscled waist. No rolls down there, for sure – part of his mind still had time to feel pleased about that. He had kept in shape even when he had to give up his favourite sport, and the day he and Wendy finally got around to removing each other's clothes, she would not be disappointed by what she found.

"Sure it was worth all those splinters," she agreed absently. She was looking across his shoulder and he turned his body around to follow her gaze. "Do you think they'll cause trouble?"

Angry shouts and jeers had begun to drift across the festival scene as the flag unfurled, but Will had tuned them out with a lifetime's instinct. The pile was built at one of those spots where the interface, a wall built deliberately to keep the two communities apart, blended with the city structure. To his left it was a solid barrier, taller than a grown man – massive panels of concrete bound together with metal staples. To his right the concrete barrier cut across what had been a road junction and merged with an iron pole fence that had once run alongside the road. You could see right through the fence to the protesting crowd that had gathered on the other side, thirty feet away, which was the source of the jeers. A black clad priest was visible through the bars of the fence, trying very hard to keep tempers down to a manageable level. Will could sense the anger over there, at the distance of thirty feet and a couple of centuries, roiling like the surface of water in a saucepan on a hot stove just before the bubbles start to appear.

"Not if they know what's good for them," he said equably.

The street this side of the interface was tidy and well looked after. The only difference between here and Agnes Street, where Will lived with his family, was the metal grilles over the windows. The terraced Victorian houses were all neat and the front gardens well tended. The kerb stones were painted with immaculate coats of red, white and blue, regularly touched up.

The other side, Will couldn't help noticing, seemed a lot more run down. It didn't surprise him – it was just one more confirmation of what everyone knew anyway, that the other side were basically lazy and couldn't be arsed to make a go of things. How could they expect to run a country when they couldn't keep their streets clean?

The train of thought was knocked abruptly out of him when someone thumped him very hard between the shoulders, and there was his elder brother, a huge grin on his face. Alan was actually a little shorter than Will, to his annoyance – a fact Will had learned not to lean on too heavily. It was bad enough that he was frequently mistaken for the older of the two. Still, the brothers' faces were clearly from the same family, though Alan's blond hair was in a neater, almost military cut, and his moustache stood out loud and proud, while Will's face still sprouted little more than bum fluff and a moustache that could almost be seen when the light was on it.

Alan cupped his hands over his mouth and shouted at the mob.

"Sure listen to the kiddy fiddler, boys!" The warmth faded out of his smile as he looked back at Wendy. "Wendy," he said with a curt nod.

"Alan."

"Good of you to come."

"Is there any reason I shouldn't?" she asked coolly.

"Oh." Alan made his face as deadpan as he could and put every ounce of inflection that he could manage into his response. "None."

The faint layer of frost on the words was almost visible, but Will had long ago grown used to the fact that his brother and his girlfriend would never be friends.

"Feck off, Alan," Will muttered.

"Ah, and if it isn't young Will!" Will gratefully recognised the new voice and turned around. The speaker was a beaming, round man with large flat glasses and thinning hair, accompanied by a woman who was basically a female copy of her husband, and two small children staring solemnly up at him.

"Good evening, Mr Mitchell," he said politely, because his employer was always Mr Mitchell, never a first name, whether at work or at church or socially like here.

"And …" Mr Mitchell held up a finger, eyes narrowed in recollection. "Wendy?" She smiled and nodded; they had met at the garage's Christmas party. "Good to see you again. And Will, thank you for the free advertising! Very smart."

Will grinned and flexed his shoulders. The back of his bomber jacket was proudly emblazoned with the name and logo of Mitchell Tyres and Services.

"Thank you." Truth to tell, Will wore the jacket because after looking at himself carefully in the mirror, he had decided it was the only thing that really worked with the jeans and freshly ironed Puma t-shirt, and the silver chain around his neck that had been left to him by his father.

"And you'll be the brother, then?" Mr Mitchell pressed on. He stepped back to size Will and Alan up together. "Ah, it's grand to see Philip Johnston's boys together, so it is – so grown up. Well, we'll be off – soon be lighting up time, and then we've got to get the children to bed. See you next week, Will."

"Have a good weekend, Mr Mitchell."

Will smiled with genuine warmth as he watched his employer and family disappear into the crowd. Sure, he liked Mr Mitchell – but it felt good to be acknowledged in public, too. He had just turned eighteen, he was an adult, and he was part of this community. He was being recognised.

"Alan!" A tall, wide and muscular lad with flaming red hair and ice-cold blue eyes pushed his way through the crowd to join them, and now it was Will's turn to feel the frost. The same age as Alan, three years older than Will, Henry would maintain to his dying day that he had only tried to flush Will's head down the toilet on his first day at secondary school as a gesture of affection. Henry's gaze slid over Will, barely accepting the fact of his existence, as he ducked his head and murmured something to Alan. Alan's face lit up.

"All *right!* Hey, Will! They want us both to help with the lighting up!"

Will's jaw dropped.

"Yeah?"

"That's what Henry says."

"Philip Johnston's boys, together." Henry put a lot less warmth than Mr Mitchell had into the phrase. "They said."

"We'll be right there. You coming, Will?" Alan's eyes darted to Wendy, who had been watching silently, and that was when Will realised he had yet to disentangle his arm from his girlfriend. "That is, if it's okay?" Alan added with a small bow and a lot of irony.

"Of course it's okay," she answered in the exact same tone, but Alan had turned away before she even finished and followed Henry into the crowd, simply assuming that Will would follow. Wendy and Will looked at each other, and he flushed under her appraising stare.

"I mean, lighting the fire!" he said lamely.

A corner of her mouth twitched.

"How old are you? Five?" But her smile widened and she nodded slightly. "Sure, go ahead. I'll catch you up." She pouted her lips and Will kissed her quickly, just a peck, before he turned to hurry after Alan.

When he looked back, she had already been swallowed into the crowd.

Alan had never understood what his little brother saw in her, or why Wendy would want to hang around with him – and, Will often thought, he would never understand that actually people like him were the reason. Wendy relied on him for protection – a girl tended to have an easier time when everyone knew her boyfriend was a six foot tall rugby player who would avenge any wrongs done against her – and he was happy to provide it. They had met at the age of eleven – on their first day at school, the same day as the toilet incident – and they had somehow just got talking. It had been lunchtime before he learned that her mother was a Catholic, disowned by her own family and shunned for the marriage with someone from the other side. By then it had felt disloyal to turn his back on her, and they had been friends ever since. Once they hit their teens, they had just kind of assumed they were doing a line, pairing off like everyone else.

The brothers and Henry had reached the foot of the bonfire, and Will had to crane his neck back to see the top. The tricolour draped over the top flapped lightly in the breeze as if it was straining to get away from its fate, but it was secured at the four corners and there was no escape.

A small film crew was setting up nearby – a reporter, a man with a camera positioned on his shoulder like an anti-tank weapon, and a fella with a microphone like a medium-sized furry animal stuck on a pole. A circle of paid minders held back the crowd around them to give them some space. The camera had the letters 'BBC' stencilled on the side and the reporter prepared himself for the broadcast.

"Okay … are we ready? Cool … Three … two … one …" The cameraman gave him a thumbs-up, the camera's light came on and he beamed into the lens.

"I'm in north Belfast … and it's Bonfire Night for the Shankill and the crowds are gathering as you can see behind me and there is certainly excitement in the air as ."

"Tomorrow is the Glorious Twelfth, marking the victory of the Protestant King William of Orange over the forces of the Catholic King James II. Tomorrow will see marches all over the province by Loyalist bands and the Orange Order, and these bonfires are lit the night before to commemorate the fires that guided King William's fleet into Belfast Lough …"

Every Ulsterman knew what the Twelfth was about, and was proud of it – though not every one of them had the same tie to the date as Will. His mother had never tired of telling him that he was meant to have been born on the Twelfth, and his Christian name had become a foregone conclusion as soon as his parents learnt his due date. By the time he had inconveniently decided to arrive a week early – eighteen years and one week ago – they were so used to referring to their second child as William that they had simply made it formal once they actually had a baby to hold.

"Not everyone regards it as a day of celebration. And – cut; okay, Pete, get some shots of the crowd over there."

The cameraman obediently swung the lens towards the interface. He was tall enough to aim over the heads of the gurning teenagers who gathered around to wave into it.

"Hey, mister!" someone shouted. "Are we going to be on the fucking TV?"

The reporter smiled.

"We might have to edit some of the recording, but sure."

"Why do you have to do any fucking editing?"

Nearby, a man was thrusting lengths of wood into a burning brazier and handing them out.

"Nearly time," said Alan, with a glance at his wrist. Will checked his own watch. It was coming up to 10.30. Will, Alan and a few other lads each took a burning torch from the man at the brazier and gathered around the base of the bonfire. Will realised he was holding his breath.

"And we're on!"

Alan thrust his torch into the base of the pile, Will only a second behind him. As one the lads stepped back and gazed into the depths of the stack, where flame was growing into life.

After only a minute, Will could feel the heat billowing back at him.

Then he could smell the smoke – the acrid, nostril-biting tang of smouldering tyres and the more chemical of wood beneath old furniture polish. Then there was a loud *crack* as moisture inside a plank expanded into steam, and the first flames began to lick their way into the outside world.

A cheer went up from the Protestant crowd, and the angry shouts from the other side of the interface grew louder. Will dug his thumbs into his belt and grinned up at the sight. He glanced sideways at Alan and his brother returned the grin. They had their differences but *this* was what it was all about.

"Da would like this," Alan said quietly, with angry pride, almost daring Will to disagree. Will felt tears pricking at his eyes and nodded up and down so that they wouldn't show.

"Aye. Aye, he would."

"Shame Ma wouldn't come, so it is."

A lone male voice began to sing, a powerful baritone with words that went straight to the core of Will's being:

"Sure, it's old but it is beautiful ... "

Immediately a dozen other voice joined in, with varying degrees of tunefulness.

"... *and its colours they are fine!*"

The brothers slapped their hands together and turned towards the interface, drawing breath into their lungs to join in with the words of the old, triumphant marching song.

"*It was worn at Derry, Aughrim ...* "

Something in the seething mass the other side caught Will's eye for a moment. Something that stood out for being different. His instincts were telling him something was there before he could consciously make out what it was.

"*... Enniskillen and the Boyne!*"

There! It was a male figure, but he couldn't make out much more than that in the street light glow. Jeans and leather jacket, and it was moving differently. It looked like someone trying hard not to be part of the crowd.

"*My father wore it as a youth in bygone days of yore ...*"

Will pushed it from his mind. If whoever it was didn't want to be part of this, they really should have thought it through better. The figure passed from view behind the concrete blocks of the interface.

"And it's on the Twelfth I love to wear ..."

Any semblance of a tune vanished as the song turned into a mass shout of proud defiance. A hundred fists punched into the air to spell out each syllable.

"... THE SASH MY FATHER WORE!"

Cheers and shouts and whoops rose from the crowd around the base of the bonfire. Orange flames reflected off a glass bottle that came curving through the air and smashed on the pavement between the brothers.

"Fuck!"

In unison, they leapt away in different directions. Jeers and laughs came back through the iron fence at them, and Will felt his cheeks burn.

"So it's like that, is it?" Alan yelled, and immediately started to look around for something to throw back. More bottles started to rain down on the Loyalist side. Then lumps of rock, which was a miscalculation by the other side, because they didn't shatter into a million pieces and they gave the Loyalists ammunition to fight back with.

The BBC crew had wisely disappeared.

"Here! Take this."

Alan pressed a chunk of rock into Will's hands, and Will's proud certainties all abruptly evaporated as he realised what he was meant to do with it. It must have been a bit of crumbled kerb stone thrown over from the other side, still with traces of green and white paint on it. He hefted it up and down a couple of times, and looked unhappily over the interface.

Sure, his people were under attack and it was the duty of every Ulsterman to defend his land. But he knew what Wendy would make of it, if she ever found out. She had people on both sides.

Alan sensed his hesitation and his lip curled.

"Ah, fer fecksake! Just throw it back where it came from, and then go back to your Fenian bint, if you have to. But throw it first. Show the Fenians who's boss!"

Will recoiled under his brother's scorn. Then, so as not to have to think about it any further, in one smooth action he drew his arm back and flung it as hard as he could, with all the strength his shoulder could put into it.

The splash of white paint made the chunk stand out as it curved through the dark air, so that Will could follow its trajectory. His brain drew a line ahead of the flying stone. A perfect curve, ending right where no one was standing, which suited him just fine …

And then the figure he had seen earlier re-emerged from behind the concrete blocks, resolutely heading back the way he had come, still trying not to be part of what was going on, but about to become very much part of it as he approached the point where the stone would land.

No! Go back! There was no time to shout a warning, and it wouldn't be heard if he did, but inside Will's head he was screaming.

Go back …

For the first time in his life he was about to hurt someone who had done absolutely nothing to him.

Go–

The stone struck the figure on the side of his head and he crumpled out of sight. Will screamed silently.

Fuck, I killed him!

Chapter 2: Transgression

"Fuck, you *killed* him!" All Alan's teeth showed in a huge grin as he slapped Will hard on the back. "My little brother!"

Will stared at where the figure lay hidden below the brick wall that was the base of the iron fence. In the distance, police sirens began to wail and Alan cocked an ear.

"Okay, Will, seriously, lose yourself. If anyone says they saw anything, we'll deny it. Go back to Wendy and have a celebration shag. She probably knows how even if you don't. Better not tell her what you're celebrating, though!"

Even the dig at his continuing virginity didn't hurt. Will's mind was still too full of the way that figure had just … dropped. *Had* he killed someone? He really might have.

"I … I'll go back to Wendy …" he stammered.

"*Ye-es!*" Alan nodded and spoke with slow patience, the way you spoke to a small child, or an adult who was scuttered out of their head but had accidentally spoken some sense. "Go back to *Wendy!*" He gave Will a gentle shove. "I'll see you back home."

Sirens were rising above the sound of the crowd as Will pushed his way back through the throng. At first it was impossible to tell which side of the interface they were coming from, but by the time he had got to where he had left Wendy, and found her not there, it was pretty obvious that the trouble was over on the other side – the side where the real riot was, he thought with righteous pride, thinking of the bottle and the rocks. He had thrown a rock back, but they had started it. He thought of Mr Mitchell's family. There had been children on this side. Sure the Taigs had had no business kicking off like that.

Through the iron bars he could see the mass of Fenians moving in one uniform direction. He had seen enough demos to recognise the way a crowd moved reluctantly when the police were pressing in, and he was pleased to see the Royal Ulster Constabulary were out doing their job.

A flash of blue light caught his eye from an unexpected direction, and he frowned. How could he see that through the interface …

Then he heard angry shouts and cries ahead of him, and suddenly the horrific truth struck him. The RUC were on this side of the barrier too! They were clearing out both sides together! That was just dirty!

Now he could see the bobbing helmeted heads of the front row of constables, pressing resolutely forward. The crowd in front of him also started to retreat, shouting angrily over their shoulders as they went. This side of the interface, they were more biddable, less inclined to fight back.

Every part of Will's being wanted to protest against the injustice. This wasn't right! They had just been celebrating the Eleventh peacefully!

But sometimes, he knew, the boyos had no choice, usually when some politician was going on about equal treatment of the communities.

Unfortunately, he didn't want to be pushed back. He wanted to go forward, get through their ranks and return to Wendy. He looked around and his eyes settled on the entrance to a side road. That would do it – but he was not the only person to have this idea and he was jostled by other people's shoulders and elbows as he headed towards it. Still, it got him away from the main street and the advancing police, and that was all that was needed. He pressed on, navigating his way left and right with a lifetime's knowledge of the area, until he was safely away from the police line but also, he realised, probably behind where Wendy was likely to be waiting for him.

So, Will walked at a fast trot by another route back towards the interface, looking no different to anyone else who was out to enjoy the night air, singles or couples. At last he could smile as he saw a familiar figure leaning against a wall by a street lamp, her back to him, eyes facing the direction she expected him to come. He crept up behind and wrapped both arms around her waist.

"Guess who!"

"*Jesus!*" He quickly let her go as she tried to pull away. Her shock turned to exasperation when she saw who it was. "And take that stupid smirk off your face. So, you lit your bonfire, then?"

"Sure we did." It seemed a strange question, until he worked it out. "You didn't stay to see?" He wasn't sure whether or not to feel hurt.

"The crowd was giving me a headache." She softened slightly and came forward to take his hands and kiss him. "Did you have a good time?"

"Ah …" One simple question, and back it all came. *The figure crumpled.* "Sure."

"Sounds like the police decided they'd had enough?"

"Aye, and on our side, too!" he exclaimed, suddenly outraged again. "They cleared out both sides! What was that for?"

She shot him a look.

"Sure I can't imagine. Come on, let's get out of here …" Still holding his hand, she started to lead him away. She stopped suddenly when she found it's very hard for a slim, eight stone girl to pull along a thirteen stone boy unless he wants to be pulled, and Will's feet weren't moving. "What?"

The figure, crumpled at the foot of the fence …

Had the charging police even noticed?

Or cared, if they did?

Was the fella even alive? Would Will wake up tomorrow to news of a killing on the Catholic side? This kind of thing could spark riots.

He had to know.

"I ... I need to go back there ..." he stammered. She dropped his hand like it was a snake and stared at him. "There's someone I need to make sure about ..."

"Oh Jesus, Will, your brother's a grown man! He can look after himself!"

Will drew back in surprise, thinking, *My brother ...?*

But then, why wouldn't Wendy assume that was who he meant? Alan was the only person back there he had any kind of personal connection with.

Will had never lied to Wendy in his life, but sometimes there just wasn't time for the truth. He took both her hands and pulled her gently close for a last kiss.

"I've got to go. Will you ..."

"I'll see myself home," she said tightly, and turned on her heel. Will watched after her for a moment, but then another vision of the figure collapsing straight to the ground spurred him on in the other direction.

* * *

The street was empty as Will poked his head out of the side road.

Down to his left, the bonfire was burning merrily, surrounded a cordon of police in riot gear and a small party of people who must have been well behaved enough to be allowed to stay. Maybe they were people who actually lived here, on the front line, in their proudly well-kept houses a few yards from the interface. The flames had consumed the pile and the tricolour pegged to the top was nothing but ashes and memory.

As far as he could see on the other side, through the iron bars, the Fenian side was deserted.

There was no one looking in Will's direction as he hurried across the street. He grabbed the bars of the iron fence and stood on tiptoe to angle his gaze as far down as possible.

A leg was down there on the ground, sticking out into view. Jeans and a white sock and a trainer. That was all he could see of the person. It wasn't moving.

Shit.

Will took a breath.

"Hello! Hello, there?" His voice was an urgent whisper, as loud as he dared make it, but it should have carried that short distance. "Are you … are you all right?"

Silence.

Shit shit shit.

He wanted to shout, but that would attract attention. The police might wonder why he was interested in a body on the other side. Or maybe Alan was one of the people by the fire, and frankly right now Will would rather explain himself to the RUC than his brother.

Okay.

Will took a few steps back and studied the iron fence. It grew out of a low brick wall that came up to his knees, but the poles were taller than a man. Could he swing himself over?

The tops of the poles looked sharp. If he tried to swing over them and got it wrong, he could gut himself, or give himself the kind of injury that would guarantee his relationship with Wendy would be forever chaste. And if anyone on the other side saw him coming, they would think they were being invaded and probably lynch him from the nearest lamppost.

But as he looked along the wall, he saw that it rose and fell at regular intervals, like very widely spaced battlements on a castle. Twenty yards in that direction, it was suddenly as high as his waist – but the poles were the same height above the ground.

He didn't allow himself time to think it through. He jogged down to the first point where the wall rose up, took a few steps back, then ran. One foot onto the low part, toes springing up, the other foot onto the high part, body momentum carrying him on. With a swift roll he was over. He felt the sharp tips brush against his groin and he jacked his body away from them in mid air, and then his feet touched down in Catholic Belfast.

A small voice at the back of his head was screaming: *the feck d'ye think yer doing?*

But he had to know.

He hurried along the interface, pointlessly crouching down, because even if he could hide from his side there was absolutely no cover at all from any lurking Fenians.

And there was the body, at the base of the wall.

A young man. Jeans and boots and leather jacket. Lying face down, legs together, one arm down by his side and the other stretched out ahead, like he was pretending to be Superman.

As Will came up close, the figure stirred and moaned. Relief made Will's heart pound.

"Thank Christ! You're okay!" He crouched down at the boy's head.

"Course I'm fucking okay." The voice was muffled as the boy spoke directly into the ground.

"You were just lying here, I thought …" Will began.

"Aye, I'm just lying here because me head's fucking splitting." The boy started to bring his arms together, to push himself up. His shoulders and arms flexed as he lifted his head from the ground, and hissed a sharp intake of breath.

The rock must have hit him just above and behind his left ear. That whole side of his head was dark with clotted blood that matted his thick, wavy, dark brown hair.

"Here, let me help you." Will slid his hands under the boy's arms and tried to lift. "You … you had a knock."

"Aye, I think I'd worked that out …"

Together they managed to get him sitting up. He sat with his arms resting on his knees, his head hanging down between them. Will studied his profile. He guessed that under normal circumstances the boy had an oval sort of face, open and friendly, the kind that made you just naturally like the fella. He also reckoned this boy couldn't be any older than he was.

The boy put a hand gingerly to the side of his head, and squinted at the blood that stained his fingertips.

"Shit," he muttered.

"You should get that bandaged …"

The boy cocked an eyebrow up at him.

"You think? You got a first aid kit on you?""

The only thing Will had on him remotely like a bandage was the snottie in his pockets, but that was probably the last thing that should be used on an open wound. Reluctantly, he realised that he only had one really clean item of fabric on him, freshly ironed that very afternoon. With a couple of quick moves, he ditched his jacket and pulled his t-shirt over his head. Street light glinted off the silver chain around his neck. The boy stared at him with eyes that were still not quite focused.

"Christ, don't get your tits out just for me."

With warm night air blowing on his skin – still carrying the smell of burning wood and rubber – and acutely aware that now he was not only alone in enemy territory, but topless in public to boot, Will folded the t-shirt, once, twice, three times, and pushed it against the boy's head. At least the cloth smelled of the Lynx that he had doused himself with before going out, which did something to clean up the air around them. He lifted the boy's hand and moved it to hold the t-shirt in place, then quickly pulled his jacket back on over bare skin and self-consciously zipped it up again.

The boy kept the t-shirt pressed to his head, sitting with his eyes closed. Will crouched next to him, biting his lip, eyes darting up and down the street in case anyone should come along and identify the enemy alien in their midst.

Eventually the boy opened his eyes and moved to get up. Will immediately put his hands under his shoulders again and helped him to his feet. The boy staggered, almost falling into Will's arms until Will caught him again.

The boy grimaced, his eyes closed again.

"Is there any chance you could point me towards Cavendish Street?"

"I – uh – don't know. Which way is it?"

The boy shot him a puzzled look, but waved a vague hand down the road. Will positioned himself next to him and together they began to shuffle along, bodies pressed together.

"Is it – uh – far?" Will muttered. He took a glance back. They had turned a corner and he couldn't even see the interface any more. The sanctuary of Protestant Belfast was getting further away with every step.

"You don't have to come …" The boy squinted sideways at him, and Will saw the moment when the eyes suddenly focused clearly for the first time.

They went wide.

"Jesus, you're a fucking Prod! What are you doing?"

He pushed abruptly away, staggering on his own feet for a moment, before he sat down hard on a step. The hand holding the t-shirt dangled limply.

Will was immediately crouching in front of him again.

"Helping you, you prick."

He took the hand with the shirt and pushed it back to the boy's head. The boy glared at him through the street lamp glow, but then he nodded, slowly and carefully, as if Will was trying to catch him out with clever words that he couldn't quite argue his way through.

"Okay … Thanks."

Will paused.

"I … probably shouldn't come any further."

"Aye, you're probably right."

"Will you, you know, be okay from here?"

"Sure." A quiet snort of a laugh. "I've a good, thick skull." He tapped his forehead with his knuckles, gently, well away from the wound. "Comes in useful in my line of work."

"What do they use you for? A battering ram?"

"Heh. That's almost funny, Billy-boy." The boy glanced up at him, then held out a hand, slowly, as if Will might slap it away. "Conor."

"I'm …" Will swallowed and his name dried in his mouth. Despite everything he had done in the last ten minutes, stuff he would never have dreamed of doing in a million years, naming himself to a complete Catholic stranger seemed to be beyond his limit.

A torn movie poster flapped sluggishly in the night breeze on a billboard a few yards away. He couldn't see all of it but he recognised the design for the summer's movie blockbuster, *The Empire Strikes Back*.

He took the boy's hand and shook it, once.

"Luke."

"Pleased to meet you." Then: "You'd better get back to your own side. They'll kill you if they find you here."

Will's eyes rose slowly above the billboard.

Oh … shit …

All the way up to the eaves, the wall was covered with a vast mural of three balaclavad gunmen in black, rifles poised at the ready, glaring down through their eye holes at the Protestant intruder.

He looked down. The kerb stones here were painted too, just like on the other side of the interface … in green and orange and white.

He stood up abruptly.

"Yeah, I've gotta go," he said, fighting down the panic. Conor just nodded wearily and waved a hand.

Will turned and trotted as far as the corner, then came to a helpless halt. The interface had come into view – and there were people there.

They didn't look like paramilitaries. They looked like locals picking up the debris after the riot – but they were there, and they would see him if he went any further.

"Hey, good Samaritan!" Conor called softly.

Will turned and fled back to him. Conor's voice was weak and he had to get down and close to hear what he was saying.

"Where you going to?"

"Agnes Street."

"Sure I have no idea where that is … But, head that way … first on the right … it's an alleyway, takes you right up to the interface, and no one will see you." Their heads were bare centimetres apart, so close that Conor's breath gusted gently on Will's face with each word. "Got that?"

"First on the right … thanks." Will braced to stand up, and some kind of autopilot took over. He had been like this before, with Wendy – a rushed goodbye, faces this close, one or the other of them having to be somewhere else. So he did what he always did on those occasions. He leaned forward and his lips brushed against Conor's, a quick kiss with a short hold. As he straightened up he just had time to see Conor's eyes fly wide open, but then the same autopilot was hurrying him away to the alley.

First priority was get the feck out of Fenian Belfast.

And only then, once he was back safely on his own side, would he allow himself the luxury of thinking, *what the feck did I just do?*

Chapter 3: Timebomb

Conor sagged gratefully against the door of the house in Cavendish Street, letting it handle the complex task of holding him upright as his key scratched awkwardly in the lock. His body cast a shadow over the door from the street light and anyway the tip wavered about before sliding in, like the lock was never quite where it ought to be. Also, he was naturally left handed, and that hand still held the wadded t-shirt against the side of his head. But at last the lock turned and he could push the door open. He almost closed it again from the other side by leaning his body weight against it – but that would make the lock click, and that might awaken the thirteen-month-old timebomb that slept in the room at the back of the house, so he took the time to open the latch, push the door gently shut and then close the latch softly. Then, he breathed deep.

He was alone in a silent, dark house – but it was *his* house, the one he had been born in, and already he could feel strength and energy returning, seeping out of the brickwork. A few inches away, the other side of the wood, was a world where people might throw rocks at his head and strange Protestant boys might kiss him (apparently), but that world would never penetrate into here.

The hallway was pitch dark but he could make his way around blindfold. Without turning on a single light or making a single board creak, he could make his way up to his room and fall into bed. Fully clothed if necessary, not for the first time. But that would be a hollow victory, because his head still throbbed and he could feel the blood matting his hair. It was probably all over his clothes too. There was no way he could keep this from the family.

So, still silently, he made his way unerringly in the dark up the stairs and to the door of his parents' room. He rapped gently on the half-open door.

Immediately a man's voice called back at him:

"That you, son?"

"It's me, Da."

His voice was stronger now, as he had expected. He hadn't been bullshitting Luke – he really did know quite a bit about head injuries, and how he reacted to them.

Luke …

He closed his eyes and tried to piece together the fragmented images of the strange Proddie boy. Same sort of age as him, but taller, a little. Lanky, almost, but also well-built, to judge from that brief moment when he had got his shirt off. Conor had felt the strength in Luke's arms when he sagged into them; Luke hadn't had to try hard at all to lift him back up. Conor was used to making an instant assessment of other men's physiques – it helped to know where to hit them and how mobile they were likely to be when they hit back –

and he guessed Luke might maybe be a rugby player. Certainly someone who worked out and took care of himself, anyway.

So what the fuck had he been doing this side of the interface? Cruising around, looking for injured Catholic boys to kiss?

Even for a Prod, that had to qualify as strange behaviour.

He was mightily grateful to Luke for the help.

He just wished he couldn't still taste the other boy's lips.

It was a problem to go over another day. Right now there was something more important to get over with.

"Are you okay, Conor?" That was Ma. He heard the rustling of bedclothes, the sound of a hand fumbling for the switch of a bedside light.

"Before you turn that on ..." he began, but too late. He squinted as light flooded the room with a loud *click*.

"Jesus, Mary and Joseph!"

They both jolted upright in bed as if the mattress had suddenly stung them. One advantage of Da's lack of hair was that he could never look dishevelled even when he was woken by his son in the middle of the night. Ma had her hair held immaculately in a hairnet.

"What happened to you–..."

"Never mind what happened to him, Michael McGarry." Ma swung herself out of bed. "Here, love, sit down."

She guided him into the one chair in the room, the one where she sat to put her face on. Conor dropped gratefully into the seat and rested his head back.

"Don't get blood on the fabric, it'll take ages to come out!" Ma automatically protested. Two pairs of round eyes turned to her. "I mean, ah, what happened to you?"

Conor sat up more straight. He knew she wasn't joking about the blood.

"Well, I locked up as usual …"

He still had Luke shirt's clamped to his head. While Ma knelt beside him and gently pried it away – he winced as the dried blood tugged at his hair – he gave a bald summary of his evening. Most of it. The unexpected denouement got left out. No one was getting to hear about that one until he had had time to work it out himself. If then.

"Son, what were you thinking, getting that close to the riot?" Da demanded.

"Maybe I forgot it was the Twelfth tomorrow."

They stared at him.

"How can you forget the Twelfth?" Da asked.

"Why should I *remember* the fucking Twelfth? (Sorry, Ma.)"

Penny McGarry would wince visibly when language sunk below a certain level and she was the only one he would apologise to. Nana Clodagh, who also lived with them, could swear any of them under the table if she was so minded.

"No, you're right," Conor went on reluctantly. They all knew it was impossible to forget the Twelfth. Everything shut down, whichever side you were on. It was everywhere. "I … may have been day dreaming. You know I've got that fight coming up …"

Da growled his opinion of day dreaming at the back of his throat.

"You *had* that fight coming up. I think we can discount it now." He crouched down in front of Conor. "How many fingers am I holding up?"

"Two, and a thumb."

Da held up one finger and moved it slowly, side to side and up and down. Conor obediently tracked the tip with his eyes, then deliberately crossed them. Da finally lowered his hand and looked straight into Conor's eyes, his face stern.

"Conor, you know that now is a really bad time to go picking up head injuries?"

"Sure I know that, Da." It had crossed Conor's mind too. They had plans which could be seriously derailed by this evening's events. "It wasn't deliberate."

Da just grunted.

His Ma was unfolding the t-shirt. She tilted her head inquisitively as she held it up, then tweaked up a corner of his leather jacket to check that he still had his own shirt on.

"So where did this come from, Conor?"

Conor felt blood rush to his face, and hoped they would excuse it, under the circumstances.

"A ... fella helped me up. He gave it to me."

"Well, that was good of him."

"Did you get his name?" Da asked.

"I didn't know him," Conor said truthfully.

"That wasn't what I asked, son."

Conor rolled his eyes.

"Luke. He said his name was Luke. That's all I know."

He was spared further interrogation by his mother.

"Up and into the kitchen," she ordered. "I'm cleaning you up."

Da was shrugging his dressing down on.

"And I'm calling Doctor McKenna," he announced.

"Da, there's no need!" Conor protested as he pushed himself to his feet. "I know about head injuries."

"Sure I thought that too, until you went and got one anyway. Go with your mother."

Da followed them out and back down the stairs, then headed for the phone as Conor let his Ma steer him into the kitchen.

Soon after that, he was having an experience that he hadn't known for at least the last thirteen of his eighteen years of life – being washed by his mother. He sat self-consciously stripped to the waist at the small kitchen table with its peeling Formica top, towel around his shoulders beneath the photo portrait of the Holy Father, while she dabbed a clean cloth in a bowl of warm water and gently mopped at the side of his head. From time to time she dunked the cloth back in the bowl, and Conor watched idly as tendrils of his blood curved and twisted in the clear water.

"Whassup?" a sleepy voice mumbled. Conor looked up at his brother-in-law Cormac, clad in his dressing gown, leaning against the doorpost. His sister Claire was just behind him, peering over his shoulder. Their half-awake looks turned to horror as they took him in.

"Jays–…" Cormac began as he took in Conor's state. He remembered just in time, with a quick glance at his mother-in-law, and moderated both his language and his volume. "Fuck. How did that happen?" he asked quietly.

"I was walking one way. A rock was flying the other."

"Is it as bad as it looks, Ma?" Claire asked, wide-eyed. Ma shook her head.

"He'll probably live."

"Well, that's a relief …" Conor's eyes went suddenly round as he stared into the far corner of the room. He held out his hand, reaching for something no one else could see. "Oh! Oh God, d'ye see that, Ma? Can you hear the beautiful music? I … I think I'm going! Grandma, Grandda, is that you?"

Cormac smothered a smile. Everyone related to Conor by blood looked at him with different degrees of exasperation.

Da poked his head around the door; Claire and Cormac moved to one side to make room. With six adults in a little house, you soon developed a sixth sense for how to get out of other people's way.

"He'll see you first thing tomorrow. He says if you walked all the way back here on your own then you're probably okay, but not to let you sleep for a few hours."

"It's nearly fucking midnight! (Sorry, Ma.)"

"Doctor's orders. I'll stay up with you." Da sighed. "And we both know you're going to be out of action at a really bad time, son."

Conor bit his lip.

"Da, I'll be fine."

"Of course he'll be fine, Michael McGarry," Ma scolded as she wrung the towel out again. "Didn't Our Lord already send an angel to bring him home safely?"

"An angel?" Conor and Da exclaimed together. Cormac and Claire just looked baffled.

"This Luke." She looked from one to the other. "Sure wasn't Saint Luke a healer? Hmm?" She dabbed again at the side of his head, while Conor and his father looked sceptically sideways at each other. Conor felt a smile pulling the corners of his mouth upwards. What would the Protestant boy make of that, then?

"D'ye think Saint Luke wears Puma gear nowadays, then, Ma?"

"Well …" She poked at his head hard enough to make him wince, as a penalty for talking back. "If he wore one of those bedsheets like on the statues, he'd stand out, wouldn't he?"

"I don't know." Even Da was starting to smile. "One of the four gospel writers – you'd think he'd wear Nike at least."

"Ohh …" she huffed.

Their voices had been getting louder without anyone realising, and then it was too late. The timebomb went off.

It began just below the limits of human hearing and then broadened out – a thin wail like an air raid siren growing louder and louder. Somehow its owner could howl "Mama!" without interrupting the constant background tone. Everyone, not least Claire and Cormac, groaned and slumped. Claire fixed her brother with a glare.

"Your fault!"

"My–…?" Conor began, outraged. But he subsided with a foolish smile, because they all knew there was nothing he liked better than playing with his little niece, who lived with her parents in the back room. "Sure I'll give her a cuddle to quieten her down."

"Not before I've got that blood off you …" Ma declared.

Conversation was suspended as Nana Clodagh appeared in the doorway in her dressing gown, favouring the room with a beatific Mother Teresa smile.

"Oh, is it breakfast already? You should have told me. Everyone's up but me!"

Da rolled his eyes.

"Clodagh, it's only midnight …"

He might as well not have bothered. She shuffled her way towards the sink and the kettle, then suddenly paused, turned, and peered closely at her grandson at the table.

"Why, Conor, sweetheart, did you bump your wee head?"

* * *

The first thing Will saw as he switched the hall light on was the dark suit on a hanger. Next to that, a bowler hat – and next to that, on another hanger, the sash.

Will stepped back and admired the montage. He knew his mother had brushed the suit to within an inch of its life, but a speck of white dust had fallen onto one of the shoulders and he carefully plucked it away. The hat passed muster. Then he moved on to the sash.

He lifted it up thoughtfully and dropped it again, letting the tassels run through his fingers, and silently whistling the first few bars of the song they had all sung back at the fire. This one wasn't as old as the one they had sung about, and it certainly didn't have the same pedigree, but the colours were indeed fine and it was quite literally the sash his father wore. And now it was Alan's, getting its first outing tomorrow for the first time in the three years since their da died.

The backing cloth was purple, and purple stripes ran down the outer edge on either side. Between them it blazed a proud, defiant orange. Tomorrow it would hang over Alan's shoulders, the two pointed, fringed ends fastened together just below his sternum.

Will bit his lip as he studied it. Tomorrow, the Glorious Twelfth, men wearing sashes like this would be marching all over Northern Ireland, snaking down historic routes like orange lifeblood pumping through the veins of a living creature. Philip Johnston would be so proud that one of his boys was following in his footsteps. His whole year had revolved around the Twelfth.

What would he make of Will's reluctance also to follow him into the Orange Order? Will would swear that he loved his country and the Protestant cause just as much, just as deeply, just as wholeheartedly as anyone tomorrow who would be marching in one of these things. And yes, he was glad that one of the Johnston boys was doing what their Da had wanted.

He had just never felt that he should be that one.

It didn't help that his girlfriend could never bring herself to accompany him to a march, because sometimes you could just have enough of too many pointing fingers.

And it *really* didn't help that while he was hugely proud of his entire Orange heritage, the nearest official Orangeman to him – Alan – was quite frankly a prick and not the Order's best advertisement. Trying to be proud of the same thing that drove his brother could be an uphill struggle.

There was a single message on the pad that lived next to the telephone on its table next to the living room door, and he turned it around to read. In his mother's writing:

11/7. 10.45 pm. Wendy for Will. Hope you're okay. See you tomorrow. Don't call if home later than 11.30.

He looked at his watch. It was almost twelve. Fine.

Then he looked at the blank paper below the message and a corner of his mouth twitched as he imagined how another call might have gone, if the caller knew his real name and his number, which thank Christ he did not.

11/7. 11.45 pm. Conor for Will. Wants to know why the fuck you just kissed him.

He honestly could not have said. He had been asking himself the same thing quite a lot as he walked home … though only once he was back in Loyalist territory, when he could afford to take his mind off immediate survival. Conor hadn't misled him. The alley did indeed go right down to the interface where it was completely sealed off by a flaking concrete block, graffitied liberally with Republican art. In a couple of places it was so crumbled that its core steel mesh was exposed, and there were a couple of holes that let you see straight through. It was very easy to find enough footholds to climb over.

Will had recognised where he was immediately he was on the other side, right opposite the bus stop and a two minute walk from the garage. No one saw him emerge from the shadows. He had set off at a quick trot …

And then it had hit him like the rock had hit Conor.

Why the FUCK did I kiss him?

He was sure it had just been instinct. Their heads had been close together, like his and Wendy's when the next thing they would do was kiss. And he had hurt this boy – he had felt guilty – he had wanted to make him feel better. Sure that had been it.

But treacherous memories had started to sidle back into his head as he made his way home to Agnes Street – things he hadn't had time for the luxury of noticing as he guided Conor away from the interface, arms wrapped around him to hold him upright in a tight hug.

The slide of muscles beneath his skin.

The sheer warmth of the other boy's body through his clothes.

At one point Conor's head had lolled near to his face, and the smell of his hair…

OH FER FECK'S SAKE!

Will had shut his eyes, thinking hard of Wendy, and almost walked into a lamppost.

He had sensed *life* in Conor. More life than in anyone else he knew, even in Wendy. For the first time he had known just how precious and fragile and irreplaceable a life was – and it was something he could have snuffed out if that rock had hit just a bit harder or at a different angle.

And if he could still feel Conor's lips against his own … well, sure that was only because he had never kissed another fella before. Of course it would make an impression.

Who knew another fella's lips would taste like that…

Will grunted angrily and pushed his way into the living room on his left.

"I'm home, Ma."

The room was dark, the only light coming from the TV screen. It was an old black and white movie he didn't recognise, the sound turned down so low you could barely hear. Ma sat in the chair that was at a slight angle to it. The chair next to hers – the one that let whoever was sitting there toast their feet in front of the fire on a cold night, as well as look at the screen directly – was empty at the moment.

It had been his father's, once, but Alan had made it very plain that now *he* was the man of the family and the chair was *his*.

She looked up and smiled.

"Hello, love," she said softly.

"Will I put the light on, Ma?"

"Oh, no need for that, darling. We've got to mind the pennies."

Will knew full well that their father had provided very well for his family; the electricity bill held no horrors for them. For a moment he had the feeling that the dark in the room wasn't caused by her not turning the light on – it was caused by *her*, it came from *her*. Darkness had wrapped around her the day three years ago when the green-jacketed RUC men had turned up at the front door, hats under their arms and expressions sombre.

"Okay, Ma." He perched on the arm of her chair and hugged her, and she leaned her head against his ribs for a moment.

"Is Alan with you, son?"

"No, Ma. We got separated."

"He'll make his way."

"Sure he will."

Will had no doubt about that. Even Alan wouldn't stay out to get hammered the night before the Twelfth, not before he was going to march for the first time.

"They had the bonfires on the news."

"Did they show us?" he asked, remembering the BBC crew and Mr Over Here.

A slight shake of the head.

"No, it was all about Stormont and Knock."

Will snorted. The reporters were playing it safe with respectable neighbourhoods where there would be no trouble.

"Did you have a good time, love?"

"Sure we did, Ma. Alan and I got to light the fire."

"Oh, that's sweet …"

Her attention wandered back to the screen, and he leaned over to kiss the top of her head.

"I'm off to bed, Ma. See you in the morning."

Five minutes later he had cleaned his teeth, washed his face, and slipped beneath the sheets. He reached over to switch off the bedside lamp and stared up at the ceiling. Slowly his eyes adjusted to the dark so that he could pick out shapes around the room. He turned over, pulled the sheets up, shut his eyes. Images and sensations swirled behind his closed lids.

The rock.

It was all about the rock.

He could have killed Conor.

But he had kissed him instead.

With an angry grunt, Will rolled onto his back and stared at the ceiling through the dark.

He might as well have gone to bed at midday, for all his chances of sleeping. His body was only a little tired and his brain was firing on all cylinders, not going to slow down any time now.

Hmm …

An idea occurred to him, and he immediately felt his body reacting with approval to the suggestion. It had already been a few days since the last time and – well, to put it bluntly, sometimes the best way to take your mind off your troubles and get into the mood for sleeping was doing to himself what he one day very much intended to do with Wendy. A visit to Pam and her five sisters, good and slow.

Will shifted his body about with the practice of long experience into the position that stopped the bed creaking or hitting the wall, and slid his hand down into his shorts. Yup, his body was definitely ready for this. It had been the right idea …

Conor's face abruptly appeared behind his eyelids. Conor as he imagined him; not the dazed boy with a bloodied head but in full health, eyes dark with an intelligence that pierced him to the core, mouth quirked in a slight, knowing smile.

Shit!

Will determinedly put his hands behind his head and continued to stare into the darkness.

Chapter 4: Machine Gun

Friday 18th July

Conor came in off the street with his kitbag slung over his shoulder. He shot a breezy smile at his surprised sister Rose behind the reception desk, and pushed his way into the main hall of McGarry's Gym before she could say anything.

The interior was still recognisable as the old linen warehouse it had once been. Sunlight poured in from the high, grimy windows, but the walls were whitewashed and the floor was laid down with durable, dark green carpet tiles. The air was warm with sweaty human activity; grunts and cries and conversation echoed around the space. The centre of the room was dominated by the boxing ring, and the walls were lined with weights and benches and bars. As someone with a stake in the business, he was pleased to see everything was in use.

Cormac was kneeling on a mat, in trackies and a white t-shirt with the McGarry's logo on his chest, spotting for an overweight guy twice his age doing sit-ups.

"Nineteen … twenty …" He looked up and smiled, happy but surprised. "Conor!" He checked his watch. "Uh – you know yer man's not here for another hour?"

"I came to warm up." Conor started to unzip his trackie top, revealing an identical t-shirt underneath. A look of alarm flitted over his brother-in-law's face.

The two of them had always got on well, ever since Claire had shyly introduced to the family the young man who had caught her eye at her sister's wedding. Cormac Whelan had come armed with flowers for her mother, a bottle of Jameson for her father, and cigarettes for her little brother, though truth to tell they hadn't been needed. The boys had just hit it off.

Now they both worked for the family business.

"You're not planning on sparring?" Cormac looked at him asking. "You know the doctor said …"

"I'll be fine, Cor. I'll stick to the bags. Even Da can't complain about that."

"Don't be betting on it." But Cormac gave him a wink and turned back to the customer. "Now, young fella, how do you feel about another twenty of those?"

Two minutes later, Conor was in front of one of the light punchbags for the first time since his accident, gloved hands raised. He fixed his eyes on the ball and sighted along his raised fists. In his mind he pictured an opponent standing there in place of the ball on its spring pole. Maybe the fucker who had thrown the rock at him? Yes, why not?

His fist connected with the ball with a leathery thud. The ball recoiled, sprang back, and his other fist was there to meet it.

Conor was back.

For the next five minutes he took it easy, letting himself slide back into the routine. Fists flying, feet dancing. It wasn't a challenge and his mind could go into neutral. This was better than lurking at home under doctor's orders, trying not to think of Luke …

Just how had that one kiss so got under his skin?

Conor's body boxed; behind the frown of concentration on his face, the wheels of his mind turned in a different direction.

He had been kissed by a boy once before. Conor had been eleven; Stephen had been fifteen or sixteen, an older teen who helped run the chapel youth group. They had always got on. Conor had gradually become aware he was Stephen's favourite but he had seen nothing wrong with it. They would go for bike rides together, kick footballs together and steal sweets from the corner shop together. He had been flattered by the attention – until the kiss. They had been alone in the equipment room. Stephen had put an arm either side of him against the wall, caging him in, and looked him in the eyes, and lowered his head and kissed him with all the tenderness and gentleness of a lover.

He had kneed Stephen as hard as he could in the balls without even thinking about it, a moment of instinctive revulsion outside his conscious control, and they never spoke of it again. Soon after, Stephen had disappeared. But Conor could still remember the look in his eyes – the tears, which were not just from the pain. The hurt, the humiliation, the panic as he realised the full depth of his miscalculation.

Not one cell in Conor's body had enjoyed the experience.

He honestly could not say the same about that stolen, unrequested kiss the other night.

A few more punches. Conor was on autopilot, his fists moving because they knew exactly how long it took for the bag to swing back at him. This was getting too easy. He let the ball slow down and stop, and took mental stock of his condition. Breathing was up, pulse was good and steady at the right sort of rate. It was time to graduate to the five-foot bag that hung on a chain from the rafters.

He stood before the dangling leather cylinder and sized it up like he would an opponent he respected. You did not take the big bag lightly. People laughed when he said it could fight back – but it could. It developed its own moves and rhythm and you had to look out for them.

He raised his fists again, and set to.

It was more of a challenge, as he had known it would be, but the thoughts that had been planted in the last session would not just go away ...

There had been kisses since Stephen, of course. No more boys, though. He had discovered girls, and girls had discovered him. It had been quite a relief to discover that girls liked to kiss him too.

Six months ago, for the first time, those kisses had led to something more. Then again a few days later, with another girl. Both girls had thought they were the first, and he had let them keep on thinking that. It wasn't big-headed to be aware that

Conor McGarry's virginity had some currency value in his community.

Of course, it was a learning experience, and one of the things he had learnt was that while boys bragged and didn't believe a word of it, girls shared information and treated every word as gospel. It hadn't taken them long to work out that they couldn't both be his first. They had accused him of treating them like meat, like boxes to tick, which he knew he had, and he had felt guilty about it – at first, until Cormac had a quiet word and he had realised their attitude towards him had been pretty much the same. He had been a scalp to claim, that was all.

But he didn't like to treat people as meat, and he had been too busy since then to really worry about girlfriends. To be honest, he didn't really miss it. It was all pretty pointless, a lot of effort for …

And he had it. It clicked into his mind so simply, so easily that he almost missed his punch.

Every kiss Conor had ever known – from Stephen, from Siobhan, from Marie – had been a means to an end, something designed to turn the rest of his body on, make it ready for sex. The kiss from the strange Protestant boy the other night had been the first from someone who cared for the sake of caring. And he had needed that care.

Conor did not scare easily, but he had been scared that night. He had grown up in a world where he knew there was violence just over the horizon, a line of dark cloud that might come near at any time. He had been nine when he came down one January Monday morning to breakfast, and found his Ma and Da sobbing as they listened to the radio reports. That was when he had learned you could be quietly going about your own business and not causing anyone any trouble, and still be shot dead by the British army.

So, when he had got old enough to venture out of their street on his own, he went carefully, and he had thought he had it. You learnt to deal with the roadblocks and riots. You developed a sixth sense for where trouble was at, and you steered away.

That night, he had got it wrong. That night, he had thought he might die. Then out of the dark came this gentle kiss.

"*Conor!*"

Abruptly he was back in the gym and he realised it was the third time his Da had called his name. Michael McGarry was standing outside the office, and with him was a tall, bulky man in a mohair coat, studying him with a critical glint in his eye. The visitor that today was all about. Had it been an hour already?

"Mr Clifford is here!"

"Coming, Da!"

Conor gave the bag one hard, final blow and turned away. And stopped.

A tall, blonde figure snagged the corner of his eyes, walking with a casual lope towards the changing rooms. Conor turned his head in disbelief. Luke?

No, not Luke, just someone who looked like him. The lad kept walking, oblivious of Conor's gaze, and the bag swung back and sent him staggering.

Face burning, he walked over to the two men. Da just looked astonished; Mr Clifford was grinning.

"Mr Clifford, my boy Conor," Da muttered.

"Tommy Clifford," said the man with a big smile. "Very pleased to meet you, Conor." He held a hand out to shake; Conor still had his gloves on so he could only raise a hand in a wave.

"Here, let me get those for you …" Da bumped his wrists together and Conor held his gloves out for Da to unlace.

Clifford's face was round and red, and his hair was Brylcreemed back over his head. Conor suddenly realised that this was the first Englishman he had met. It felt weird to hear a flesh and blood man speak with that accent, even though he had heard it a million times before on the telly.

In fact, Conor realised, he sounded like one of the weekly guest stars on *The Sweeney*, which his Ma liked to watch – so maybe this was a London accent?

"Did you have a good flight over, Mr Clifford?" Conor asked politely.

"Very good, thanks, yes." The Englishman cast an appraising eye around the building. "Interesting place. Is it all yours, Michael?"

"Aye, it is that …"

Da gave Clifford a brief history of McGarry's as he led him towards the office. Conor trailed in their wake, hopping and wriggling as he pulled his trackies back on.

"… The linen company went under – the boss took the money and ran – and me Da – he was the warehouse manager – he just scraped together enough to buy the lease up – the Council owns the property but they're …" He coughed. "Friendly …"

Clifford pursed his lips and nodded politely, and Conor wondered if he understood half of what he just heard – not the words, but the meaning behind them. The majority Protestant Council were hardly *friendly*. McGarry's was in a predominantly Protestant area but there were enough Catholics to be noticed. The Council tolerated McGarry's as they knew no one else would be interested and they were happy to take the few pounds they got out of it. But the fact was, a working class *Catholic* had managed to acquire the lease of a *Protestant*-owned property in a predominantly *Protestant* area, *and* hold the business together, *and* it was still going, even though the McGarrys had to sink every penny they had into it, and work for almost nothing so that now they barely had any pennies left to rub together – and, in Da's case, somehow still find enough cash to pay for three daughters' weddings.

"We're very handily placed," Da went on, "right on the borderline between communities, so we do a lot of cross-events, which keeps us in the public eye on both sides."

Conor translated in his head: *it's a no man's land*.

"Yes, I can see that would be handy," the Englishman agreed, sounding a little more interested, though Conor knew he couldn't conceive of the fragility of the unspoken truce that made McGarry's an island in the Troubles. But if McGarry's had any future at all, it had to lie in the good work it did across both communities.

Da had made the office ready. The curtains were drawn, a film projector stood ready on its stand, and he had taken down the noticeboard so that the far wall was a blank white screen.

"Sit yourself down, Tommy. Conor, get Mr Clifford a cup of tea. Now, we did explain to your assistant that sadly you won't be able to see young Conor in action in the flesh …"

"Yes, that's all understood, though it's a disappointment. How's the head, Conor?"

"The doctor says a few more days, Mr Clifford."

"Please, call me Tommy. So – what happened exactly?"

"A roof tile hit me, Mister … Tommy." Conor turned his back as he filled a mug from the urn. None of the McGarrys liked lying, but they had hit on the story because even though

Conor had been an innocent bystander at the riot, just the word 'riot' on its own might undo all the good they hoped to do.

"Bummer. I'm glad you're okay."

"Conor, get the lights ..."

Da fiddled inexpertly with the projector, the reels began to spin with a mechanical clatter and moving pictures flashed silently onto the wall. Clifford settled back in his chair, eyes fixed on performance. Conor settled down in a chair at the side of the room while Da stood by the stand.

"This was last year ..."

There was no sound, but Da had finally learnt to use a tripod rather than just hold the camera and the images were steady. Looking only a little younger than he now was, with a more schoolboyish haircut, Conor came out of his corner and the fight was on, to the sound of the whirring reels.

Clifford said nothing until the end. The fight had been inconclusive, a set number of rounds and that was it.

"Last year?" he asked.

"September, that's right. Now, this was in January ..."

Again, Clifford was silent. He lit a Hamlet and the smoke drifted up to twist and curl through the projector beam. The Englishman's face was unreadable, but his eyes darted left and right, taking in every bit of every scene. A few times, Conor shifted in his seat, opened his mouth to speak, to explain what he had just been doing, but Da caught his eye and gave the tiniest shake of the head.

And Conor realised it was best that way. If the fight didn't speak for itself then words were just a waste of time.

"And last of all, this was in April. There was a bit of a mix-up and we didn't realise until we got there that it was a proper knock-out competition – Conor's first …"

"Oh?" Clifford hitched himself a little further up in his seat.

This fight was twice the length of the last two. Conor took his first serious hit just after the halfway point. It had been enough to knock him backwards but not enough to bring him down, and he winced as he watched it happen again. He remembered it all too well. It had been like his consciousness was on an elastic string – the blow had knocked it out of his head, and thank God it had snapped back before his body noticed and fell over.

But now he knew there was better to come. He and his opponent had been well matched and it had come down to sheer attrition. The fittest one would win, and that one was Conor.

The other boy was wilting. He let his guard down just for a moment, and even though he knew what was coming, Conor grinned in anticipation. On screen, his younger self suddenly darted forward and his rival wilted under a barrage of blows, left-right-left-right-left-right, almost too fast for the camera to see. His rival staggered back as if he was shot. He was still recovering when Conor dealt the final, knock-out blow that sent him to all fours.

Conor glanced sideways to see how the Englishman was taking it. The visitor was on the edge of his seat and the cigar hung limply from his lips."

"*Wow!*" he breathed.

"I call it the machine gun." Da switched the machine off and turned on the lights. "I went to pick our lad here up from school …" He gave Conor's hair a friendly ruffle.

"Da," Conor protested, knowing the story that was coming.

"… and I saw him in a fight in the school playground."

"A fight, eh?" Clifford murmured, with an appraising glance at Conor.

"Davy James was a prick," Conor murmured, flushing. "He kept lifting up girl's skirts and making them cry."

"Ah." Clifford nodded. "I didn't go to a mixed school, myself, so we didn't get that problem."

"Oh, we were all Catholics," Conor explained helpfully, and there was an awkward pause while they looked at each other and each realised they had a different understanding of what is meant by a mixed school.

"Anyway," Da pressed on after a moment, "our Conor looks like he's going under, because this Davy James is built like a brick shit- … Uh, a very big …"

"I think that's one expression which does work for both of us," Clifford said dryly.

"Well, Tommy, you get the picture. But out of nowhere, acting purely on instinct, Conor comes in with the machine gun. Finishes him off, only thing is getting him to stop. A natural. And I thought, I can work with that."

"You weren't wrong." Clifford was looking at Conor in a whole new light, with a gleam in his eye. "Machine Gun McGarry. Oh, yes. *I* can work with *that*."

He leaned forward, stubbed his cigar out, turned to face them both. His hands were clasped in front of him as he began to speak, emphasising his points with a double-fisted jab.

"Can I assume you gents have heard of Mr Barry McGuigan?"

"Uh-huh."

"Sure."

They certainly had heard of Barry McGuigan.

At the age of fifteen, four years ago, the skinny boy from Clones had boxed his way to victory in the All Ireland Amateur Championship. Two years later, McGuigan had fought in the Commonwealth Games, representing Northern Ireland. And, later that same month, now aged nineteen, McGuigan would be at the Olympics in Moscow, fighting for Ireland.

Like most successful Irishmen, it didn't matter which side of the border he was from. If you were born on the island of Ireland then you claimed him as your own.

"Here's how I work," Clifford went on. "I'm not a sportsman, I just happen to work in sport. I'm not a trainer, I'm not a coach, I'm a promoter. In my business, you're always looking ahead, always asking, who is the next big thing? A few years ago, young Barry was the next big thing. Now, he is the *current* big thing. By being successful, he has created a vacancy. Who's *next*?"

He tapped his chest.

"That's my job. I look for who's next, and I may just have found him …"

Conor flushed and his heart began to pound under Clifford's thoughtful gaze. His father tilted his head slightly.

"Go on."

"I'll be frank, Conor, I'd hoped to see you fight live, as you know. Well, I'll be back and forth for a while still. I'm travelling all over the UK. You're not the only lad I have my eye on. But, I have funds to select a handful of hopefuls, no more than that. If you turn out to be one of them then I will pay for you to come over to England, I will get you sponsorship, I will get you trained up to a level that this place – no offence, Michael …"

"None taken."

"… could ever manage. I will get you fights, I will put you in front of people who will see you do your thing with their own eyes and draw their own conclusions."

Da's eyes narrowed.

"And what happens when Conor is no longer the next big thing?"

"Ah!" Clifford laughed and held his hands up in surrender. "You see right through me, Michael. Yes, the day will come when Conor is neither the next big thing nor the current one, and yes, come that day, I will drop him like a hot potato. *But*." He held up a finger. "By that time, he will be in a place where he can dictate his own destiny. Look at it this way – whatever happens in Moscow, do you think McGuigan will be going back to his paper round in Clones any time soon?"

Da smiled.

"No."

"Neither do I. Yes, my interest is in Conor for a very specific window of his life, and what Conor does after that is his problem, but I can get him to the point where he can make any choice he likes, and after that we part as friends, no hard feelings."

Clifford left those words hanging for a moment. Then he fished into an inside pocket and pulled out a business card.

"Give me a call when Conor's fit to fight again," he said. He didn't hand the card to either of them but laid it down deliberately next to the ashtray. "Now, is there any chance you could call me a taxi?"

There was time for a cup of tea before the taxi arrived, and then they were all out on the pavement outside to see their visitor off.

"Have you been to Northern Ireland before, Tommy?" Conor asked as the car pulled up. The visitor smiled.

"A few times, a few times. It's always better than the image we get on the TV back home, and it can always surprise you." He laughed and pointed at a bit of graffiti on the wall across the road: FUK THE QUEEN. "I mean, if I hadn't seen it, I would never have thought anyone could misspell that particular word." He climbed into the back, and threw them both a cheery wave, and a wink at Conor. "Look out for those punchbags!"

He turned away into the car so he didn't see Conor's smile grow fixed or his face burn. They waved the Englishman off until his ride had turned the corner, and then father and son turned to face each other.

"England?" Conor said quietly.

"England," Da replied, just as quietly.

Conor had always known it was a possibility – in fact it had been the whole point of Da inviting Tommy Clifford over in the first place. And Conor had no particular beef against the English. It wasn't them who kept the Catholics of Ireland subjugated – that was the fucking Protestants, and Conor was genuinely baffled how the Prods couldn't see that the English treated both sides equally like dirt. Now he had actually met an Englishman, they had got on and Conor was prepared to give him the benefit of the doubt.

But still ... England.

Da seized his shoulders and suddenly burst out laughing. "*England!*" He pulled Conor into a hug. "Oh, son, I knew it! I knew you could do it!"

"Let's … not … tell … anyone … yet …" Conor gasped between thumps on his back.

"For sure, for sure. It's not in the bag yet." Da let him go, straightened up. "Come on, then. We've got a gym to run." He turned to push the door open, shaking his head. "Look out for those punchbags …" he murmured, and chuckled.

Conor followed him in, his face set, his smile already fading.

If you'd cost me that fucking interview, Luke …

He had to find out who this Luke was.

Chapter 5: The Tufty Club

Monday 21st July

The cafe was humid with steam and thick with frying smells. Will had to lift the tray up to navigate his way through the crowded tables to where Wendy waited by the window. He had bought tea for the two of them, and his usual bacon roll. The roll's scent just below his nose was making his stomach rumble.

"Too late to change your mind," he said cheerfully as he set the tray down. She smiled as she took her mug.

"I'll be fine. Does your ma not feed you properly?"

Will had already demolished half the roll with a single bite and was making appreciative noises as he chewed. He tried to smile without displaying a mouthful of chewed crumbs, and swallowed with a single duck of his head.

"She feeds me fine. I just work up an appetite walking to work." They usually met for a mug of tea before work, and the roll did make him feel maybe a bit too full – but it was just too tantalising to sit within easy reach of frying food and not eat some. He washed the mouthful down with a mouthful of the cafe's thick, strong tea. "So, how was kids' club last night?" She pulled a face, and sighed. "Oh. That good?"

Another sigh.

"We were doing road safety with the Tufty Club," she said. "You know Tufty?"

"Isn't he yer rat who teaches road safety to bairns?"

She rolled her eyes.

"He's a squirrel – but yes. Tufty is this nice behaved English squirrel who always looks left and right before he crosses the road and never plays out in the street. He has an eejit friend called Willy Weasel who keeps getting hit by cars. Every time it happens we get a little lesson about what Willy Weasel did wrong and what Tufty did right. So, we showed the girls this film, then I have to ask are there any questions? And it's all …" Her hand shot up. "'Miss, Miss, why does Policeman Badger wear a blue uniform? Is Policeman Badger from the South, Miss?'" She lowered her hand again. "Because we all know where the policemen wear blue uniforms, don't we?"

Will smiled over his mug.

"So Policeman Badger's a Garda?"

She nodded wearily.

"Policeman Badger's a Garda, Tufty's a Taig and they're not going to let any Fenian tell them what to do about road safety. So let the little feckers get run over, I say."

"You probably should learn not to call them that. You know, if you're going to be a teacher."

"I've got until September to learn."

Will just grunted and hid behind another swig of tea.

Even without the recent unwelcome intrusion of Conor into his thoughts, he had been spending more and more time in his head on this particular issue. The future of Will and Wendy. Come September, Wendy would be going to Queen's to train as a teacher. Ten years from now, she would probably be headmistress of a primary school somewhere.

And him?

Still at Mitchell's garage?

Will was under no illusions as to which of them had the brains. Their O-level grades had shown that, if nothing else. It had always been a foregone conclusion that he would drop out of school after that, but she had successfully defied her father's conclusion, foregone on her behalf, that she would do likewise. She had stayed on at school for A-levels, and aced every exam she took. Now he could picture her career just taking off from here, blazing up and away like a brilliant rocket, while he stayed doing the same thing for the next fifty years.

They weren't kids in the playground anymore, and he wondered how long they might coast on the illusion that they were. Supposing they got married? What would he have to offer her?

Just tell her you love her. That was Alan's advice for any situation requiring a woman to be won over. Will wasn't sure who that said more about: Alan, or the kind of women his brother liked to go out with. The words had always dried in his throat when he tried to say them to Wendy – for the simple reason they weren't true.

Once again she displayed her supernatural ability to pick up on the slightest nuances in his expression, and she took it as a cue to open up with her own thoughts.

"Will, back on Bonfire Night, I was maybe a bit cold with you?"

He frowned.

"You were?"

"I just … I just wanted to make sure I didn't spoil anything between us?"

Will frowned harder and ran through the sequence of events of that night – at least, the sequence of events that Wendy would have known of. Turned up. Sang 'The Sash'. Lit the fire. Got separated. Met up again. Split up again as he went back to find …

Well, anyway, that was all that Wendy could know about.

"Sure I don't think you were cold. I mean …" He thought back. Okay, she had been fed up, but this was quite usual in anything that included her and Alan. "If you were, then …" He had learned to say this even when he couldn't quite see how, and it might even be true because who knew exactly how girls' minds worked? "Then I'm sure I deserved it."

She made a head movement that was neither a shake nor a nod, so he had no idea how she was taking it.

"It's just that since then, you've been a little … I don't know. Distracted?"

Will buried his face in his mug. *Shit!* Was it really that obvious?

"And there it is again," she said promptly. Will sighed and put his mug down, so that he could reach over the table with both hands and take hers.

"Okay," he said. It was a delicate act, making it up as he went along, trying to tell the truth without saying all of it. "It was a weird night. I'm still …" He twirled a finger at the side of his head. "Still trying to make sense of some of it. It's nothing to do with you – I mean, I promise, it's not about anything you did.

She held his gaze, then smiled a slow, wan smile.

"This is why I like you, Will Johnston. You don't bullshit me. Sometimes you're a bit of a dick but you don't bullshit me."

He grinned, more out of relief than anything else.

"And I like you too, Wendy Robbins."

Turned out neither of them was going to admit to loving the other that day. But *like* – yes, they could both do that in all sincerity.

He glanced up at the clock above the counter, and quickly stuffed the rest of his roll into his mouth.

"Shfit." Crumbs sprayed out which he tried vainly to contain, muffling his words. "Go'a ge'a wor'."

Mitchell Tyres and Services was a two minute walk from the cafe, past the bus stop and the sealed-off alley where Will had climbed back to Protestant safety on the Eleventh. The shutters were being rolled up as Will reached the forecourt and the first customers of the day were already lining up. He nodded to some familiar faces, and took his time card from the rack to punch himself in for the day on the machine by the entryway. Then he headed quickly out to the back to change into his work overalls.

"Ah, Will! Just the lad!"

A beaming Mr Mitchell intercepted him as he came out into the work area. The garage owner was in his usual immaculate three-piece, stomach straining against his waistcoat. He tossed Will a bunch of keys which Will instinctively snatched out of the air.

"Will, son, I've promised a friend a special favour. There's a blue Nissan out back that he's trying to sell. Give it the works, will you? Engine is fine, but it could do with a full valet, inside and out. Take as long as you need – don't worry about the paperwork – I'll handle that. Oh, and change the tyres. I think we have some new Firestones in? They'll do nicely. In fact, do them first of all, before they all go to other cars."

"I'll get right onto it, Mr Mitchell."

They both knew Will could do much more than give a car a valet job. He could strip the engine down to its basics and put it back together again – but, if this was what Mr Mitchell wanted today, this was what he got. Anyway, it never hurt to be picked for special one-offs by the boss.

There was only one blue Nissan out back – a Cherry, four or five years old. Will drove it into the service bay and quickly snagged four of the new Firestones – Mr Mitchell had been right about how quickly they would go if you weren't careful. He got the car jacked up and spent half an hour getting the tyres fitted and filled up and balanced. Then he could free up a servicing space by driving the car back into the rear yard, and that was where he spent the rest of the morning vacuuming and scrubbing and polishing.

The day was muggy, and before he was halfway through he had to roll his overalls down to his waist, tying the empty sleeves together as a belt to keep them up. Sweat made his t-shirt cling to his body and his hair was damp, but by the end of it the Nissan looked fine. It was a small car with a surprising number of tight nooks and crannies, and several times he had to contort his lengthy body quite uncomfortably to get at everything.

Doing the outside was easier. A gentle power wash followed by a machine polish brought the paintwork to a lustrous shine; then he scrubbed the windows down with white vinegar and water, and buffed them dry by hand. At last he could step back and take a final look at his handiwork, pursing his lips with approval. He shrugged his overalls back up to his shoulders and went to report a successful conclusion to the morning's work.

Two men were walking in from the forecourt as he came in from the back. He recognised one at once, and even though the other was a complete stranger, Will immediately guessed what he was.

Sergeant Moore of the RUC was a familiar face in the neighbourhood. His calm, affable face and his stolid figure in his immaculate uniform radiated authority, and there wasn't a boy for miles around – including Will – who hadn't had their heads cracked or ears clipped for some kind of misbehaviour. Just being seen with him immediately vouched for the bona fides of the other fella.

Not that he needed it, because he was so obviously a British army officer, despite being in civvies. Short, neat hair, a green Barbour jacket, and a spine so straight that his wife could have inserted a broomstick up his arse before waving him off that morning.

Mr Mitchell shot out of his office and made a beeline for them before they were barely five steps inside. The three men conferred and Mr Mitchell hung his head, deep in thought, every now and then nodding. Will made his way over to wait his turn to report on a successfully valeted Nissan, and the garage owner's round face split into a big smile.

"Will! Perfect."

"Mr Mitchell, I've –…"

"Yes, yes," Mr Mitchell waved him to silence. "Now, gentlemen, tell young Will what you were just telling me. Will, you know Sergeant Moore, of course, and this is Captain Woolley of …" He paused, to make it an announcement. "The Army Intelligence Corps! Go ahead, Captain."

"Thank you …" The Englishman paused and looked around them all, seeming to suspect something – Will wasn't sure what – but he got three innocent looks in return. "As I was telling your manager, ah, Will, there was a shooting incident last night. Some gunmen – we believe, Loyalist gunmen – attacked one Gerard O'Hughes. He was shot and badly wounded in front of his family."

"Sure that's a shocking shame," Mr Mitchell put in.

"Thank you."

"I mean, the man's a known shill for the Republicans. An inch in the right direction and they might have done away with him altogether."

There was a pause. Mr Mitchell had kept his genial smile on as he delivered his sentiments.

"We know exactly what sort of man O'Hughes is, Mr Mitchell – but the fact is, a crime was committed."

"And there was a sighting of the gunman's vehicle," Sergeant Moore put in. "They didn't get the number but are almost sure it was a blue Nissan."

Will suddenly felt very cold, but years of practice of putting up with Alan let him keep his face calm.

"And the gunman very kindly parked on O'Hughes's front lawn," Woolley continued, "giving us a perfect set of tyre prints. Now, we are checking in all the nearby garages …"

"For sure, for sure." Mr Mitchell seemed to think for a moment. "A blue Nissan …" He looked Will in the eye. "Will, isn't there that Nissan out back right now? I think it's blue. You know, the one you were going to start work on next?"

Captain Woolley looked as though someone had just told him he was getting a medal.

"Yes, Mr Mitchell, there is," Will agreed, his face perfectly straight as he took the cue. "I was just about to start work on it."

"Well, why don't you bring it through to the service bay and the Captain can take a look …"

"Ah, no!" Woolley stepped in quickly. "No offence to your man here, but any forensic evidence could be corrupted. No, I'll go and look at it in situ, with your permission."

Will had never heard 'with your permission' sound so like a stated fact before.

Mr Mitchell gave a shrug and a nod.

"This way …"

Captain Woolley's good mood evaporated the moment he saw the gleaming blue vehicle parked against the wall in the back lot.

"This is the car you were *about to start* work on?" His eyes bored into Will's.

"Yes, sir."

"I take responsibility for Will's work," Mr Mitchell interjected, "but you can check the time sheet if you don't believe him."

The Englishman's shoulders slumped.

"Okay …" he murmured, and Will could hear the sound of hope departing. Still, just in case, Woolley pulled a sheet of paper from his pocket and unfolded it to show a very clear tyre print. He crouched down by the nearside front wheel and clocked that he was looking at a brand new Firestone. He hung his head for a moment as if to clear it, then looked up the others.

"I thought you lot were on our side?" he said quietly.

Three stony Protestant stares glared down at him in response, and Mr Mitchell drew himself up to his full height.

"Sir, every man in my employ will defend the interests of the Union with his life!"

Woolley stood slowly back up to his own full height, which was slightly higher than Mr Mitchell's. The two men were as nose to nose as they could get with the garage manager's stomach getting in the way.

"And who decides what those interests are?"

There was a tense moment of silence, and suddenly Mr Mitchell smiled.

"You know, Captain, what I've always admired about the British army is its skill at picking its battles wisely."

The Captain was just far enough forward that the other two men could exchange a few words.

"I'm sorry, Arthur, I delayed him as long as I could …"

"Don't worry, Ian. Young Will did us proud!"

Sergeant Moore nodded approvingly at each of them, then set his cap square on his head and marched out to rejoin the Englishman.

"Nicely played, Will, nicely played," Mr Mitchell murmured.

"Thank you, Mr Mitchell." Will wasn't sure if he should be flattered by his boss's trust, or angered at just how easily he had been played. Mr Mitchell patted him on the shoulder.

"When you go home this evening, don't bother punching yourself out. Let me take care of that when I lock up."

Will's eyes went wide and he immediately decided being flattered was the appropriate response. Mr Mitchell always stayed a couple of hours longer than anyone else, to handle the paperwork and probably fix the books, so Will was getting a couple of hours extra pay for nothing except a bit of discretion.

"Thank you, Mr Mitchell!"

Chapter 6: Observation Point

Wednesday 23rd July

The alleyway was damp and smelled of the different kinds of waste, human and animal, that had been deposited in it.
Just what the fuck am I doing here?
Well, he already knew the answer to that question.
Just what the fuck are you doing here, spending time looking out for a Protestant boy who kissed you?
That was harder.
Conor pressed his face to the crack in the concrete and peered out onto an alien world, framed with rusting rebar. The Protestant side of North Belfast. He was where Luke would have climbed back over that night, hidden down the end of a blind alleyway. Now Conor could also benefit from the fact that it was very hard to be spotted down here from his side. By moving his head, Conor could take in perhaps a fifty yard stretch of the other side.

The chances of Luke walking past any randomly chosen fifty yard stretch of Belfast had to be quite thin. But he had been a bit more scientific than that.

Conor had woken up in the middle of the night with a name in his head, clear as day. It happened sometimes: a word or a phrase buzzing around in his thoughts with no idea where it had come from. Sometimes he woke up humming a bit of music that then took days to dislodge. On this occasion it was a street name.

Agnes Street.

He was almost certain that Luke had said those words.

Was there even such a place? Or was it just some garbled bit of junk knocked out of random memories by a flying rock?

As soon as he could the next day, Conor had dug out a street map of Belfast and flicked his way to the index. He ran his finger down the A's.

Adelaide Street.

Agincourt Avenue.

Agincourt Street …

… Agnes Street.

It existed.

He had looked up the grid reference and turned to that page, and there it was – a half mile stretch of road running north to south between Crumlin and Shankill Roads, both of which he *had* heard of, and not favourably.

Somewhere in that half mile was Luke.

Conor had smiled slightly. Now all he had to do was search in an ever-increasing circle out from there until he had all of Belfast covered, and sooner or later Luke would be found. Easy.

But it was made easier by the fact that his memory had also, eventually, coughed up another name.

"Good morning, Mitchell Tyres and Services?"

The name that had been all over the back of Luke's bomber jacket. All Conor remembered was 'Something Tyres and Services', but he had leafed through the Yellow Pages and there was only one name that matched.

Pip-pip-pip-pip-pip ...

The clunking of a coin tumbling into the phone mechanism.

"Oh, ah, hello." Conor's throat was so dry that it barely came out as more than a whisper. What the fuck was he doing?

Hey, it's only a phone call. They can't get you down the phone line.

"*Hello? Can I help you?*"

"Ah. Yes. Hello. I wonder … could I speak to Luke, please?

A pause.

"*I'm sorry, can you say that again?*"

More confidently now:

"Could I speak to Luke, please?"

"*Luke? L – U – K – E? I'm sorry, we don't have a Luke here … Hello–?*"

Conor had already slammed the receiver back into the cradle. He stared down at it, hating it as though it was personally responsible for the let-down.

Fuck!

But once he had cooled down he had to admit that if he was stranded the wrong side of the interface, he might not give his real name either.

He had given it a day – enough for the memory to fade. And then he had called back, only this time he made himself speak breezily, like Da talking to a salesman.

Pip-pip-pip-pip-pip …
Clunk … whir …

"Oh, hello there! I wonder if you can help me. You fellas sorted my car out the other day – no, no, it's fine, absolutely – in fact you did such a good job, maybe you could pass my thanks on to the fella who handled it? He did an excellent job but I didn't get his name … Ah, tall, young lad – fair hair – well built …"

That immediately triggered another memory. Luke stripping off his t-shirt and giving Conor an eyeful. Street light gleaming off metal at his neck.

"Wears a fancy chain thing …"

"*Why, that sounds like our Will Johnston. Sure I'll pass that on – I'm sorry, I didn't catch your name …?*"

Click.
Brr-rr-rr.

He had a start point and an end point. Luke a.k.a. Will Johnston lived in Agnes Street and worked at Mitchell Tyres & Services. A quick look at the street map showed that if he had any sense at all – which admittedly, given that he had come over the interface and kissed a complete stranger, was not at all a foregone conclusion – then there was only one sensible route he would take to get to his job.

It would take him past the alleyway.

A final phone call established the garage's opening and closing times. Conor could estimate when Will would pass this point.

He was there half an hour before the garage was meant to close.

Five minutes after closing time, Will came walking by across the street, one hand in his pocket, the other holding a cigarette, sauntering along without a care in the world, utterly unaware of the hidden eyes that were seeing him in daylight for the first time, devouring every detail.

Until that point, Conor had almost been prepared to believe Luke really was a miraculous intervention sent by Our Lord, like his Ma had said. Even all the talk on the phone hadn't actually proved anything.

But the evidence of his own eyes now said that the Protestant boy who had kissed him was real. Amazing how much of what he saw actually matched his jumbled memories. A shade under six feet tall, Conor guessed – which meant he was probably taller than Conor was, but never mind that. And yes, he was well built but not large with it. Conor guessed he was a naturally slim fella who had bulked up with exercise. Jeans and the same bomber jacket with the garage name on it. Dirty blond hair which looked far too well looked after for

Conor's taste – hair was just something stuck on the top of your head, and you might give it a brush at the start of the day to keep your mother quiet but that was all. A square jaw and a square face above it – open and honest, the kind of face you couldn't help trusting, feeling yourself warm to.

Look, all he did was kiss you …

Well, that wasn't quite true. He had earned Conor's gratitude in a big way. Maybe he had even earned the kiss. Conor might not have made it home without him.

But that couldn't be why Conor so badly now wanted to know everything he could about him. They lived in two worlds separated by a barrier even more solid than the interface, built on four hundred years of mutual suspicion and loathing, but that kiss had drilled the tiniest little pinprick, even smaller than the hole Conor was now looking through. Tiny, but enough to open a channel that let the two worlds start to mingle.

Conor was there again the next morning, to watch him head to work.

And go home in the evening.

And the morning after that …

Now, Conor leaned his head against the cool concrete.

This is fucking ridiculous. What am I going to do? Watch him come and go until one of us dies of old age?

No.

That evening, he would wait until Will appeared … and go after him.

Every braincell he had shrieked that this was a fucking stupid idea, but it was the only way to resolve this that Conor could see.

Climb over the barrier – thirty seconds, maximum. Run to catch Will up – another thirty seconds. And then …

Get his phone number?

Jesus, this wasn't a fucking date.

And if people saw the Fenian climbing over the interface and took offence?

Well, sure he'd bluff it out, or something. Will seemed to know people over there. He'd vouch for him … wouldn't he?

Anyway, after what Will had done for him, the risk he had taken, it was the least Conor could do.

He checked his watch. It was coming on time. Sod's law, this would be the day Will took another route …

Conor's heart pounded as the now-familiar figure loped into view. He braced himself for the scramble over the interface, took one final look to reassure himself …

And stopped.

What?

Will's body language was different. He wasn't walking past.

He was slowing … and stopping.

Will pulled out a cigarette, put it in his mouth, ducked his head to light it … and just stood there as he smoked it. His head moved as he looked absently from side to side. At one point his gaze swept over the interface but showed no sign of lingering there.

A small queue of men and women and children stood nearby to him, and Conor scowled suspiciously as he suddenly twigged why Will might have paused here. With a queue of people. At a bus stop.

Conor groaned as Will suddenly drew himself up and chucked the cigarette down and ground it out with his foot, and then he was hidden from view as the bus pulled up in between them.

Oh, you've got to be fucking kidding!

Chapter 7: VCP

"Ah, will you look at that!" A beaming Alan clapped his hands as he surveyed his men. "It warms the cockles of your heart, so it does!"

The rest of the section – and Will – grinned happily back as they climbed down from the Land Rovers pulled up at the side of the road.

Even Will had to admit Alan cut a fine military figure in his camouflaged battledress and polished boots. An Ulsterman planted squarely on the soil of Ulster. He had the single tape of a lance corporal on each arm, which put him in charge, and the Maid of Erin cap badge of the Ulster Defence Regiment gleamed from the black beret placed precisely on his head. The others – Ronnie, Marcus, Charlie, Tom, Johnny, Sidney, Lewis, Sandy and, unfortunately, Henry – were all geared up the same way. Only Will was different, yet to earn his uniform, but Alan had found him some green overalls and a woollen watch cap which, from a distance, looked sort of military.

Will had ignored the comments about the cap mussing up his hair. He was proud to be out here and he didn't care.

They had changed in a room lined with metal lockers that smelled of sweat and gun oil, in the UDR barracks a thirty minute bus ride from Agnes Street. If you joined the UDR then you could make enemies who might turn up on your doorstep, so you patrolled away from your own community, and as it was too dangerous for anyone not on duty to wear the uniform in public, everyone got changed on base before and after each patrol.

Inside the base, Will had felt like he was in a fort in a Western movie. Maybe the Alamo, with John Wayne, if you left out how that actually ended. It was a complex of low-lying buildings surrounding a central square, all ages from crumbling Victorian red brick to modern prefab, which would have looked completely at home in this sort of neighbourhood – apart from the massive three-storey-high concrete wall surrounding them, topped with razor wire, that made it very clear this was a place under siege. A manned watchtower poked its head above the top of the wall to give a view of the locality.

Rows of rifles, machine guns and mortars were laid out on tarpaulins in the square, being cleaned and serviced by more army men in their shirt sleeves, and a row of dark green army Land Rovers was parked over to one side. One of them had the bonnet up, with the top half of a man in overalls buried in the innards of the engine, which immediately told Will there would be a job for him in the UDR if he decided to join.

If? He had cracked a half-smile. Technically he was only here as an unofficial guest, getting a taster for what life in the Regiment might be like, but Alan had already met it pretty plain where his expected destiny lay and Will himself had never really doubted it.

The section had piled in to three of the Land Rovers. The massive metal gate had shifted aside just slightly more than the width of one of the vehicles, and they they had headed out into the wilds of Belfast.

And here they now were, pulled up on the Mullaghglass Road, a B-road lined with trees and fields running south west from the city into the countryside.

Alan stood with his hands on his hips, feet slightly apart, pivoting at the waist as he peered up and down the road.

"Aye, this'll do nicely. Ronnie, Tom, you have the flank – there, and there. The rest of you, we'll set up here, so get the gear out. Will, look out for the razor wire – it can give you a nasty cut. Lewis, give my kid brother a hand."

The Ulster Defence Regiment mostly consisted of part-timers like Alan, even though it was the largest infantry regiment in the British army. Will already knew some of the lads at least vaguely by sight and he knew every one of them held down a day job too. Tom and Ronnie, for instance, the two flank sentries, were respectively an accountant's assistant – Tom and Alan worked together in the same office – and a plumber. They headed off to either side of the road and withdrew into the tree cover, just far enough that no driver would see them easily, their eyes scanning around them with a casual, practised, radar-like intensity. They both toted the standard, slim, black metal SLR rifles, cradled in their arms with casual familiarity, aimed down at the ground but leaving no doubt in Will's mind that they could be brought to bear in an instant.

"With you, Will …"

Lewis slid a pile of stacked orange traffic cones out of the back of the Land Rover. Will scooped them up and staggered across to where Alan was standing.

The UDR had been set up when it became clear that the RUC needed military support, rather than being expected to act like an army in its own right. In practice, this meant light military duties like that evening's agenda. Its squads patrolled, they gathered passive intelligence, they were positioned to guard key points and areas – and they manned mobile vehicle checkpoints.

Nine times out of ten, Will knew, those checkpoints passed off peacefully. Once in a blue moon, purely by the law of averages, they could net something. They might even end in shooting and loss of life. Alan had been very firm that at the first sign of anything like that, Will should dive into the undergrowth and wait. Alan liked to rule the roost at home but their mother still had powers of veto over some things, and this was one of them.

Under Alan's direction, Will and Lewis laid out staggered lines of traffic cones from both sides of the road, creating a chicane that traffic from either direction would have to swerve to get through. To discourage anyone trying a more direct charge, they then carefully uncoiled lengths of razor wire and draped them around the cones. The other lads spaced themselves in two distinct lines on either side of the VCP, the front and the rear barrier parties, a clear and visible armed presence.

Alan pursed his lips with approval.

"Grand, grand, grand. Now let's see if we can scare the shit out of some Fenians!" He patted Will on the shoulder. "Sorry you can't officially do anything, but watch and learn, watch and learn. Why not pass the tea around?"

Will got the thermos out. Despite the vigilance, the patrol was friendly and informal; they all took their cups with a smile and a nod, and they chatted together. Will was with familiar faces, and the familiarity and friendliness helped dispel any nerves he might have felt. The evening was overcast but pleasantly warm.

For this, Will had passed up an evening with Wendy, but she had understood. He was not alone. Charlie, Marcus and Sidney wore wedding rings, and he knew there was at least one proud father already in their ranks because Sidney had been passing around baby photos during the ride.

Everyone would much rather be at home with their women, or down the pub, or doing whatever normal people did when they didn't live in a community under siege. But this was what Ulstermen did to protect their world and Will was proud to be part of it. He had been brought up to pay his way in life and if there was something you wanted – peace, stability, freedom – then you damn well earned it through your own hard work.

Will's ears pricked up the sound of a car, and abruptly the atmosphere changed. Cups were put down, everyone stood up a little more straight and alert, tightening their grips on their rifle handles. Sidney had the job of stepping into the road brandishing a large red STOP sign on a pole. A suddenly grim-faced Alan gestured with his eyes that Will should back over to the far side of the verge.

It was a silver Vauxhall Viva estate with County Down plates. It duly pulled over, and Alan strolled over as the driver's window wound down. Try as he usually did not to be too impressed by his elder brother, Will had to admit that Alan had balls. His rifle was aimed at the ground and he walked as though he hadn't a care in the world. He was covered by a squad of trained and armed soldiers who all knew exactly what to do if things turned bad – but that wouldn't protect Alan if the driver suddenly pulled out a pistol and opened fire, quicker than Alan could bring his own weapon to bear.

"Good evening!" Alan said cheerily. "Sorry to have to bother you but would you have any kind of identification on you …?"

They were a middle aged couple with kids in the back, and they did. It all took thirty seconds and a bit more friendly banter passing in either direction. Alan stepped back and gave the nod, Sidney reversed the sign to the green GO, and everyone parted on good terms.

"D'ye see, Will? Piece of piss! Any more of that tea going?"

The next car came from the other direction. It was an Escort with Fermanagh plates, and immediately Will sensed a little more tension in the air. Fermanagh was a stone's throw from the border.

But these were two girls, both blondes, and both – like all sane women – resistant to Alan's idea of manly chat, even when Alan leaned down extra close to put his head through the open window. His body blocked Will's view of exactly what happened, and the words were muffled, but Alan stepped slowly back with a swagger in his hips, the Ford's wheels screeched and the car pulled away. Will just had time to clock the two dagger scowls from the occupants before they were out of sight.

Alan sauntered back to rejoin Will and Lewis.

"You wouldn't think lesbians would be allowed out together, would you?"

"What did you say?" Will sighed. Alan looked surprised.

"You know, the usual chat. Hey, Will, why do blondes were knickers?"

"It keeps their ankles warm," Will replied dutifully, and Lewis snorted back a laugh. "Why was the blonde so pleased it only took her three months to finish the jigsaw?" Alan shrugged. "The box said three to four years."

Alan actually paused before Lewis guffawed, then laughed himself now that he knew it was funny.

"Car coming!" Sidney called, and at Alan's nod they went back to the usual positions, Sidney in the middle of the road with the STOP sign raised.

Antrim plates, Will noted, and the squares lines of a Volkswagen Polo. If a car can have body language, this one showed reluctance. It seemed to him that it slowed down just a bit too slowly, and Sidney was on the verge of jumping out of the way before it pulled up in front of him. A man and a woman, in their mid twenties.

Alan did his usual saunter over.

No, Will noted, not his usual saunter. His thumb was brushing back and forth against the rifle grip, just millimetres from the safety catch.

"Good evening!" The greeting had less of the usual cheer. "Would you mind pulling over, turning your engine off and getting out?"

He indicated the side of the road where the Polo should go. Will frowned, trying to guess what had tweaked Alan's antennae. Had he maybe seen the driver's face on alerts distributed to all garrisons? Had the number been listed as one to look for?

The car pulled over in front of him. The woman in the passenger seat looked worried and the man was grim faced, his jaw set. They certainly looked like people who expected the worst. So, people with guilty consciences?

And then Will realised that no, it was nothing like that. He saw what Alan had seen and four hundred years of culture sent a shiver down his back, even though he knew it was ridiculous, and even though he had kissed one of these people recently and now couldn't stop thinking about him.

The only thing these people had done wrong was to hang a set of rosary beads from the rear view mirror.

The woman got out and stood, hugging herself, expecting the worst. The man more assertively propped his backside against the car and folded his arms.

"So, Corporal, how can we help you?"

Alan stood just a bit too close to him, and smiled a smile that barely passed his nose.

"Very sorry to bother ye, but a car matching this description …"

"Where?"

Alan blinked.

"I beg your pardon?"

The man shrugged.

"Where was this car matching our description? I can account for my movements pretty thoroughly over the last few days."

Alan's smile had faded altogether and his eyes narrowed. Catholics who talked back were not part of the script.

"Where were you on Friday the twenty-first of October, 1977?"

Eh? Will shot him an astonished look. That date was sacred to both of them and not one to be bandied about lightly. The man's eyebrows went up.

"Really?"

"Oh, yes."

"You expect me to remember my whereabouts nearly three years ago …"

Alan moved even closer.

"There was a car crash on that date," he almost whispered, "with fatalities. A Catholic driver was involved."

The man shrugged again.

"I'm very sorry."

"Now, if you can't account for your whereabouts on that …"

"I was in Dublin, in the Exam Hall at Trinity."

Alan only let himself be thrown for half a beat. He raised an eyebrow.

"That's a very specific memory for, as you say, a day nearly three years ago …"

"It was the day The Clash played there."

Several of the lads smothered laughs and Alan's jaw worked silently for a second. He seemed to be adjusting to the concept of lippy Fenians, but Will doubted it was doing his sense of humour any good.

"D'ye tell me that? You saw The Clash at Trinity?"

"I was *studying* at Trinity. For my Law degree." A pause. "Which I passed." A slightly longer pause. "With a *very* high grade."

"Ah, well. A lawyer. Ye'll be knowing all your rights, then."

"I've a pretty good idea."

"And ye'll be knowing all of ours."

The man stepped forward so that he and Alan were literally nose to nose – as close as Conor and Will had been when Will had–… He pushed the memory away. It wasn't helpful and he really did not see that scenario repeating itself here.

"I know you need something a little more specific than 'a car matching your description'," the man said.

"Hey, Henry," Alan called, not taking his eyes off the man, "remind me, was there anything else in that car alert?"

"Aye, there was." Henry didn't smile. "Said there was something hanging off the mirror. Something like a necklace."

All eyes went to the rosary, and the man seemed to slump.

"Tchk." Alan pulled a face. "Not your day, is it, sir? We'll have to conduct a search but fortunately we brought along someone who knows all about dismantling cars." He walked over to Will and jerked a thumb at the Polo. "Reduce it to kit form," he instructed through his teeth.

Will felt himself flush under the gaze of the harmless Catholic couple as he studied the car to size it up.

"I can't."

Alan paused, froze, then slowly turned back round to him in disbelief.

"*What?*"

"You need special tools to dismantle a car properly. We don't have anything like that."

"Just … just …" Alan struggled to find the words. "Just tear the fecker apart! You can do that, can't you?"

Now it was Will's turn to step up close to his brother.

"For sure I can, but I'm not doing an arseways job on a car." Will kept his voice low, so that from a distance it might just look like they were conferring. Loyalty was loyalty; Alan might be a bullying shit but he was a *Protestant* bullying shit and Will was not going to show him up in front of the Fenians. "Not for you or for anyone."

Alan drew a couple of breaths.

"Well, *your Majesty*, what *can* you do?" he grated. "Can you get the wheels off?"

"Not all at once. Not without putting it up on a ramp."

"How about removing the door linings? Can Sir do that with the tools to hand?"

Will thought. If the right tools weren't in the Polo, they would be in one of the Land Rovers.

"Aye, I can do that."

"Well, then." Alan jerked his chin at the car and marched away.

Ears burning under the owners' glare, Will jammed the flat end of the crowbar into the gap between the inside lining of the door and the metal, levered. More conventionally, Sandy was checking underneath the vehicle with a mirror on a stick, but Will was the one they glared at and he couldn't blame him. This had stopped being fun. They all knew this had nothing to do with gathering intelligence to defend his people and his home. They all knew this was just bullying.

The man had stopped complaining. Maybe he knew his rights, but if he knew that much about the world then he also knew better than to argue with a group of armed men who … Well, there was no other way of putting it. Who were in charge, whatever the law said.

But his wife, or girlfriend, was suddenly not so reticent.

"Why are you doing this?" she blurted. To Will's relief she aimed her frustration at Alan, the one in charge, not at him. "What have we done to you?"

The man tried to calm her with an arm around her but she slapped his hand away.

Alan just seemed to be energised by the confrontation. His smile grew broader and he spoke with the casual arrogance of a man who knows that everyone, from the armed men backing him up here and now to the sympathies of anyone in authority who might be complained to in the future, was on his side.

"We'd all rather be at home, Ma'am, but you know how it is. There's a war on and we have to protect our communities."

"You people! You're disgusting! Don't you know we're all on the same side?"

"The same side, is it? We wouldn't be defending ourselves if we didn't need defending, now, would we? Maybe you should have a word with *your* people. If they would just appreciate being looked after …"

"*Looked after!?* Maybe we want to be equals, not *looked after!*"

Alan snorted and turned away.

"How you doing there, Will? Find anything? Let's take a look …"

Will stepped back so that Alan could peer into the exposed innards of the door. Alan took his time while Will looked away, so he caught the movement half a second before his ears picked up the distinctive engine noise. Another army Land Rover was coming around the bend along the road. The Catholic couple just rolled their eyes at the thought of more reinforcements turning up to support the patrol, but Will noticed Alan and the rest draw themselves up a bit more smartly.

He realised why when the vehicle pulled up and the two men who got out were a sergeant and an officer. Two pips on his shoulders, which Will was pretty sure made him a lieutenant. Alan saluted smartly.

"Good evening, sir."

"Evening ..." The officer took in the situation. "Report, Corporal Johnston?"

"Just a routine check, sir." Alan gave the Catholic couple a significant glance which very clearly said they would keep quiet if they knew what was best for them.

The man ignored it and stepped forward.

"Apparently my car matches a description in an alert," he said brightly, "but I'm not allowed to know in what way or where my car is meant to have been, because it's more fun if I guess."

Will winced. Alan's expression turned to ice and the officer's voice went low, like Will's earlier. There was right and wrong but there was also loyalty to your own kind.

"You do have a record of this alert?" he asked. Alan didn't blink or speak. "If I radioed base right now, there'd be a record of it?"

Still no answer, and the lieutenant finally noticed the discrepancy in the whole scene.

"And why is that man not in uniform?" He nodded at Will.

"He's ... ah ... a civilian specialist, sir."

"A ... specialist?"

"In vehicles, sir."

The lieutenant gazed at Will with dark eyes that had seen it all.

"What's your name?"

"Will Johnston." Will didn't say 'Sir'. The man wasn't his superior.

"In other words, he's your kid brother along for the ride, Corporal? Jesus Christ, do you know the trouble we could get in, bringing civilians out on this kind of thing? Johnston, get into the Land Rover. We're taking you back to base."

Oh great, Will thought. *Alan is going to be in a foul mood now for the rest of the week and you're not the one who will have to live with it.*

He drew himself up.

"With respect – sir – I'd rather put the car back together first. I wouldn't want to leave it to a non-specialist, so I wouldn't."

The officer looked surprised and Will caught a twitch in Alan's face that might just have been respect. So he had possibly defused the foul temper. A little.

"Of course," the lieutenant said abruptly. "Do it and then get out of my sight."

Quite how Will was going to do that second thing while sitting in the back of the man's Land Rover was not a question he was going to ask. He quickly set to putting the car door back together, the officer turned towards the civilian couple to be as apologetic as he could be without actually admitting anything, and half an hour later Will was back at base on his own. He changed quickly and caught the last bus back home.

Chapter 8: Thanks for Being A Prick, Alan

The sun was long down by the time Will jumped off the bus opposite the interface. The bus pulled away and its red tail lights proceeded in the direction of central Belfast. He zipped his coat up and jammed his hands into his pockets, and set off for the five minute walk home, head down, gazing at the ground, mind still full of just how much of an arsehole Alan was likely to be when he got back from patrol.

He turned a corner and suddenly a dark figure blocked his way, an angry silhouette against the lights down the street, his whole stance hostile.

"William Johnston?"

"Yes …?"

Adrenaline surged. Lingering memories of the patrol coloured everything Will saw and heard. This had to be an angry Republican and there could only be one way this was going. He started to pull his hands from his pockets to defend himself, but the figure moved so quickly they were only halfway out before the fella caught his wrists, one in each hand, and pressed forward, pushing him into the shadows.

And suddenly the figure was kissing him. It wasn't much of a kiss – short, perfunctory, almost angry, like his assailant was making some kind of point. It lasted seconds, if that, but seemed to go on much longer, even as the other fella stepped slightly back, still holding on to Will's wrists in a grip Will could never break free of.

"Takes you aback, doesn't it?"

Will stared. Now his eyes had adjusted, he could recognise the face, but he had known from the moment their lips met.

"Conor?"

If Conor had just stepped out of the shadows and talked to him, Will would have been surprised. He would have stammered, not been sure what to say or how to take it, very definitely on the defensive as he spoke to a Fenian. But as soon as Conor kissed him, somehow it seemed perfectly natural that they should be here now, talking.

"Aye." They gazed at each other.

"You're …" Even in the dark, Conor's figure seemed more powerful, stronger, than the stumbling, half stunned boy Will had helped along. "You're okay, then?"

"Oh? That. Aye. I just have to take things easy for a while, doctor says."

"Good. I … I'm glad."

"So, who the fuck's Luke?"

"Luke …?" It took Will a moment to remember. He had forgotten that he had given a false name. "Oh. You know. *Star Wars*. There was a poster …"

He saw Conor's teeth as the other boy smiled.

"*That* Luke? So why the fuck didn't you just give your own name?" Then, as Will drew a breath to answer, "Nah, forget it. I'd have done the same, probably. Mind you, you hadn't kissed me at that point."

Will took another breath to start saying, "I'm sorry," and maybe give an explanation of some kind.

But he let it out again. He didn't have an explanation, and he wasn't sorry.

They stared at each other in the darkness. Will tried to match the Conor of the here and now with the one that grown inside his head over the last two weeks. The one in his head had always been based on the dazed figure he had held in his arms. He had never pictured a Conor fully restored to health, as this one appeared to be, and it was a million times better.

I keep on thinking of you ...

... were six words he was determined not to say.

But then, what was Conor doing here if Conor didn't feel the same?

He wondered how long it would take Conor to realise he was still holding onto Will's wrists.

"How did you find my name out?"

At last Conor let go of him, but only so he could tap the side of his nose. It was a slow movement, gently releasing Will, and their fingers brushed together as their arms fell to their sides.

"I have my ways."

Another pause.

"Were you waiting for me?" Will asked.

"Aye." Conor paused, then smiled again. "I told myself if you weren't on the last bus then that would be it – but here you are."

Will grinned back. Conor would never know how easily he could not have been on the last bus. The deal had been that Alan would drive him home at the end of the patrol – until he got sent home early, because the officer had said so, because Alan had been a prick.

Thanks for being a prick, Alan!

"I think we need to talk."

Will's heart pounded.

"Okay." He forced himself to be nonchalant. "What about?"

Conor ducked his head in a way that told him not to ask bloody stupid questions – he knew perfectly well.

"Unresolved business." They looked at each other – two boys, ancestral enemies, neither really knowing what to make of the other, both knowing that something needed making. "Too long and too complicated for here. But ... we can't *not* talk, can we?"

Will slowly shook his head. There was not the slightest chance of arguing. Conor was making perfect sense in a way that no one else could have understood.

"No. So ... where? And when?"

Both of them were running through possibilities in their heads. It would have to be somewhere safe, somewhere neutral, somewhere where no one would raise an eyebrow at a Protestant and a Catholic boy meeting up.

It was not going to be easy.

"I'm clever. I'll think of something. You got a phone number?"

"Sure, it's …"

"Hold on." Conor pulled out a slim diary from his back pocket, and saw Will's surprise as he produced it. "It's where I keep track of my training." *Training for …?* Will wanted to ask, but Conor was poised with the pencil he had pulled from the diary's spine, so he just gave the number. "And that's Belfast, right?"

"For sure it's feckign Belfast!" Will laughed, and Conor actually looked surprised for a moment, before he laughed too, surprised at himself.

"Of course! I wasn't thinking." He pushed the pencil back into the spine and the diary back into his pocket. "Give me time. I'll be in touch."

Conor turned to head off. Will instinctively took a step to follow him, and then they both stopped. Conor looked back at him, head tilted.

"Probably better if you don't?"

Will nodded, and pulled back into the shadows. He watched Conor trot back across the road to the alley, and scramble over the interface with impressive speed, and drop down out of sight.

He looked at the blank end of the alley for a long time, before finally turning for home, and even the thought of the bad mood Alan was going to be in didn't seem to matter so much anymore.

*　*　*

The moment his feet touched Catholic ground, Conor gasped and sagged against the mouldering brickwork of the alley, drawing in deep breaths like he had been holding them in all the time he had been over on the other side.

"*Fuck fuck fuck fuck fuck fuck fuck!*"

He could still feel the electricity drawing him to Will – a current that seemed to run through the blind wall of the interface and out into Protestant territory. It was like a static charge that had built up and had to be discharged, even if it hurt. Yes, they needed to get together badly. They had to sort this out once and for all.

A cold wave ran through his body despite the warmth of the summer evening, enough to make him shiver, and he recognised the feeling from his training. When your system was all fired up with adrenaline, you could get a severe chill unless you wrapped up and warmed down to let it drain naturally. He hadn't realised how keyed up he was. He set off home at a slow trot, just the right pace to restore equilibrium.

But, thinking of training gave him an idea.

They could probably meet at the gym safely – as in, they could be in the same place at the same time without arousing too much comment. It catered for both sides. But, actually having the privacy to say the things that had to be said … No, not there.

He had a better idea.

Anyway, he'll probably turn out to be a complete arsehole, and that'll get him out of my head and I'll never see him again.

It was a comforting thought to be heading home with.

Chapter 9: Car Freak

Thursday 24th July

"Oh, no!" Wendy moaned and clasped her hand over her face. "Oh no, I can't watch …"

But she still seemed to be peeking through her fingers. Will laughed and slid an arm around her, cuddling closer on the sofa but not taking his eyes off the telly, where a middle aged couple in a hotel room were getting ready for bed. The woman sat in her underwear, brushing her hair in a mirror. The dark window behind her showed it was nighttime.

Here in Belfast, in the real world, the phone started ringing in the hall. Alan grunted and pushed himself up from his chair.

"That'll be for me." A gust of cold hallway air blew in as he slipped out of the door. The more bad tempered Alan got, the more head-of-household he liked to act, and he was still coming down from getting his head bitten off publicly in front of the Papists on patrol. So, naturally the call had to be for him.

On screen, John Cleese's face slowly emerged from the darkness, and Will began to laugh, along with his mother and the studio audience. The woman and the husband both stared in disbelief at the apparition. John Cleese began to tap at the window with his hands, as if he was testing it for something. Then he slowly began to topple backwards and Will howled with laughter as he disappeared back into the darkness.

"Oh, that Basil Fawlty's a fool!" his mother cackled. Will smiled for a different reason. He was happy when she was happy.

Alan slipped in through the door, letting in another gust of cold hallway air, and fixed Will with a dour gaze.

"It's for you," he said, as if somehow Will had committed an act of treachery. "Luke?"

"Luke …?" Will went blank for half a second. "Luke!" He leapt up so quickly that Wendy almost fell over. "Uh – thanks. I'll get it." He shot Wendy an apologetic glance.

"Better be quick. He's on a payphone."

As the door closed behind him, Will heard his brother asking, "Who's Luke?", and he winced at the thought of Wendy's honest bafflement. But then he had picked up the receiver.

"Hello there, Luke." He held it in both hands, his mouth close to the speaking end, glancing behind to check that the living room door was properly shut, like this was a lovers' assignation that someone might overhear.

There was a moment's silence, and then someone was imitating a broken respirator down the line at him.

"*I AM your father!*" a voice intoned, followed by more heavy breathing, and Will felt himself grinning even more widely than he had at the misfortunes of Basil Fawlty. He lowered his voice further and once again checked all was clear behind him.

"Luke's the son, you eejit," he murmured.

"*Well, anyway.*" Will closed his eyes and savoured the sound of the voice. "*I thought of something. You still want to meet up?*"

"Yes."

It seemed far too easy an answer – it didn't come close to saying just *how badly* he wanted to meet up. But he couldn't say it any louder. It was perfectly possible, as he knew from experience, to follow conversations on the phone if you stayed close enough to the door, even with the telly on.

"*Could you do it this Saturday?*"

Will felt a gust of relief. Wendy worked all day on Saturdays and he only did mornings. He wouldn't have to hide this from her.

"Sure, in the afternoon."

"*And ... do you have any running gear? Anything like that?*"

Will stared at the phone, surprised into a more conversational volume.

"Running gear?"

The rest of the conversation was short, with Will's part mostly saying "yes" or "no", in case of flapping ears at his end. Finally he hung up, his mind whirling with possibilities.

* * *

Well, that's done it.

Conor hung the phone back up and briefly leaned his head forward, resting his forehead against the back wall of the phone box.

But the plastic managed to be clammy and sticky at the same time, and the smell of the box made it somewhere no one wanted to linger, so he stepped back out into the evening air and began the brisk walk back home. He dug into his pocket for some fags and ducked his head to light up, looking up from under his brows to mind where he was going. Two burning eyes behind a balaclava mask glared back at him.

Twenty feet high, the mural covered the end of the terrace ahead. Above the mask was a black beret, and for background, Irish colours were furled over a pair of crossed Armalite rifles.

Conor drew in on the cigarette and breathed out twin jets of smoke.

"What the fuck are you looking at?" he murmured.

* * *

Will's hand rested for a moment on the wood of the door. Basil Fawlty's barked, clipped ranting tones came through from the other side. He closed his eyes and drew a breath.

He had always been pretty sure he was a good boyfriend. He did not mess around with other girls. He had never cheated on Wendy (unless wanking to the pictures in Alan's magazines counted) and did not think he ever would. But he was about to lie to her.

Well, of course you're going to lie to her, because how could you ever explain the truth?

And anyway, he decided, he was not cheating on Wendy, he was helping her. This was all about clearing his head, getting Conor out of his system, pricking the bubble, so that then he could be a better boyfriend without the distraction.

He went in.

Basil Fawlty was rapping furiously on a bedroom door, inviting someone to come out. An old lady appeared out of the room, the audience shrieked, and Wendy, his mother and Alan convulsed with belly laughs. He had no idea what the joke was, except that the old lady was clearly the last person Basil had expected to see.

"I guess I missed that," he commented.

Wendy was looking quizzically up at him, an effect spoiled a little by her involuntary giggles. He pretended not to notice as he took his place next to her on the sofa again.

Alan had slipped back into their da's old chair and was leafing through the *Radio Times*. Which also had always been their da's job. The family had always watched what Philip Johnston wanted to watch, and now it was Alan's turn to assume the mantle.

"Next, *Last of the Summer Wine* – feck that – Ah, Ma, you missed *Dallas*! … Chuck me the *TV Times*, Will?" Will flicked over the magazine for UTV, and Alan fixed his eye on him. "So …"

"Who's Luke?" Wendy asked.

Shit!

He had been expecting the question to come from one or the other of them, and had been preparing the best answer for whoever asked. By splitting it up between them they had somehow created a pincer movement that cut straight through his defences.

"He's, uh, a fella."

"Aye, I'd worked that out." Now Wendy and Alan were both sitting up a little more alertly, a rare moment of unity and agreement, both of them aware something was up. Neither of them knew what it was, but they could both recognise when Will was squirming about something.

"He's not that Luke Harris that was at Sunday School?" Ma suddenly asked.

Shit again. Why didn't I think of Luke Harris?

For half a second he thought of saying that yes, Luke was Luke Harris from Sunday School, who he hadn't seen since he was six years old when the family moved back to Scotland.

But that would just open the door to more questions. Are they back then, how's he doing, should we invite him round …

"No, Ma, he's not Luke Harris."

I think. I mean, I don't even know his surname. Conor was one up on him, in that regard.

"So who …" Wendy started.

"He's just a fella!" Will exclaimed, far louder than he intended, and he saw the surprise and hurt on her face. "Sorry, sorry, sorry …" He felt for her hand and squeezed it, while the lie formed in his head out of different ideas and concepts that whirled together in half a second into a concrete whole that came tripping out of his mouth.

It came more easily if he pretended he was talking to Alan, even though he was looking at Wendy. He had developed this skill with his brother, after all, and never once felt guilty about it.

"He is a total eejit," he explained. "Total, total … I mean, all he talks about is cars."

"Cars," Wendy said without expression, and sounding far too like Sybil Fawlty when she was listening to Basil's latest bullshit explanation. He took the hint. A whole long explanation was backing up inside his mouth, but he reeled it quickly in and went straight to the end.

"I worked on his car and we got chatting … and Mr Mitchell says we should always be polite to the customers, whatever we think of them … so I agreed with him a lot and now he thinks I'm really into cars too."

"You *are* really into cars," Alan pointed out.

"Oh, aye, I know my way around a car but I'm not a car freak! You know, big, imported American convertible jobs …" He bit his tongue. The lie was getting too specific.

Alan just pursed his lips and rolled his eyes. Wendy smiled slightly.

"And this car freak calls you at home because …?"

"Oh, he wants to meet up. I said we'd do it this Saturday. You know, get it over with."

"You looked pleased to hear it was him, though? You got up quickly enough."

A pause.

"Aye, well, like I say, I wanted to get it over with."

"So if you didn't want him to call … why on earth did you give him your phone number?"

Will shut his eyes, drew in a breath.

"Because," he said heavily, *and please make me stop lying to you.*

She searched his face, but then smiled, and nodded.

"Saturday, then." She snuggled back close and his arm went automatically back around her. "I'll think of you when I'm serving prescriptions in Boots."

"Oh, aye."

"And you can tell me all about him on Saturday night."

Chapter 10: Black Mountain

Saturday 26th July

Will's ears popped as the bus trundled its way out of the city and up Black Mountain.

Most Belfast dwellers could simply tune out the Belfast Hills, the thousand-foot-high, ten mile long ridge of ground that loomed over the city from the west. It was always there and you only had to lift your eyes slightly to see it, so most people didn't.

Will knew he probably had been up here before, but he couldn't remember when, and he had forgotten it was quite so high. He could feel himself tilted back in his seat, and the bus engine was labouring. Revs dropped as the driver downshifted for a second time and the bus lurched forward again.

The buildings of Belfast had fallen away a long time ago and the road was lined with scrubby gorse and stiff grass, dull dark greens and browns in every direction – all that would grow up here in the elements that came in straight off the sea, outside the protection of the lower ground. Will's city-dwelling mind immediately reacted against it. He liked streets and corners and road signs. How else could you find your way around a place?

Though it would be very difficult to get lost on a sloping stretch of moorland with a single road cutting through it.

Conor had said there was only one bus stop, which you could see from miles around, and he would be waiting there.

The bus began to drive a bit more easily, the engine purring more happily as it pulled itself off the top of the slope and on to the level ground which as far as Will knew ran all the way down to Donegal. Off in one direction, the ground flowed smoothly for a couple of miles before rising suddenly up into the summit of Divis, fenced off and with massive antennae and aerials sprouting high up into the air, property of the British army. And yes, there by the side of the road was a bus stop, and a figure waiting by it, arms folded, leaning against the pole and watching the bus draw up.

Will, not to his surprise, was the only one to get off. Conor slowly unfolded himself from the pole and they waited in silence for the doors to hiss shut and the bus to pull away again. For the first time, in daylight, Will could properly take in the boy who had inhabited his thoughts for what seemed like forever.

Conor was in grey cotton trackies that made him look like a professional athlete. It wasn't just that he wore them, he *inhabited* them, like an extension of his skin, moving as naturally in them as Alan in his UDR uniform. Will remembered the broad shoulders but he hadn't realised Conor's form was so compact – not an inch wasted in achieving the act of being Conor. Will remembered the strength and the warmth bursting through when he supported him.

He remembered Conor's hair as brown and wavy, but that had been in the dark. He hadn't quite realised the chestnut sheen of it, the rich, thick texture which he suddenly knew would be fascinating to feel, to run his hands through. Though at the moment the sweatband around his head would spoil that.

Conor jutted his chin forward, a kind of upward nod in greeting. His oval face was forever tilted slightly back, like its owner was on the verge of an argument, but there was humour and intelligence in the eyes that were dancing over Will, appraising him in turn.

"You made it, then."

"Aye."

A racing bike was chained to the pole. Bikes weren't really Will's thing and he couldn't make a guess as to its age and value, but he knew enough to recognise a machine that might be old and scuffed, but was well loved and cared for by its owner.

"Didja cycle up here on that?" he asked, remembering the slope that had challenged the bus.

"Aye. Well, I'm used to it. I come up here a lot." Conor bent down to check the chain with a tug of his fingers, then swung a small rucksack from the rack onto his back. Now that was he was seeing Conor clearly and fully restored to health, Will saw that the other boy rolled his shoulders whenever he moved, and kept his arms braced and fists clenched, like he was forever on the edge of a bruising. That, and the way he kept his face angled, seemed to say he was forever angry about something – in fact seriously, seriously pissed off – and didn't even realise it.

Conor looked at him thoughtfully, up and down, the way Will would size up a fine girl from a distance. His heart started to pound …

Until he realised it wasn't his body that Conor was admiring in – it was what the body was wrapped in. Conor's smile was one degree short of derision.

"The fuck's that?"

Will plucked at the cheap blue nylon of his school tracksuit.

"You said bring running gear," he said defensively.

"Aye, I did."

"It's my school sports kit." He hadn't played sport recently enough to have anything more modern.

Conor smiled more widely. He really seemed to find it funny, and apparently expected Will to feel the same.

"Oh, aye. Well, it'll do." He bounced up and down on his toes a couple of times. "Let's see what you can do in it." Somehow, on the last bounce, he rotated one hundred and eighty degrees in mid-air, and was off jogging down a narrow path through the heather the moment his feet touched the ground.

Will stared after him for a moment. Okay, the request for running gear should maybe have alerted him …

They really were running?

Apparently so. And since the choice was go after him, or wait here for the next bus going the other way, he set off after Conor.

Somehow, he couldn't catch Conor up, though he tried. Will was not unfit. He could sprint and weave and dodge with a rugby ball in his hand, but somehow just heading in a straight line was too difficult for his legs. However much strength he tried to use, however hard he lifted them up and kicked his feet down, he couldn't catch up with the boy ahead of him, who seemed to be borne on his way by the heather beneath his feet. Will could feel his lungs start to burn, a stitch start to form in his side, while Conor just kept floating ahead.

"How you doing?"

Conor had suddenly switched around again without slowing down. He was jogging *backwards*.

"I'm fine," Will said grimly. He couldn't catch up, but he wasn't falling behind either. Conor winked.

"Soon there. Another five minutes."

He danced around to face the other way and then was flying along the path again.

By the time Will caught up with him, Conor was sitting on a boulder, his legs out in front of him, fishing a tartan Woolworths thermos and a pair of cups out of his bag. He shifted up so that Will could plonk down next to him, and passed him a cup.

"I wasn't wrong, then. You looked like someone who worked out."

Will nodded and mimed lifting a bar with his hands as he swallowed the tea. Conor had made it strong and sweet, just like it should be.

"Weights. I played rugby at school until I had to give up …" He saw Conor cock his head, and answered the inevitable next question with a roll of his eyes. "I hurt my back in a pile-up, I was flat in bed for weeks and the doctors said, well, I'd better not play again if I enjoy not being on crutches for the rest of my life."

"Shit, that must hurt." He saw honest sympathy, not pity, in Conor's eyes. Conor raised his cup in a mock salute. "Well, it's good to meet you properly, Will Johnston."

Will returned the gesture.

"And you, Conor …?" he let the pause turn expectant, and Conor seemed genuinely surprised at the gap in Will's knowledge.

"Oh! McGarry."

"Conor McGarry." They studied each other as if they were each seeing the other boy for the first time, and then they looked away and sipped their tea.

The streets and sprawl of Belfast was spread out below them on the flat ground of the valley, all the way to the lough that was steel grey in the distance. The giant cranes of the Harland and Wolff shipyard, Samson and Goliath, were like a pair of yellow Lego pieces.

"I can see your house," Will said suddenly. Conor's head whipped around.

"You know where I live?"

Will smiled.

"No. Well, you said Cavendish Street, but apart from that." He studied the urban sprawl below them. "But if I knew where it was, I could see it, and you could see mine."

"Aye, you're not wrong," Conor agreed, after a moment. "If we'd both thought to fly a great big flag outside our front doors, we could probably pick them out." He looked sideways at Will. "I did look Agnes Street up. It's less than a mile away from us."

Back down there, in the city, you could be just either side of the interface and still a million miles apart, to all intents and purposes. You never even stopped to think about how close something was as the crow flies. But up here, nothing but air between them, for the first time ever it made Will think. He held his thumb and forefinger slightly apart, and studied Belfast through the gap.

"Probably about that far, with the wall in between."

Conor nodded silently. He put down his cup, drew himself up, spread one hand out over his heart and held the other out towards the city.

"Two households!" he declaimed. "Both alike in fuckwittery, in fair Belfast where we lay our scene, from ancient grudge break to new mutiny where civil blood makes civil hands unclean."

Will cocked his head.

"Is that a song?"

Conor stared.

"That's Shakespeare! William fucking Shakespeare! You should know that. Good Protestant writer, so he was."

"Like Seán O'Casey." It was the first name that came to Will's mind. He hadn't even heard of Seán O'Casey until the man's name had recently popped up in some radio programme that he and Alan had heard, along with a titbit of information that had made Alan burst out laughing and exclaim, "*Seán O'Casey was a fecking Protestant!*"

Conor scanned Will's face for the slightest hint of a wind-up. Then he snorted and turned away.

"Fuck off Seán O'Casey was a Protestant."

"He was," Will insisted. "He was Church of Ireland. You know, a pisky-palian."

Conor slowly turned his face back to him, eyes going wide as he recognised Will's sincerity.

"Seán O'Casey was a Protestant? Jesus." He shook his head and sipped his tea. "Keep that under your belt. You could restart the Civil War."

Will smiled and tried his own tea again.

"Did William Shakespeare really say 'fuckwittery'?"

"Oh, aye. Terrible foul mouthed, so he was."

After that, they lapsed into silence. Will finally hit on something to break it with.

"You said you come up here a lot?"

"Aye, to train. It's all I'm allowed to do at the moment for a while, until the doctor says." He tapped the side of his head, where the stone had hit him.

"So …" Will took in the grey trackies with a new understanding. "You're a proper athlete?"

"Sure I'm a …" Again, Conor seemed surprised that Will didn't know something. He chuckled. "Sorry. I just feel like …"

A pause, and Will's heart began to pound.

"Like we already know so much about each other?" he risked saying. *Even though we hardly know each other at all.*

"Aye," Conor said quietly. More loudly: "Anyway. I'm a boxer."

"Oh, aye? Like Barry McGuigan?"

It was the right thing to say. Conor flashed him an approving thumbs-up.

"Barry McGuigan! He's yer man. Mind you, he could do with a few more bacon sandwiches. There's nothing on him."

"He's a …" Will tried to remember. "Featherweight?"

"Aye."

"And you're not?"

Conor snorted.

"Do I look like a fucking featherweight? No, I'm a middleweight." He drummed his fists on a taut stomach. "Eleven stone exactly, not a pound over."

"How did you get into boxing?"

Conor pulled a face.

"What else is there to do?"

From anyone else it could have just sounded like a casual remark, and Will almost took it at that. Until he thought: Catholic boy from the Falls Road area …

Conor was right. What else was there to do?

Another couple of pieces of information fell into place in Will's head.

"McGarry … Are you anything to do with that gym?"

Conor nodded cheerfully and pulled the sides of his trackie top open. Underneath he was wearing a t-shirt with the word 'McGarry's' in a curly handwriting style.

"Me da owns the place." He let the top drop and pulled out a packet of fags, holding it over for Will to take one. "You've heard of it?"

"My girlfriend said we should maybe get membership. Something to do together."

Conor was just about to flick his lighter. He paused and cocked his head.

"You've got a girlfriend?"

"Uh-huh."

There was a distinct further pause, before Conor flicked the flame into being so Will could light up.

"So, you get sex whenever you like but you still kiss guys?"

Even though neither of them had moved over the last few minutes, Will had been feeling the distance between them shrinking down to a hairline gap. Suddenly it sprang wide open again. So, now they were finally coming to it. The reason they had wanted to meet. And Conor had opened with a question Will wasn't comfortable answering.

He didn't need to. His reaction was answer enough.

"Ah." Conor grinned and drew on the fag. "No sex."

Will felt his face burning.

"We're just … waiting for the moment."

"Ah. The moment."

He seemed to be enjoying this far too much.

"So what about you?" Will asked hotly. "Mr Experience?"

Conor gazed into the distance and puffed out his cheeks. Then he glanced sideways at Will, and with a shy smile held up three fingers.

"But only two girls. Marie McCarthy wanted a second helping, but to be honest the first course wasn't that great."

Will was struck by a sudden, absurd jealousy of Marie McCarthy, and whoever the other was. To cover it up he quoted a bit of his brother's wisdom.

"You don't look at the mantelpiece when you're stoking the fire."

"Very true. So. One of us does it with girls, one of us just …" Another sideways glance, and a smile. "Chokes the bishop a lot, I guess. And kisses guys."

"What, and you don't?" Conor's eyebrows went up. "Choke the bishop, I mean." Conor ceded the point with a duck of his head. "Anyway, I just went with the moment."

"So … the moment to kiss another guy came before the moment to shag your girl?"

"I … Oh … Feck off."

They smoked silently. Will's face was still burning and he couldn't say why. He had known – hoped – when he came up here that they would get round to this.

"Of course," Conor said suddenly, "it was easier with Marie because at least we were in her bed without any clothes on, which kind of makes it easier to get it up. Siobhan was a knee trembler against a wall, and that's not a lot of fun. Word of advice – when you and your girl finally find the moment, try to find a bed too."

"Thank you," Will said with heavy courtesy. "We will."

"But here's my one true love." Conor pulled a wallet from a pocket on his rucksack. "My heart is currently owned by this particular young lady, lock, stock and barrel."

To Will's horror, he began to take out a Polaroid photo.

Will studied the small square slip with loathing as it approached. Conor was going to show him his girlfriend and he was going to have to pretend to like her. But he didn't want to offend the other boy, so he mentally began to prepare a selection of neutral responses.

Then he saw the picture and his heart suddenly melted. "Naw!"

From the depths of a frilly bonnet and a high sided pram, a little baby girl beamed out at him.

"Katie." Conor smiled fondly at the photo, before tucking it back in. "My sister Claire's little girl, thirteen months next week. I'm her uncle and godfather. 'Scuse me, I need to go and have a piss."

He pushed himself up from the rock and Will looked around for any kind of cover. There was none. Conor simply walked a few paces away and stood with his back to Will, unzipping. Will looked away until the sound had finished. When he looked around, Conor was coming back, zipping up again.

"That was private," Will remarked.

"Heh." Conor held out his arms and slowly turned around, like Julie Andrews about to burst into song. "Who's going to see? Apart from those fuckers." He nodded towards the army base on Divis. For a moment he looked thoughtful as he took his place on the boulder again, trying to decide whether to say something. "Okay," he remarked, "our earlier topic of debate, and to show you how private it is up here … One time, I was up here alone and I realised I was just *so* alone, no one for miles around … So I just lay back and unzipped and …" A note of awe crept into his voice. "I had the – best – stress reliever – *ever*. I mean, *ever*. At the end …" He shook his head. "I could have brought down a low flying aircraft, so I could." Will's shoulders began to shake with silent laughter. "Some of it must have come down in Andytown, so it did."

Will laughed louder.

"Here is the weather forecast. Scattered showers moving in from the west."

Conor threw his head back and laughed out loud for the first time.

"That's a good one, so it is. Okay, so now you know a bit more about me." He held his head to one side as he studied Will. "So. What else can we tell each other?"

There were only inches between them, Will realised, and their faces were on the same level. He just had to lean forward and he could kiss Conor again before Conor even realised what was happening.

Suddenly that was what Will wanted to do more than anything else.

He couldn't think of a better way of ruining everything they were trying to achieve.

A blood vessel beat in Conor's neck, a tiny regular twitch in the skin just above his collarbone. Will looked away, pretending to think.

"I guess you went to a Catholic school?"

Conor held up both hands.

"Jesus, May and Joseph, the boy's a genius."

He was smiling, so Will did too.

"Did you leave after O-levels?"

Conor's face went blank.

"What's an O-level?"

He left it just long enough for panicked uncertainty to grow in Will's mind. Was that a joke, or …? Then he burst out laughing.

"Aye, I left after O-levels. You?"

"Aye, me too. I went straight into an apprenticeship at the garage."

"Huh. No chance of me becoming a mechanic when my best subject was Literature …" Conor snorted. "English Literature, of course, because sure why would they ever teach Irish Literature?"

"Is there any Irish literature?" Will asked deadpan, and Conor spun on him, eyes blazing.

"Of course there's fucking Irish literature! W.B. Yeats, James Joyce, George Bernard Shaw, Eugene O'Neill …"

Will grinned.

"Seán O'Casey …"

"Seán O'fucking Casey! Of course there's …" He trailed off as Will's grin grew wider. "That was a fucking wind-up, wasn't it?"

Will just nodded.

"You fucker." Conor looked like a thought had suddenly hit him. "You're a mechanic … Here's a question for you. Me Da drives an Anglia. It runs okay but it sounds like someone's letting off a fucking gun as it goes – which isn't the best look in our neighbourhood. What's that about?"

"A gun?" Will immediately ran a dozen mechanical scenarios through his head. "Like … *bang-bang-bang-bang*, all the time?"

"Well, not really. More like … you know when it runs properly, it's like *brr-brr-brr-brr-brr-brr* … But now it's *brr-brr-brr-BANG-brr-brr-brr-BANG* … But faster than that, and it gets faster if you rev up."

"One of the cylinders is bust," Will said straight away. "I'm guessing it's got a burnt exhaust valve. If you brought it in, I could do a compression test to tell you which one. It'll need replacing."

"Shit. More money."

If your Da brings it in, I'll do it for the cost of the parts.

The words were on the tip of his tongue, but Will bit them back. He had a sneaking sense that Conor would resent being a charity case – and he could never swing it with Mr Mitchell anyway. The garage boss was pretty liberal when it came to doing favours for friends, and he let his staff do the same. Do it at mate's rates, or sometimes even at cost – but he liked to know why.

And also …

Conor hadn't heard any of his thoughts but he put his finger on the problem.

"Does your garage serve …" He coughed, and spoke more formally, like a BBC news reader. "'Both sides of the community'?"

"Oh, aye. But they'll fleece you with a nice, itemised bill you can't argue with."

"Guessed so."

An idea struck.

"D'ye have that wee book of yours?"

Conor looked surprised, but he delved into his rucksack and produced the little diary. Will turned to a blank page at the back, thought, then wrote quickly for half a minute and handed it back.

"I've put down what needs doing, and the parts you'll need, and the cost. Take your car to a good Catholic garage …"

"Personally blessed by the Holy Mary," Conor agreed solemnly.

"… and tell them these are Protestant prices, and they can do better. Don't let them charge you a penny more."

"Oh, aye." Conor smiled as he tucked the book away. "That's nifty. Thanks, much appreciated. What got you so into cars, anyway?"

Will shrugged.

"What got you into boxing? I've always been interested. And then …" He paused. He rarely talked about this with anyone, even Protestant friends, but there seemed to be a general amnesty on holding things back. "When I was fifteen …" *Friday the twenty-first of October, 1977.* "… My da was killed in a car crash."

Conor pulled a face.

"Shit. I'm sorry."

"So I guess I just like to make sure cars work properly." He smiled slightly. "The other driver was Catholic."

Conor scowled.

"Sure you don't blame us for that?"

"No." Will shook his head gently. "Anyway, all the witnesses said it was his fault, even the Protestant ones, and one of them was from his Lodge." He paused a beat, thinking of Alan. "But I know someone who does blame you, anyway."

"Well, that's a shame, but tell this someone that the rain falls on the just and the unjust alike."

"Is that Shakespeare again?"

"Jesus." Conor looked away.

"Okay, I was only asking!"

There was sad patience in Conor's eyes as he turned his head back.

"No, it was Jesus who said that, in the Bible ..." He paused, head cocked as Will grinned from ear to ear. "You're fucking winding me up again, aren't you?"

They had to head back. This time they walked, enjoying the day, the view, the weather – and each other's company. At least, Will knew he was enjoying Conor's. Was Conor enjoying his?

Well, if he wasn't then all he had to do was run and leave Will behind again. He seemed happy to stroll side by side. Anyone who saw them from a distance would assume they were two old friends. There was no contact, no physical touching, apart from once when the backs of their hands brushed. After that the boys ambled along with their hands in their pockets. Which didn't stop their elbows sometimes touching instead. Cloth against cloth, a fleeting contact sending a thrill down Will's arm.

Talk and secrets flowed naturally and easily, more than they ever did when they were with people from their own side.

They were both the youngest child of their parents. Conor was at the tail end of a series of six babies, the two in the middle miscarried, and the only boy. ("So when Ma and Da finally got the son they wanted all along, they stopped making them ...") Will learned the names of the three surviving sisters, and their husbands, and Conor's nieces and nephews. Conor learned about Alan, and Wendy, and her intention to become a teacher, and Will's fears that it could be a career choice that just pulled them apart. Conor offered no opinion, but started to hum a tune which Will recognised from the radio, Joy Division's 'Love will tear us apart', at which point he elbowed Conor to make him stop.

They shifted on to happier stuff. The first girls they had fancied, the first cigarettes, the first time they went on the drink. They were both proud of Ireland's sporting stars – Mark Lawrenson, George Best (they both had his poster up in their rooms), Sean Kelly – and of course Barry McGuigan. In the current top ten there was not a single song that either of them enjoyed, though they both agreed that if Kate Bush ever showed up on their doorstep, they would. Feargal Sharkey sang like a girl, but the Boomtown Rats, now …

They accompanied each other tunelessly belting out the chorus to "I don't like Mondays" across the hillside; it sort of fizzled as they both had to accept they didn't really know the words of the next verse.

Neither of them had a high opinion of Margaret Thatcher, who they both agreed was clueless about real life in the Province, and even Will didn't think much more of the Reverend Ian Paisley.

"The people of Ulster," Will intoned, "WILL NEVER SURRENDER!"

Conor shuddered.

"Jesus, you sound more like him than he does."

By the time they were back at the bus stop, Will had yet to find a single good reason why they couldn't be friends.

Apart from the obvious, which was *so* obvious neither of them was going to waste time and say it.

Conor checked his watch.

"Yer bus'll be along in a moment." He crouched down to tackle the combination lock on his bike chain. "One, six, five." He looked up. "My birthday, the sixteenth of May. One more thing for you to know."

Will smiled. "I don't know how old you are, though."

Conor straightened up as he coiled the chain.

"I'm eighteen."

"Born in 1962?"

"Aye, it was a deadly year."

"You're two months older than me, then."

Conor smiled as he wheeled the bike across the road to the eastbound stop. Will ambled along with him, hands in pockets

"I Sure I'm the older, wiser one, but I think we both knew that."

They stood, looking at each other. All Conor had to do was swing his leg over his saddle and he would be away.

"Well."

"Well."

Conor bit his lip and gazed into the distance. His mouth began to shape a sound. "Wh …"

Will went suddenly tense. He was about to hear Conor say his name.

"Wh … hy, exactly, did you kiss me?"

Will choked out a laugh. Then he flung his hands up into the air and gave the only honest answer he could.

"Honest to God, I don't know. I wish I hadn't."

"Aye. Me too."

"Because …" Will felt his heart begin to pound again, but they were being honest. "I haven't stopped thinking of you since."

Conor didn't smile, or laugh. His face was … blank? No, Will thought, not blank. This was Conor at his most honest, sheltering from nothing.

"I haven't stopped thinking of you either," he said quietly. Then suddenly the Conor that Will had got to know was back. "But that's all behind us now, isn't it? Still, it's a habit you want to keep an eye on. Could get you into trouble."

"I will," Will promised, and they were back to looking at each other again.

"Here's your ride." Will turned round. The bus was half a mile away. "Nice to have met you, Will Johnston."

"Nice to have met you, Conor McGarry."

Conor smiled, and nodded, and swung himself onto his bike.

"When can I see you again?" Will blurted.

Conor stopped moving. His feet went down to the ground and his head slumped. Then he slowly looked up.

"Ah, life would have been so much easier if you'd just shut up there."

Will held his accusing gaze.

"No, it wouldn't."

Conor sighed and swung his rucksack around, neither agreeing or disagreeing. The little book made its appearance again. Unsmiling, Conor tore out a page and passed it over.

There were two phone numbers on it. Will frowned, not understanding.

"Call the top one," Conor said, expressionless. "That's my home number. Let it ring twice, then hang up. Ten minutes later, call the other. That's a phone box, where I called you from last time." His pressed lips relented, a little. "If I'm at home, I'll hear you call, and I'll head out and take the second call. So. You want us to do this again, your turn to think of something. Surprise me."

"I will ... Hey." Will held the paper up. "You already had this written out. You'd already thought of it ..."

"Ah, well." Conor let slip the slightest glimmer of a smile. "Plan for the worst and you're never disappointed." And suddenly he was facing the other way and heading off down the hill as fast as gravity could pull him. "Surprise me!" he called again over his shoulder, and if he said anything else then

Will couldn't hear it over the sound of the bus pulling up behind him.

Chapter 11: Bad Pie

<u>Tuesday 29th July</u>

A rat was gnawing through his intestines and Will pushed his face into his pillow, trying not to howl. He squeezed himself into as tight a ball as he could, knees up against his chest to crush the life out of the wee beast. A faint smell of sick still hung in the air from the first time he had thrown up but he was past caring.

"Here you are, my sweetheart." His mother cleared stuff off his bedside table to make room for a washing up bowl and a jug of water. She stroked his damp hair, and risked a quick kiss on his cheek. "It's probably all out now but …"

"Thanks, Ma," he murmured.

The pains had struck round about two in the morning. He had hurried to the bathroom and just had time to pull his shorts down before squirting the foulest smelling shit ever into the bowl. The smell would have been enough to make him throw if he hadn't already wanted to. He had flushed, and lingered by the bowl until he was almost sure he wasn't going to be sick.

So he had gone back to his room, just in time to hurl all over the bed clothes.

His mother had stripped and remade the bed and he had fallen back into it, not daring to sleep again, for the next six hours. He couldn't help noticing that with one of her grown-up sons as helpless as a little child again, she suddenly seemed a lot more recovered and back to normal.

"I've phoned Mr Mitchell for you and said you're poorly." Will groaned again, this time with the humiliation. "Alan's just off to work and I'll be out shortly, so you'll be on your own …" She looked worriedly down at him. "I could stay …"

"I'll be fine, Ma," he insisted weakly.

"Well, if you're sure …."

Another kiss, and she was gone.

But Will was not alone. He opened one eye. Alan was leaning against the door jamb, arms crossed and smirking with a malice that was entirely at odds with his austere work suit and white shirt and tie, the epitome of the smart book clerk.

"Not the first time you've got nasty sticky stuff all over your blankets."

"Feck off."

"Shall I leave you some hankies too?"

"Feck. Off."

"You wouldn't have to do that so much if you'd just –..."

"*Feck ...*" Will groaned again, and gritted his teeth as another pang fired itself off through his bowels. *"... Off."*

"I mean, just do her or dump her. I don't know why you arse around like this."

The story about meeting a car freak on Saturday had not really borne up under questioning as to why he had had to wear a tracksuit for the occasion. So, he had admitted that the car freak story was not entirely true – and in fact he had gone training with Luke because he was thinking of rejoining the rugby team.

This had immediately earned derision from Alan, and united both of the women in his life, who were unanimous that he should think of no such thing, remember what happened when you put your back out, you were on your back for a month and the doctor said never again.

So he had sincerely promised never again to meet someone called Luke for rugby training.

But Wendy was still angry with him, which of course Alan had noted.

"You know what? You're right," Will mumbled into his pillow. "Call her and tell her to come round and I'll shag her in between throwing up."

Alan's smirk just grew wider, but he at least went away.

After a while, Will heard the front door shut. The house was made in such a way that for some reason even closing the door quietly sent a shock throughout the building. It was impossible to come and go without people knowing.

A few minutes later, it happened again, and he was alone in the house. He closed his eyes and tried to sleep while his body did its stuff, slowly pushing the remains of that bad meat pie out of him by whichever turned out to be the handiest exit.

He dozed for a while, on and off, every now and then jerking suddenly awake at some noise. A car outside, the pipes in the house next door, the rafters creaking in the attic as they readjusted themselves under a warm roof. All familiar sounds, but also different. The echo, the vibration was altered. Somehow you could tell you were in an empty house.

Will smiled weakly into the pillow. Empty house. That had always been how he assumed it would start, the day he and Wendy finally did it. Now all he needed was Wendy, and a stomach that wasn't trying to crawl out of his body.

Well, it would have to be *someone's* empty house, wouldn't it? However much they wanted it, neither of them was going to cough for a hotel room. And Conor had advised him to do it in a bed, and he was the one with the experience, and Will always believed in listening to the voice of experience.

Conor …

Will smiled again, and at the same time groaned. That was funny. Apparently it took a bad dose from a dodgy pie to get Conor out of his mind. He hadn't thought of his Fenian friend all day.

But now …

Conor was back in his head.

Where was Conor now? Will didn't really know what he did with his days, apart from train and help out at the gym, and he wouldn't be training because he was off boxing until the doctor said, because of …

Moving swiftly on. Not training yet. But Will suddenly realised he would really like to see Conor box.

He had Conor's two numbers in his wallet. If Conor was at home, he could call now. Conor could be round in minutes …

Except that he wouldn't. He would still have to get across the interface, and in daylight, and Will had to admit that right now he wouldn't be the best company.

Shame. Waste of an empty house.

Then it stuck him so suddenly that he gasped out loud. Empty house … Now, why hadn't he thought of that before? It was perfect–…

Except that suddenly he knew he needed to be in the bathroom again, about thirty seconds ago. He hurdled from his bed and fled the short distance down the little landing. His shorts were down before he was even through the door and, thank you God, his arse was just about pointing in the right direction over the bowl before he released a few more gallons of stinking slurry.

But, once it was all over and he was slouching back to bed and had tumbled back onto the mattress – and hey, he really did feel a bit better, maybe that had been the last of the pie – he knew what he was going to do.

Will lay on his back and felt a warm glow in his stomach. Which was of course the absence of poison, and nothing at all to do with excitement at the thought of seeing Conor again.

* * *

Conor came out into the yard backwards, his hands full of a stack of musty cardboard boxes. He tipped them onto the pile that he and his Da had built up and dusted his hands.

"And that's the rest of the crap. Just the heavy stuff to go now."

Da grunted with satisfaction.

"They'll be here soon."

The extension was a single storey construction of breeze block and plasterboard, built onto the original back exit to the old warehouse. Four small rooms including a toilet, two on either side of a short passageway that led to the door into the gym. Metal window frames and walls painted a dingy, neutral colour that went with the carpet. It was pretty clearly a property that had never been loved. It had been put up in the last dying days of the linen business and used as offices, but Michael McGarry had no use for it as the gym only really needed one office, and that was a room in in the main building.

But it was dry and weathertight, and there was no reason it couldn't be made to shine.

Conor and Da went back inside just as the inner door opened and Cormac stepped in, holding the door open so that Claire could push Katie's buggy after him. The little girl looked around with wide eyes but then they settled on two familiar faces, her grandda and her favourite uncle, and she gurgled with delight, holding out her arms and kicking her legs.

"Ga-da! Nuhnuh!"

"Bang on, me oul' flower, the one and only!" Conor unbuckled her and lifted her up to bounce her on his hip, while he listened to what his father had to say and she tried to push a curl of his hair into his ear.

"So – what's this about, Da?" Claire asked, cheerfully but maybe just a little suspicious. It was meant to be Cormac's day off and they always tried to get out of her parents' hair on those days; to find a little time for themselves, to make up for the fact that home for them was still the back room of the house where Claire had grown up.

"Well, then." Da rubbed his hands together. "You'll see that your brother and I have just been clearing this old place out. You know that Lafferty used to store his junk here?"

"Aye," Cormac agreed. "Nice little earner for you."

"And did you know Lafferty has decided to take his custom elsewhere?'

"Ah, shit!"

Conor drew in a sharp breath and turned to Katie in mock outrage.

"Did you hear the rude word your Da used?"

"He's moving the rest of his stuff out this weekend," Da went on. "So, what will we have then? Four empty rooms." He gestured at each door in turn. "There's plumbing for the toilet, so we can easily a bath in there too, and get the pipes extended into the next room, and there's already a water boiler, so we can put in a small kitchenette with a sink, and we could probably swing a telly too. And the wiring will handle a fridge and maybe even an electric cooker. And that leaves two rooms next to each other this side …

He stepped into the nearest room, where a row of dented grey filing cabinets stood against one wall.

"… That could easily be two bedrooms. In short, a wee flat for a young couple I know who could really do with a home of their own."

Claire and Cormac looked stunned.

"Michael … really?" A smile spread of pure joy spread over Cormac's face. "*Really?*"

Claire seemed a bit more canny.

"And of course, Da, it'll be good for you to have someone living on site, right?"

"I won't deny there are benefits from an insurance point of view," Da agreed solemnly. "Not to mention getting our back room back. And you would be paying a wee bit of rent."

"And …" She frowned. "Isn't the back door a fire exit? So there'll be people traipsing through …"

"Only if there's a fire. We can fix it so it can be opened by anyone this side but has to be unlocked by anyone coming in from the outside. For the door through to the gym, we'll stick a big sign on it saying 'Private, no admittance' and while the gym's open you know there'll always be someone on duty to look after it, and you'll only need to lock up after business. Does that work for you?"

Claire put her hands on her hips and surveyed the room.

"The paint could do with some work," she observed.

"*Claire!*" Cormac protested. "Seriously, Michael, thank you …"

"Well, it does …"

"Already taken care of!" Michael laughed. "We have our decorator standing by. An eejit who was stupid enough to get his brains bashed in and who needs to keep occupied until he can fight again."

All eyes turned to Conor, who gave them a friendly wave with his free hand.

"Just tell me what colours you fancy. Once Lafferty clears out, I'll get onto it."

Cormac opened his mouth. Claire cut across him.

"Nothing too fancy … White will do."

"And I'll help out when I can, of course," Cormac added.

"Sure white's fine for the main rooms," Conor agreed, "but this little girl here deserves a nursery of her own. What do you think, sweetheart?" He jiggled the baby up and down, and waved his hand expansively. "This is going to be your very own room. We can paint it with pink and blue and green … lots of beautiful colours for a beautiful princess."

Katie jabbed a stubby finger at something only she could see on the nearest wall. Conor followed with his eyes.

"Exactly what I was thinking," he agreed. "We'll put something special there. A, what d'you call it, mural. A rainbow or a teddy bear or something that will keep you quiet while your Ma and Da get busy making you a brother or sister in the next room."

"Conor!" But Claire smiled and rested her head on Cormac's shoulder as he slipped an arm around her waist. "Are you sure it won't be too much for you on your own?"

He shrugged.

"I'll do as much as I can and if we have to get the family in then that's how it goes. But for now, what else have I got to do?"

Chapter 12: Escaping The City

Saturday 2nd August

This time it had been Conor on the bus, clutching his backpack on his lap like it was a lifebelt on a small boat rocking in a rough sea, and wondering just what the hell he was getting into.

A fresh, salty breeze blew into his face as the doors folded open and he stepped down onto the pavement. The bus pulled away with a hiss of hydraulics and a gust of diesel fumes, and he was committed. At least, until the next bus back to Belfast.

He slung his backpack onto his shoulders and stepped smartly across the road to the grassy bank. Beyond that the golden sands of the beach came into view, heaving with bodies on this warm Saturday afternoon. And beyond them, the sea. Conor had no choice. He stood and admired it, grinning like an eejit.

Somehow the air and the light did something to him inside that just made it good to be there – relaxed, free from care and worry. Clean salt air blew in his face as he took in the scene, dispelling the last of the diesel. Laughing, shouting kids; grown-ups trying to find enough shelter behind windbreaks to manage a picnic; kite flyers; ball game players; mums and dads pressed into sand castle building duty; a few hardy souls venturing out into the waves that were rolling in straight from the Hebrides.

Sure he had been to the seaside as a kid, but visits were few and far between and the last had been years ago. He made a mental note that whatever happened, they were definitely going to walk on the beach – maybe even dip into the sea with their trousers rolled up.

But if *they* were going to do anything at all, first he had to find Will.

The system Conor had set up – and he allowed himself a pat on the back for his brilliance – had worked just fine. Will had rung the home number twice, then called the phone box ten minutes later. Will had given him all the directions he needed to get this far – bus to Coleraine, connecting bus to Downhill on the coast – and now he was on the last stretch. Conor turned and set off down the road, fishing and unfolding the bit of paper from his pocket. He studied it, stopped and turned around to retrace his steps.

"Turn *left* from the bus stop …" he muttered.

The house wasn't hard to find. There weren't many to choose from – just a single line of them on the side of the road opposite the beach, with the high ground rising up immediately up behind, straight out of their back gardens. Unlike Cavendish Street, where the houses were terraced and every one looked the same, every house here was different and stood in its own small grounds, usually behind a lawn of scrubby, sea-breeze-hardened grass. Most of them were bungalows, all different shapes and sizes. The one he was after was the least sized of the lot.

He studied the house from the road. It could have been based on a kid's drawing, plain and simple with a window on either side of the front door. He could imagine a squiggle of smoke growing out of the chimney and a family of stick people poised in front of it. It was painted white, like its neighbours, but unlike them it looked …

Conor, the son of his mother, who kept her house like a pin, could find no other word for it. It looked *tatty*. The walls were off-white through age rather than aesthetic choice. A couple of the roof tiles hung loose. The paint on the window frames was peeling, and there was a hole in one of the panes, patched up by one side of a cardboard box taped over it from inside. No one *here* got down on their knees every morning to scrub the doorstep to within an inch of its life.

The corner of his mouth curled in a sardonic smile.

If you're going to occupy and oppress half the population, least you could do is live better than us …

The number on the door was the one he was after, though.

Conor put his head to one side and asked himself one last time: was this what he wanted to do?

But he knew the answer already.

He had got onto the right bus, after double checking the number and destination on the front. He had almost got off again when had casually asked the driver how long the trip was, and the man had just as casually said, "Oh, ninety minutes …"

Conor had gaped in surprise. The driver himself looked surprised that someone could be surprised. He had looked Conor up and down, and taken in the backpack.

"You running away from home, son?"

So Conor had muttered something, and taken himself and his pack to the back.

Ninety minutes! Was anywhere in Northern Ireland ninety minutes away? It was probably the longest journey he had ever made.

This better not be your idea of a joke, Will …

But because he was Conor McGarry, quietly confident inside his own skin wherever he went, he allowed himself to get over himself and observe it all with detached interest. At the very least, he should have a story to tell about his wild adventure.

The bus had pulled onto the M2, heading away from Belfast. A road sign loomed up in the distance, and flashed past almost before he had had time to catch the names. Antrim, Ballymena … Place names he had heard of, for sure, but never seen.

And he didn't see much of the places anyway, from inside the bus, though there was enough to tell him that he wasn't in Belfast any more. He certainly saw enough in Antrim to tell him that he would not be getting off the bus here – not at a bus stop where the kerb stones were painted red and white and blue. Just passing through. Keep going.

After Antrim the bus rolled along the A26 and the journey became more leisurely. Ballymena seemed pleasant enough, though the murals were distinctly reminiscent, as were the army patrols and the patrolling RUC men in their green uniforms, and the civilian population, ordinary people happily going about their business and pretending none of it was happening. He knew straight away that he was clocked as a Catholic when a group of lads got on, because it was simply an instinct that anyone born in Northern Ireland possessed. And they knew he was Fenian just as sure as he knew they were Prods.

Conor had once heard it explained that the difference was in how far apart your eyes were – even if you couldn't consciously see the difference, your subconscious knew. What spoiled that theory was he could never remember which way round it went, which side had their eyes closer together, but fuck that, he just *knew* and so did they.

He returned their stare levelly, not challenging and not submitting, and they just acted like he wasn't there. He had already observed this in other passengers on the bus. You paid your fare and you instinctively sat with your own people, and after that you were just another passenger and had every right to be there, so long as – Heaven forbid – you didn't talk to anyone.

If he did ever have to talk to someone, he made a mental note to check out how they pronounced their H's, and say it the same way. It was another known giveaway.

He had gazed out of the window as the bus began to move again, and slowly breathed out, and allowed himself to smile. He had to admit he was looking forward to seeing Will again. Even if they had only met for an hour or so, and even if that meeting had actually been intended to get the big Protestant eejit *out* of his head, not further in. Which it might have done, if Will hadn't said those last words right at the end …

When can I see you again?

… The words which Conor had to admit he had been hoping Will *would* say.

That kiss was still there, somehow, at the back of Conor's head. It had planted something, which their meeting on Black Mountain was meant to have rooted out. Instead, it had been watered and had grown into something, and Conor, who was usually no slouch at using words, couldn't describe what.

Of all the boys he knew close to his own age, the one Conor got on with best was his brother-in-law Cormac. Cor was like a friend and a brother – Conor assumed that last bit, as he had never had a flesh and blood one – rolled into one. If Conor was ever going to admit to loving another boy, it would be Cormac.

But Will wasn't a friend like Cormac. Conor had already told him things he had never mentioned to Cormac, and it hadn't felt strange.

Conor was popular with the girls and he got on well with them, but, he had never got close to being in love, and he had found that sex was an awkward, time consuming complication that got in the way of friendship and good conversation, which was why he hadn't particularly looked to do it again after Marie McCarthy.

But Will wasn't a friend like any girl he knew, either.

He couldn't put a name to it; all he could do was describe what it meant.

Quite simply, it meant that seeing Will would make him happy. And why should he not be happy?

You don't grow up as a Catholic in Belfast without very soon realising you are not always going to get what you want. And Conor was used to denying himself, in the name of his training. But when you actually had the chance of something you wanted, and taking it wasn't going to hurt anyone, just what the fuck would be the point of turning it down?

And with that resolve fresh at the front of his mind, Conor walked up the short concrete path and pressed the doorbell.

For good measure he rapped on the frosted glass window too.

Then he stepped back and waited.

There was movement behind the glass, and then the door opened, and there was Will grinning down at him, and Conor had to bite the inside of his mouth to stop himself grinning back.

"Couldn't you find somewhere a bit further away?"

Will looked at him knowingly, then stepped back to let him in. He closed the door behind them, and Conor found himself in a narrow hallway with a threadbare carpet and peeling wallpaper.

"So …"

Will was in a t-shirt and jeans torn off at the knees, and sandals. He looked fit and happy and relaxed. Far more relaxed than the last time they had met, anyway – but then, Conor supposed, they were on his home turf this time. It was his turn. And there was a warmth in his smile that soaked into Conor's bones like sunshine on a hot day.

By necessity, they were only standing inches apart, and Conor knew with sudden absolute certainty that if Will was a girl, he would move in to give her a hug and probably a kiss. He brought his backpack around his shoulder and carried it in front of him with both hands.

"Who the fuck owns this place, then?"

Will opened his mouth to speak, then looked abashed.

"It's … uh … mine."

Conor's mouth dropped.

"I didn't know you were master of a property empire."

"Throw your stuff in there … You brought a sleeping bag? Grand … D'ye need the toilet? It's through there … Come on through."

Will led the way into the lounge. Like the rest of what Conor had seen, it looked like it had been decorated by someone who just about cared, back in the sixties. Fadedly garish upholstery on the two chairs and the sofa, and not one of the three matching either of the others. A TV on four spindly legs next to the fireplace, opposite the sofa. Will had already made provision for hospitality with a couple of six packs of Tennents laid out on the coffee table. Conor took a can gratefully and it hissed as he pulled back the tab. They tapped their cans together in salute.

"Sláinte," said Will.

"The Queen," said Conor, in a terrible attempt to imitate Tommy Clifford's accent.

"So, yeah, this place …" Will gestured at the two chairs, side by side, and they dropped themselves in. "It belonged to my Granda. He died a couple of years back and it's stayed empty because …" He waved a hand to indicate the size of the problem. "Well."

Conor nodded. Finding the time, energy or money to do a place like this up, once it had been allowed to get into this state, would be a big commitment.

"So we just use it for weekends and things like that. But," Will went on, "Granda left it to my brother and to me, once I turned eighteen, which I have done, so it's both of ours."

Conor grunted, and took a swig of the Tennents to quell the sheer, molten anger at injustice that suddenly swelled within him. Everything Conor had, he had worked for, while this place had fallen into Will's lap by sheer fate. The Johnstons had this precious asset and they couldn't even look after it properly.

He couldn't resist it. He had to let it out somehow.

"Shame you're not ten years older. You could have used it properly."

"Huh …?" Will took a moment to think what he meant. "Oh! Aye. Well."

"I only just turned eighteen," Will added, "so I haven't done it yet."

Conor smiled.

"Aye, I know, but I was talking about voting."

Will spluttered into his beer, and laughed, and the brief awkwardness was passed.

"Your brother's not going to turn up, is he?" From what Conor had heard, Will's brother was a specimen of pure Orange and he had exactly zero desire to engage with him on his own turf.

"No, I can guarantee he won't."

Conor raised his eyebrows in a silent question; Will bit his lip and shifted in his chair.

"Because ... he thinks I'm here with Wendy and tonight is the night we do it."

"Ah!" Conor looked up at the flaking ceiling. "You'd better come back smiling, then."

"Aye ..." Will scowled at his can. Conor glanced over at him and felt himself about to reach over to touch Will's wrist.

"Will," he said sincerely. He kept his hand firmly planted on the arm of the chair. "I really don't want to be a problem for you and Wendy."

Will shook his head.

"You won't. You won't. I really hope that ... that one day I can introduce you to her, because ... well, I get on with her, and I get on with you, so you should both get on, right? And we'll be three friends together, right?" Conor raised his can to acknowledge the logic. "But first ..."

"First you'll have to explain me to her." Conor sighed. "I know. I know."

He didn't want to ask what story Will had spun for Wendy, because whatever Will thought about their relationship, the moment you start hiding things from your other half – well, as far as Conor had been able to tell, it's not a good sign. So, there was already a crack between them, and he didn't want to widen it, or even draw attention to it.

"What did you tell your folks?" Will asked. Conor shrugged.

"I said, Ma, Da, I'm going away for the night, and they said okay, and Ma loaded me down with half a ton of sarnies. I've still got some left, if you want." He jerked a thumb at the wall to indicate his backpack, lying on the bed in the next room. "They trust my judgement."

"Hmm. That must be nice," Will mumbled into his can. He knocked back the rest of his beer and crushed the empty can in one hand. "So, what do you want to do?"

Conor smiled.

"Funny you should say that …"

They walked along the edge of the sea in bare feet, shoes dangling from their hands and Conor with his trousers rolled up, while the last gasps of freezing cold waves surged and ebbed around their knees.

"You look happy," Will observed with a smile. The sea breeze ruffled his hair and Conor laughed from sheer joy.

"It's just fucking amazing!"

"It's fecking cold, is what it is."

"Ah, just enjoy it, you ninny."

No one paid any attention to the two lads strolling in the surf. Why should they? The beach was full of people just having innocent fun. Conor glanced down. You could barely see air between their free hands. He could so easily reach out, even just extend a finger, and they would be linked.

He casually transferred his shoes to that hand instead.

A group of children rushed into the sea ahead of them, and straight out again, shrieking. A beachball came bouncing across the sand and Will booted it back to its owners with a casual kick.

Then he realised Conor had stopped and was looking out to sea.

"What's that?" Conor pointed with his head.

Most of the horizon was clear, sun and sea merging at some invisible point through the haze. But over to the left, the north and west, you could see just see dark land above the bay, barely visible through the haze.

"That's Donegal," Will said. Conor's frown deepened.

"Donegal's in the South."

"Aye."

"And we're on the north coast."

Will's smile widened to match Conor's growing confusion.

"Aye."

"So, that's to the north of us."

"Aye." Will laughed. "The most northern part of Ireland … is in the South."

Conor twitched his head like he was trying to shake a flea out of his ear.

"This country!" He perked up. "Hey, does that shop sell Jammie Dodgers?"

* * *

The Jammie Dodgers were on the table, along with two cups of strong, well-sugared tea and the rest of Conor's mother's sandwiches.

Will couldn't see them because he stood in the middle of the room, holding the seat cushion in front of his face.

"Ready?" came Conor's voice.

"Aye …"

The cushion tore loose from Will's grip as a mighty blow struck it from the other side. It flew back into his face and he staggered back against the wall, letting the cushion drop.

"Jesus!"

Conor stared at him in concern, his fists still half raised.

"You okay?" he asked.

"Aye …" Will took the cushion up again. "That was just harder than I expected."

Conor laughed and raised his fists back into a fighting stance while his feet danced back and forth.

"As Wendy will one day say …"

Will stuck his tongue out. "Feck off! And do it again. I'll be ready."

He raised the cushion again. If he looked down, he could see Conor's feet, still dancing, moving back and forth, side to side. And this time he was ready when the blow came.

"And again," said Conor. Another blow, from a different direction. "Keep them guessing. Yer man, Muhammad Ali? He said, 'float like a butterfly, sting like a bee', and that's what I do." The cushion shook again, and again. His feet danced in a slow circle and Will turned himself to face it.

"Doesn't the other fella know about Muhammed Ali too?"

"Sure he does, so he just puts his hands up in front and absorbs the hits, because he wants to wear me out and then he can start hitting back. So I have to get into his head. I have to make him think, is this really worth it? Tempt him out, try to make him hit back even though that wasn't his plan …"

Blam – blam – blam, each one from a different direction.

"And sooner or later, he's the one who's tired, and he starts letting his guard down, and that's the beginning of the end. You get in the knocks, let him get confused as to what you're planning …"

Blam.

Blam.

"And then …"

The cushion shook under a sudden volley of blows with barely a gap between them, pushing Will right back against the wall.

He lowered it cautiously and peeked over the top. Conor was poised in the middle of the room, beaming in triumph. His shoulders were a little more pronounced as they rose and fell, but apart from that he barely seemed tired.

"And that, my friend, is the machine gun!"

* * *

They had cleared the last crumbs of the sandwiches and Jammie Dodgers, and the empty plates were pushed over to one side. The boys sat either side of the kitchen table and Will handed Conor the deck of cards. They were soft and slightly sticky – an old and much used pack that never left the holiday home.

"Shuffle."

Conor sliced the pack a couple of times and handed it back. Will began to deal. Seven rows of three cards each.

"Okay. This is the story of a real prick of a boy. I believe he was a Catholic but he went to a Protestant school. No one knew what to do with him because he was an arsehole. Maybe you know someone like him."

"Maybe I do."

Will set the pack aside. Twenty-one cards were laid out in three columns of seven.

"This school only had three classes in it."

"And twenty-one kids."

"Aye. Choose which card is our boy, but don't tell me which it is."

Conor mentally picked out the three of clubs.

"Okay."

"But you can tell me which class they put him in."

Conor tapped the middle column. The three of clubs was the third one down.

"Well," Will sighed, "they did their best, the teachers, but honestly, it just didn't work. So they decided to rearrange all three classes."

"This is a pretty shit school."

Will gathered the columns up, one at a time, with the chosen column in the middle of the stack. Then he dealt seven fresh rows into three new columns.

"Some kids were in the same class, some were in a new one. Which one is our boy in now?"

Conor tapped the left hand column.

"Well, these teachers were saints, I tell you. Maybe they were nuns."

"If they were nuns, I promise you they weren't saints."

"But try as they might, it still didn't work. So they said, I know, we'll rearrange again, just once more."

Again he gathered up the cards into a stack. The right hand column, the left hand column and the middle column. And again he dealt out the twenty-one cards into three fresh columns. Before he could ask, Conor tapped the second column again, where the three of clubs was now the fourth one down. Will nodded, and smiled, and stacked the cards up for a third time with that columns again in the middle.

"But the little shit was *still* so disruptive, they decided, feck this."

"Maybe they were nuns after all, then."

"They decided it was just going to be impossible to put the boy into the right class. Just impossible. I-M-P-…"

He started to deal out the cards from the top of the pack, face down, one on top of the other, one card for each letter.

"…O-S…"

He paused.

"Two S's," said Conor.

"...S-I-B-L-E. And so they decided to put him in a class …"

He turned over the next card face up. It was the three of clubs.

"… All on his own."

Conor stared, and gaped, and burst out laughing.

"Fan-fucking-tastic!" He clapped his hands together loudly. "Okay." He wriggled closer to the table on his seat. "Do it again but without the slabbering."

Their heads hung over the table, their hair almost touching.

"Slabber, slabber, slabber." Will dealt out the cards.

"I've chosen one and it's in the right hand column."

Will smiled and started to gather the cards up. Middle column, right hand column …

Conor's hand shot out and caught his wrist. It was the first time they had touched that day and Conor could feel Will's pulse hammer beneath his fingertips.

"You always put the column I choose in the middle."

Will looked up, and the corners of his eyes creased.

"Maybe."

"Continue."

Conor let go of his wrist, and sat back while Will redealt.

"Slabber, slabber, slabber …"

"So," Conor said when he was done, still staring the cards. "You know it's one of seven cards. If it's in this column, it's one of these two, if it's in this one it's one of these three, if it's this then it's one of these …"

Will's face was deadpan, apart from a very slight upward curl to the corners of his mouth.

"If you say so."

"Continue …"

Conor leaned forward and scrutinised the next dealing with eagle eyes. His hair brushed against Will's.

"And because there were only two cards it could have been in that column, they're now next to each other …" He looked up, eyes shining. "They're each the fourth one down. So whichever column goes in the middle will have seven cards on top of it …"

Will's face could not have been straighter.

"So then it will be the *eleventh* card down, and 'impossible' has ten letters, so when you deal out ten cards the eleventh will be …" He tapped his card. "This one." He sat back and stretched, hands behind his head with a grin that took up up his whole face. "Pretty good! I mean, it could get you burnt as a witch but still pretty good."

And if ever they were going to kiss again, Conor thought, it was surely that moment. So he sat back a little further and let the moment pass.

Smiling, Will knocked the cards back together into a pack. "So, what else can you do?"

Chapter 13: The Spark

"Ready?" Will called, his face up to the closed bedroom door.

"Ready." Conor's voice came through the wood.

"Okay then." Will turned the key in the lock, and stepped back.

First, nothing happened.

Then a rustling sound drew his eyes downwards.

A yellowing, fragile page from the cottage's archived pile of the *Belfast Telegraph* was sliding out from under the door. It stopped, showing half an advertisement for Dunnes and a filled-in crossword.

Now metal scratching sounds started to come from the area of the door handle, accompanied by some mild and muffled cursing from Conor. The key was wobbling in the lock. And, very slowly, turning.

Will began to smile as he saw how this was going. He thought of taking away the newspaper, but that would be unkind.

The key wobbled some more, and the loop slowly turned vertical. And then it fell backwards, out of the lock and onto the sheet of newsprint.

The paper slowly withdrew beneath the door, taking the key with it.

A few seconds later, Will heard the sound of the key clicking in the lock, and the door opened to reveal a beaming Conor.

"Ta-dah!" He waggled a tightly rolled-up five pound note. "All you need is something thin and stiff enough to push the key around in the lock from the other side. Only works with this kind of lock, of course. Not a Yale."

Will laughed.

"So, how did you ever discover that's a useful skill?"

Conor shrugged.

"I'd be more worried about why your grandda liked to keep his bedroom doors locked."

* * *

They went out again, to buy fish and chips. The evening breeze was picking up cold so they went back to the cottage to eat them. They sat side by side on the tatty sofa with their food on their laps and open cans on the floor by their feet, and watched Sean Connery save the world again in *Thunderball*.

The sofa had been made for people in an older, smaller generation and it wasn't quite big enough for two boys to sit in without very lightly pressing into each other. Conor discreetly tried to wriggle into the far corner on his side. Will leaned away from him and tried to angle his legs in the opposite direction, as much as the high sides of the sofa would allow.

On screen, a woman made the mistake of opening her own car door, immediately tipping off 007 that in fact this was a man in disguise.

"Jesus, that's embarrassing. Getting beaten up by an Englishman while you're dressed like a woman."

"He'sh not English, he'sh Shcottish."

"Shtill a fucking Prod."

Bond killed the bad guy and ran out onto the balcony of the chateau to escape the dead man's goons.

"So, he just happens to have a jetpack tucked away in case he needs it? How did he get it there in the first place?"

"That's how he got there ahead of the fella he just killed. He flew it in."

"Sure it makes enough noise to wake the dead. Wouldn't the guards notice?"

"Why are they even trying to kill him? Haven't they noticed their boss is dead? So they're probably not going to get paid."

007 landed and bundled the jetpack into the boot of his waiting Aston Martin.

"How d'ye think James Bond gets his car serviced? I mean, he couldn't just take it into any garage. You'd think they'd notice the machine guns and all the gadgets. I would."

The sofa was just the wrong shape. Conor knew his body well enough to tell that spending an hour and a half sitting like this would result in a knot at the base of his spine. He slowly let himself relax back into the middle, and found that Will had already given up the uneven fight. Their hips and their knees dusted lightly against each other, and it was far more comfortable.

The Aston Martin opened up on the pursuing bad guys with two high pressure water jets squirting out of the exhaust

"Why don't the fellas just move out of the way?"

And that was how they watched the rest of the movie.

* * *

Conor stood poised with a tea towel. The calced-up geyser over the sink was slowly discharging water and the sink was filling with bubbles. Will casually switched the radio on while they waited.

Conor perked suddenly up.

"Oh, turn it higher!"

Will's thumb twirled the dial and the pulsating bass notes filled the cushion. Conor's hips began to wiggle to the beat, Will nodded in time as he pulled the first plate from the suds, and Debbie Harry sang the song of a woman who was very clearly looking forward to a night of amazing passion. The rest of the band faded away and for a few key seconds the music was just bass and drum machine. Conor rapped with a knife and fork on the counter top in time as the drums came back in.

Catching eyes and pausing the spark was undeniable, or so Will felt.

* * *

Conor sat back, his arms resting on the chair's arms, fingers coiled over the arm ends.

"Okay. Ready."

Will stood in front of him and solemnly raised one finger.

"One word."

Will held a hand up next to his face, and moved the other hand in a circle next to it.

"It's a fillum. Of course it's a fillum. You don't read any fucking books."

Will held up a finger again.

"I know, one word."

"No, that was me telling you to feck off."

"The long Saturday nights just fly by in the Johnston household, don't they?" Will tapped three fingers against his forearm. "Something that druggies do. Heroin. Shooting up."

"It's syllables, you prick!"

"Aren't you meant to be silent? Okay, three syllables."

Will tapped one finger.

"First syllable."

Will paused, thinking, one hand on his hip.

"Oh! Who's your man. Ah – nancy boy. *Generation Game*. Larry Grayson!"

"I'm thinking!"

"And you're talking again."

"Okay." Will tugged at his earlobe.

"Ear ring. Pierced ear." Will angrily jabbed a finger into his ear. "Ear wax. Blackheads."

"Sounds like!"

"And you're still–…" Will aimed a finger at him in warning. "Okay. First syllable sounds like …?" Will raised a single finger again. "I know. One word. What does it sound like?"

Will rolled his eyes, then mimed firing a shot at Conor out of his forefinger, thumb cocked up to the ceiling.

"Gun. Oh, it was *one*! Sounds like one. Or gun. Ah … Ton. Sun. Bun." Conor began to murmur his way through the alphabet. "A-un. Bun. Cun. Dun. E-un … Fun? It's fun! First syllable is fun! Unlike this game."

Will cut him off with an abrupt wave of both hands, then tapped three fingers against his arm again.

"Third syllable." Will described a circle in the air with both hands. "Circle. Sphere. Oh, was the first syllable sun, then? No, but this is the third." In desperation, Will repeated the gesture. "Round. Roundabout. Planet Earth. Planet Mars? Ball? Football!"

Delighted, Will jabbed a finger at him.

"Football?"

Will made a gesture that was meant to tell Conor he should rewind a little.

"Rugby ball? Cricket ball?"

"It's *Thunderball*!" Will shrieked, at a frequency that could stun dogs. "*Thunder*-fecking-*ball*! We were watching it half a fecking hour ago!"

Conor sat back and stretched with a big, easy smile, hands behind his head.

"Sure I guessed it a million years ago, but you're so easy to wind up."

Will's eyes narrowed in a scowl. He seemed to be wrestling with some idea, fighting his way to a decision. Conor waited to see what it was.

Then Will took hold of his right wrist with his left hand, and held his right arm out. Conor watched in puzzled interest.

"Okay, so you can … OH JESUS NO, WHAT ARE YOU DOING?"

Will bit his lip and slowly pulled his arm so that his elbow bent … in completely the wrong direction.

"STOP IT!" Conor shrieked, unable to tear his aghast eyes away. He started to wriggle backwards in his chair – anything to get away from the unnatural sight. Will gladly let his arm go back to normal.

"It's called hypermobility," he said. "Or just you know, double jointed."

"Jesus!" Conor stared at Will's arm. "No wonder you conquered us."

* * *

What was I hoping would happen?

Will lay in his sleeping bag on a bare mattress and stared up at the cobwebby ceiling. His room was at the back of the house, away from the road, but the curtains barely fitted and enough light came through to show everything in shades of grey.

He had wanted to see Conor again. And he had. He had wanted to enjoy spending time with Conor. And he had. He had got everything he had hoped for out of the day so far, and somehow it just didn't feel as much as it could have been.

And, Jesus, the sheer self control he had needed to not try and put his arm around Conor while they were on the sofa … It would have felt so right.

Scenes from the day replayed in his mind. The sheer joy he had felt when he had opened the front door, and there had been Conor. The innocent pleasure on his friend's face as they walked along the sea. The charge that had hung in the air as they washed up to the music of Blondie.

If Conor had been Wendy and he had felt half as turned on … He could feel a stir between his legs at just the thought.

And then there was the sound of someone fumbling at the door, and he stared as it opened to show the outline of Conor. In shorts and t-shirt. Carrying his sleeping bag.

Oh ... Jesus ...

"There's a fucking hurricane blowing through the broken pane. How big's that bed?"

"Uh …" Will croaked. "It's a double."

"Budge over, then."

Will wriggled his sleeping bag over to one side. Conor lay his own bag down next to him and climbed in – top to toe, his head down by Will's feet. The bed shook a bit more as Conor zipped his bag up and Will felt him turn away from him. Slowly, Will turned himself away to face the wall.

They lay in the stiff silence of two people trying very hard to fool sleep into coming by faking it.

"There's a draught around my head."

Will rolled his eyes,

"No draught at this end …"

He felt the mattress shake again, and kept his face to the wall as Conor wriggled around so that their heads were at the same level. Then Conor turned over so that again they lay back to back.

"Still not warm, is it?" Conor asked suddenly.

Irritated, Will squirmed himself around to stare at the back of Conor's head.

"Are you going to complain all night?"

A pause, and then Conor turned towards him. Their faces were bare centimetres apart and Will could feel the gentle touch of Conor's breath on his skin. The last time that happened, Will had kissed him a moment later.

"Turn back over," Conor said, and Will grumpily turned back to face the wall. The mattress shook once more as Conor also turned over, and Will's eyes flew wide open as he felt Conor snuggle in close behind him. The boys lay spooned together in their bags, Conor's front to Will's back.

"This is how you keep warm," Conor mumbled sleepily. Still Will lay there, wondering, waiting.

A few moments more, and – his heart began to pound – Conor's arm slid protectively over him. Will lay still, his body stiff as a board, but Conor made no more moves. Will slowly, tentatively, crooked his arm so that their fingers could twine together.

And that was how they lay, Will's heart slowly calming down while he sensed Conor slip into sleep. Sleep crept in on him too, and his last waking thought was that he had never felt so safe.

And if this is as far as their relationship was to go, in physical terms, well, actually he was okay with that.

Chapter 14: One Mighty Explanation

Sunday 3rd August

"The fucking plug's broken!" Conor called through the bathroom door.

"Sure it works just fine!" Will called back.

"Water runs out as soon as you pour it in!"

"Jam your cloth into it and wash fast, then!"

After that there was only muffled grumbling and the sound of splashing water. Will smiled, and turned back to making breakfast.

Conor had been the first to wake up. By the time Will got his eyes open, he was back in the running gear he had worn on Black Mountain. A cheery smile, and a wink.

"See you soon!" The front door closed seconds later. Will had got up and attended to business in the bathroom, and he was dressed by the time Conor was knocking on the front door again, breathing hard and glowing with a satisfied sweaty lather.

Will slid a couple of slices of lard into the frying pan and waited for them to start to melt. He also put the radio on, and together with the bubbling fat it drowned out the sound of washing, which also helped him get over the thought that Conor was naked, just a few feet away from him–…

It hit him like a slap, enough to make him draw in his breath. He scowled at the lard as it slowly slid across the pan. Will slowly let the breath out again, and turned and craned slightly so that he could peer back down the hall, all the way to the closed door of the bathroom at the other end.

"I fancy Conor," he murmured beneath his breath.

And now he had – sort of – said it out loud, it seemed so obvious, like remarking that water was wet. *Of course* he fancied Conor. It just hadn't occurred to him because – well, he just hadn't thought about it, that much.

He knew he *liked* Conor. He knew he wanted to see him, to be with him. But he wasn't the kind of guy who *fancied* guys … was he?

There was Wendy. He had a girlfriend. When he was alone and enjoying his own private company, he thought of girls. Naked girls.

Well, to be sure, he thought of naked girls shagging naked boys, but wasn't he mostly thinking about the girls?

He cracked eggs into the pan and slid them about with the scraper, and remembered how his body had reacted to the thought of Conor, last night, before Conor came into the room. When was the last time he had felt like that with Wendy?

But hadn't it gone down again?

He had woken up with a hard-on like a handbrake, but that was nothing unusual, it just meant he needed a piss.

Will chucked in some bacon to go with the eggs.

He had started all this by kissing Conor on Bonfire Night, and he still wasn't sure why he had done that. All the time he had wanted to see Conor again, it had been Conor's company he wanted. Not his body.

And there was another question to ask on top of all of this. What did Conor feel?

Conor had been the one to track him down, and come and find him. Conor had been the one to take things beyond that first kiss. He obviously enjoyed Will's company as much as Will enjoyed his. Did Conor also fancy him in return?

Had there really been a draught coming through the window last night? But after Conor had laid down next to him, he hadn't made any kind of move apart from putting his arm over him.

Will smiled and shook his head. He knew that what he wanted was impossible, and if Conor wanted the same then he would also know it. It was hard enough for a Prod and a Catholic boy just to be friends. There was no way anything else was going to happen, so best forget about it.

The bathroom door opened and there was Conor, clad only in a towel that hung low from his hips around his waist, mussed hair, powerful shoulders, strong arms, a sleek torso, and straight away Will's body was telling him again that whatever his head said about Conor, it had other ideas.

Conor was only there for half a second – "Bathroom's free" – before he disappeared into his own room to get dressed.

* * *

Neither of them said much over breakfast. It wasn't awkwardness, it was just that eating food was serious business. After that it was another walk on the beach.

Will stopped suddenly in his tracks as a thought struck him out of nowhere. Conor walked on a few paces before he noticed and looked back, his head cocked in curiosity.

"I don't know why I didn't think of this …"

Conor was starting to look worried.

"What?"

"It's Sunday morning. Do you … you know …"

Conor grinned.

"Go to church?" A small shake of the head. "The family will be at the ten-thirty service but I've not been on a Sunday since I was fifteen, sixteen. Everyone knows Saturday night Mass is shorter so that's fine."

"But … you didn't go to Mass last night either."

Conor elaborately slapped his brow, once with each hand.

"Well, shit, I must have forgot." He laughed. "And if this has just occurred to you, I'm guessing you don't either?"

Will drew a breath, puffed his cheeks as he let it out.

"We did, every Sunday – until Da died."

"Ah." Conor looked deliberately from left to right. The beach wasn't crowded, maybe because of everyone who actually was in church. Then he reached out, in public, half a mile of sand on either side of them, and took Will's hand. He squeezed. "I still think the Big Man's probably out there, somewhere – He's just not very interested in Northern Ireland."

Will gave a wan smile.

"Why do you think He's out there at all?"

Another squeeze, and a shy smile from Conor.

"Took a miracle for us to meet, didn't it?" Conor abruptly let Will go. "Still, if He's real, he owes Northern Ireland one mighty explanation."

"Aye. You're not wrong."

Then it was back to the cottage to grab their things and clean up and head out to the bus stop.

* * *

Their bags were packed. Will's was at his feet by the front door. He rested his hand on the door latch.

"Will …"

Conor's voice was rough, uncertain, enough to make Will look back in surprise. Conor reached out and took his hand. Then the other. And then he pulled Will gently towards him and suddenly they were kissing.

Oh, sweet Jesus, they were *kissing*, there, pressed together in the narrow hallway, in front of the frosted glass window while cars passed by only feet away outside, and now there was nothing perfunctory, nothing unexplained, nothing angry, this was what they both wanted, wanted so much. Conor's hands started at his waist and slowly moved up his back, holding the tight embrace until they arrived at the back of his head. His hand cupped Will's head and guided him as they kissed with complete control, intensity and intimacy, their lips moving over the other's, exploring, gently probing, caressing.

They came to a natural halt, their heads bowed, their foreheads pressed together.

"You had to leave it until now to do that?" Will murmured, feeling half drunk.

"Aye." Conor raised his head and they kissed again, slowly, tenderly. "Call it curiosity."

"Curiosity."

"Same reason I held you like that last night. I knew I wanted to … and I might not get another chance."

"Huh?" Will blurted in protest without thinking. Conor's eyes were tender but his face was set as he delivered harsh facts.

"If one of us was a girl, we'd have shagged last night."

"That's probably true." *But if you were a girl, I wouldn't have wanted you like I do …*

"Now, let me just explain a couple of things that might have passed you by. We are two fellas, in Northern Ireland, and what we just did …"

"… was fecking fantastic!" Will interrupted with a shy grin. Conor acknowledged it with a nod.

"… could make life very unpleasant for us, and also very unlong, if the wrong people saw it, unless, we both go very, very carefully. And I have absolutely no idea where we go now."

Will twisted his mouth. He did not want to hear it said out loud, but he also knew it was true.

"And …"

"And?" *There's more?*

Conor tapped his own chest. "*I* am young, free and single." Then he prodded Will, just hard enough to make him sway back. "*You* are not. So here's the thing. I will not mess Wendy around and I don't think you want to either, because you're a decent fella and not a shit. So, you need to decide – are you her boyfriend or not? And if you are, that's grand, I'm happy for you, and we're not doing this again."

Heart pounding, mouth dry, Will dared to say the unsayable.

"Supposing I decide I'm not her boyfriend?"

"That still leaves us to work out something. We can see each other, maybe, but life's about to get busy for me and I'm not going to spend the rest of my life sneaking around to catch the odd moment with you. I'm certainly not coming all the way to fucking Downhill just to kiss you again. So, yes, this might have been my last chance." Conor smiled wryly, though his eyes still shone as he shouldered his backpack. "And now we've got a bus to catch."

Probably no one noticed the two boys who got on at Downhill, then changed at Coleraine. They obviously knew each other, but on both buses they sat on opposite sides of the aisle and only exchanged a few casual words. The brown haired one spent most of the journey gazing out of his window, and if there was anything on his face it was only a vague frown, looking like he might be running something over in his head.

    The blond one also spent a lot of time looking out of the window, and on his face was a big, half-circle smile.

Chapter 15: Irrational Behaviour

Monday 4th August

"Here you are, darling … sweetheart …"

Alice Johnston set the breakfast plates down in front of her two sons, Alan first of course, and then Will. Will was in jeans and t-shirt as he would be putting overalls on after. Alan was in his suit trousers and white shirt, open necked.

"Thanks, Ma."

Will smiled happily and naturally as he attacked the bacon with knife and fork, but it grew more fixed as he became aware of the predatory gleam in Alan's eye. They hadn't seen much of each other since Will got back from Downhill, and Will had kept it that way, going straight up to his room and making sure he only emerged at times when their mother was likely to be around.

But they both knew that this was the point each day where she would go upstairs to fix her hair and her face, and they would be alone and there was no diplomatic way out of it.

"So." Alan's mouth twisted into a smirk the moment they heard her foot on the stairs. "What was it like?"

Will shook brown sauce over his fry-up.

"What was what like?"

Alan leaned closer.

"You know perfectly well, you dirty fecker, and don't tell me nothing happened, because you've been smiling ever since. You got your wick wet with Wendy over the weekend, didn't you? And about time. So, what was it like?"

Will casually popped a slice of bacon into his mouth.

"You've done it yourself."

Alan pulled his head back in surprise.

"Aye, once or twice."

"So it was probably like that."

Alan clicked his tongue in irritation.

"How many times?" Despite himself, Will felt a smile start to spread over his face, and Alan took it as vindication. "Ha!" he crowed triumphantly. "Three times? Four?"

Will just shook his head, still smiling as he attacked his fried bread and doused a slice in tomato juice.

I am smiling at the thought of your face if I told you I spent the weekend with a Catholic boy, and my lad got hard when we kissed, and I think I could feel his too, and that probably means he could feel mine.

But the smile vanished at the thought of what would immediately follow Alan's expression.

"Did she scream? Or cry?"

Will stared at Alan and wondered just what the feck kind of sex life his brother had.

"Huh?"

"Did you use johnnies or did she not give a shit?"

Will looked him in the eye and spoke very distinctly.

"No one got up the pole." He had the satisfaction of seeing Alan flush and look away.

Thank God, their Ma came back downstairs, and if she detected a slight tension, she didn't show it. Will was almost certain she still didn't know how close she had come to being a grandmother two years ago; Alan had had to spend some of his inheritance from their father for his then-girlfriend to take the trip to England.

Alan beat a retreat upstairs for a final piss and Will finished off his breakfast, hoping to get out of the house before Alan was back down.

No such luck. They met at the bottom of the stairs, Alan doing up the buttons of his suit as Will was taking his Mitchell's jacket off the hook. Will shot him a warning look and Alan held up his hands.

"Okay, okay, maybe I've got no business."

"Maybe," Will agreed. He reached out for the latch and pulled the door open. Alan bounded forward to be first out of the house, blocking Will's view of the road.

"What matters," he said over his shoulder, "is my little brother spent the weekend shagging his girl and he's a proper man at last … oh, hello!"

He stopped suddenly. Will peered over his shoulder. And there, on the doorstep, her finger outstretched to press the doorbell and her face a mask of shock, was Wendy.

* * *

"And then what?" Conor asked, his voice tinny down the phone line.

Will closed his eyes and leaned against the side of the kiosk.

She had only been there because she had thought it would be nice for them to walk to the cafe together. There *hadn't* been tears, there *hadn't* been recriminations or accusations. Just a mask of ice that had appeared in an instant which he knew was laid over a wound a mile deep.

"Nothing," he said dully. "She just … walked off."

"Did you go after her?"

"Aye … sort of …"

He shut his eyes, remembering.

"I swear I wasn't–…"

"So what were you doing?"

And then that indrawn breath; that hesitation, because how the *fecking feck* was he meant to give a meaningful answer to her question in just a few seconds, out there in public?; and her catching it, and knowing that there was something he was ashamed to tell her.

"I couldn't think what to say."

A pause.

"Aye," Conor agreed. "I can see that would be complicated."

Will had gone through the system in his lunch break, more out of hope than anything else. Call the McGarrys, let it ring twice, wait by the phone box. Ten minutes later, to his surprise, Conor had called back.

He didn't even know how Conor spent his weekdays, or whether he would have been at home or not. But he had had to talk.

"I mean, I could have said I had not been shagging any girl."

"Which would have been true."

"Aye, but what would I say instead? Alan wouldn't believe me, but feck what he believes, but Wendy … she'd still know I'd kept something from her. And Alan … Well, he worked out straight away that whoever I had been with, it wasn't her, and he just headed off laughing. I think he actually admires me even more for cheating on my half-Fenian girlfriend with a pure Orange girl."

"You see." Conor was deliberately making his voice sound like a stern teacher pontificating on the blindingly obvious. "This is why you shouldn't go kissing strange boys during riots. You have no idea where it will lead."

Will smiled, though his eyes were blurring.

"No." He glanced around, as if he might be overheard. "But … I'm glad I did."

A pause.

"Aye, So am I."

"I just have to …" *Sort it out. Somehow.*

Well, to be honest, he didn't *have* to sort it out. But he felt anyone with any kind of integrity *would*. Wendy deserved better.

Pip-pip-pip-pip-pip …

At his end, Conor pushed another coin into the slot and the line cleared. Will checked his watch.

"Sorry to make you spend another. I'd better get back."

"Aye, I've got to be off too. Doctor's appointment."

"Oh?" Will suddenly perked up. He had actually forgotten that Conor was, technically, unwell.

"I'm hoping Doctor McKenna will give me the all-clear to go back in the ring."

"That's fantastic!"

"Aye, well, we'll see. Every now and then I bang my head against a concrete post just to see what will happen and it hasn't reopened, so I'll probably be okay."

"I really hope so," Will said sincerely. "So …"

"Aye."

"Until next time."

"Aye."

"Thanks for … listening. I just … wanted to hear you."

"Aye. Well …"

"Conor ..." Will's mouth was suddenly dry and it came out as a croak, while his heart went into overdrive so hard he wondered if Conor could hear the beat. He could sense Conor waiting at the other end of the line, an interrogative silence that echoed. Could he guess what was coming?

I love you.

Could he say it?

Will worked his mouth and tongue until there was enough moisture and lubrication to speak.

"I ... think I'm falling in love with you."

Immediately he said it, he bowed his head and squeezed his eyes shut and pictured the words winging their way along the wire. A long silence with just crackles and hiss over the line; then Conor, making a reply to words Will hadn't said.

"I love you too ..." Somehow Will could tell that wasn't the end of the sentence. It was his turn to wait while the line crackled gently at him. "... You big eejit."

* * *

Conor sat in his underwear on the examining couch while Doctor McKenna probed his skull with his fingers, made him stick out his tongue, had him follow his fingertip with his eyes and shone a light into them, tapped his knees with a light hammer, listened to his breathing through a stethoscope, front and back.

Then he dangled his legs while the doctor went back to his desk to scribble notes, his head hunched over the paperwork.

"Any headaches?"

"No."

"Blurred or double vision?"

"No."

"Instability? Do your legs feel wobbly? Do you feel like the ground is on a slope or moving?"

"No."

"Confused thinking? Loss of memory? Inability to follow thoughts through? Irrational behaviour?"

I've fallen in love with a Protestant boy – does that count?

"No."

"Of course …" McKenna glanced up with a friendly smile. They had known each other all Conor's life. Eighteen years and three months earlier, the doctor had delivered him screaming into a waiting world. "Irrational is a subjective term and I'm talking to someone whose chosen path in life is to have trained apes pay to bash his head in." Conor smiled back. "Oh, get dressed, Conor, you'll be fine." Conor slid off the table and reached for his shirt. "Now then." The doctor sat back, lightly tapping his pen on his desk. "There's no reason you can't resume boxing, but don't just throw yourself back into it. Train yourself back up – and train yourself lightly. I know you're used to training all day and that would be a mistake. Try to break it up with something less intense."

"I can do that." While Conor buttoned his shirt up, he briefly told the doctor about the redecorating project for the gym extension – the new home for Claire and Cormac and Katie. "So you see – train mornings, decorate afternoons – that should do it, right?"

McKenna nodded approvingly. "That's perfect – and what a fine idea of Michael's, so it is. About time those three had a proper home of their own."

Conor finished dressing and they shook hands.

"Take care, Conor," McKenna said gravely, showing him to the door. "I don't just mean the boxing. Whoever hurt you in the first place is still out there. There's someone walking around and breathing our air who thinks it's acceptable to throw rocks at his fellow human beings."

Conor shrugged.

"Aye, well. This is Belfast."

"Hmm. I'm from Kilkenny." McKenna pressed the folder of notes into Conor's hand. "Give this to Sister at the front desk, and take it easy."

Conor smiled.

"Do I still get a lollipop?"

* * *

Pour two capfuls into a bucket of warm water …

Conor squinted at the directions on the bottle of sugar soap, then up at the expanse of blank wall in front of him, which now that the room was completely empty suddenly looked the size of a boxing ring standing on its edge.

"Me and my big mouth …" he murmured. He turned slowly on the spot. And this was just one room. There was another like it, and the hallway. At least the bathroom and the kitchen were going to be done by professionals, but still.

And he had gone and promised Katie a pretty mural in her room on top of painting the flat, which was more work, and even though she hadn't understood a thing he said, he was determined to keep his word.

And first – apparently – every wall needed rubbing down with sugar soap, otherwise the paint would look fine at first, but it would start to peel and soon his sister's family would be living in a run-down hovel and everyone would be saying Conor McGarry didn't care enough to do a proper job.

So he carefully measured out two capfuls into a bucket, and carried it through to the next room to fill up from the hot tap.

The foam rose up in the bucket, and he suddenly realised he missed Will.

Only a couple of hours since they had last spoken, twenty-four hours since they had kissed, and the absence was a sudden spike of sorrow in his heart. He wanted that lanky, gormless body with its goofy smile *here*, right next to him, in this room, now, breathing the same air, sharing the same space.

On the phone, neither of them had mentioned their conversation in the cottage, in each other's slack embrace in the hall, after that fantastic snog – and yes, Conor had felt Will's arousal, just like he was pretty certain Will had felt his. With their bodies pressed together like that, there hadn't been much room for error. Of course, just getting a stiff because someone was pressed against you didn't mean anything – the same thing could happen when he cycled down a bumpy road. But there had been no doubt what it meant this time.

Conor had told Will it was 'curiosity'. In fact, he had made up his mind on his morning run that he was going to kiss Will before they left, if Will would let him, which he felt he probably would. Do it properly. He had almost done it on the beach, but that would have been jumping the gun and way too public. He had wanted to find out what it was like when there was no one else about, no pressure or danger, just two willing fellas who both wanted it and could take all the time in the world – apart from the constraint of needing to get a bus, so if they both got carried away with what they were doing, there was a built-in time limit.

Turned out it was pretty good.

He turned the tap off, took the bucket back to the first room, dunked the sponge in the water, and began to scrub the walls.

He didn't regret what they had done, and he didn't regret a single word that had passed between them afterwards, because every word had been true. They both knew the situation they were in. They both knew the difficulties and the dangers. The only difference between them was that Conor would probably find giving each other up easier. It would mean hardening his heart, but he was used to that and this would be just one more thing he couldn't have.

He wasn't sure Will had had that same experience.

So far, they been leaving the ball in the other's court. It was up to Conor to think of Black Mountain. It was up to Will to think of Downhill. Now they both had thinking to do. Will needed to get himself straight with Wendy, but longer and harder would be them thinking through their chances of any kind of future, which from where Conor was standing just looked impossible.

I-M-P-O-S-S-I-B-L-E. Ten letters and two 'S's.

Conor smiled faintly. He would have to show that trick to the family.

The internal door opened and shut out in the hall passage, letting in a brief snatch of noise from the gym. It was a proper fire door, and together with the thick brick walls of the old warehouse it made the extension pretty well soundproofed. It would be a good home, here.

"You're in here, son?"

"Through here, Da."

A moment later his father appeared, looking approvingly round.

"So, what did Doctor McKenna say?"

Conor gave him a brief report as he continued scrubbing the walls. It used muscle groups that he didn't generally exercise – his arm was starting to ache – and he made a mental note to see to that.

"That's grand, grand."

Michael McGarry had his hands stuffed into his pockets and seemed to be taking an interest in almost anything that wasn't Conor. Conor recognised the body language because he had used it often enough himself. It was the McGarry way of saying there was a delicate subject to broach.

"So, light training, working yourself back into it …" Da said.

"Aye." Conor kept his voice neutral as he moved on to the next wall. Da would spit it out eventually.

"How are you up for a friendly match? Next Saturday?"

Chapter 16: Community Event

Saturday 9th August

"A friendly match?" Will asked, and he hadn't even got round to closing the front door behind him yet. Alan had pounced on him the moment he came back from work.

"Aye, a friendly!" Alan chuckled as he checked his watch. "Well, that's what the Fenians think anyway. We're all going to support and that includes you. And why are you back so late anyway? You're usually straight home for lunch. We should be going."

Saturdays for Will were half a day at work and then an afternoon of leisure, which usually involved Wendy one way or another.

"Aye, well, I had … stuff." He didn't want to say he had been hovering outside Boots, where Wendy worked. Trying to find the courage to go in. Trying to find the right words to say if he ever did. In the end he gave up and just wandered. He had bought fish and chips for his lunch, which had been a mistake because it just made him remember his last fish and chips meal, and who had been there with him to share it.

Alan studied his face carefully.

"What happened to Mr Smiley? I'd say you've been out shagging your new girl but you don't exactly have that look."

"I have not been shagging my new girl," Will muttered. Any feelings that showed on his face, he tried to hide by hanging his coat up, but there was only so long he could stand facing the wall.

He and Conor hadn't talked all week. Will had tried the two-ring system a couple of times, but there had been no call back to the phone box. Conor had said his life was about to get busy. Will didn't know what was taking up his time.

He hadn't seen much of Alan either that week, due to careful management of his own time and Alan's UDR commitments, which had suited him just fine.

Understanding suddenly dawned for Alan, closely followed by a patent smirk.

"She's already dumped you! Ah well, she lasted long enough for you to –…"

"Time for a cup of tea, love?" their mother called from the kitchen. Will didn't particular want a cup of tea, but he saw Alan's impatience and this would be a good way of making him change the subject.

"Thanks, Ma!" He went on through to the kitchen and Alan had to follow. "So what's this friendly match, then?"

"Well …" Alan spoke with forced patience, and another glance at his watch, as the tea was poured. "Henry's da is on the Council."

"Aye, I know that."

"He happened to overhear a conversation – thanks, Ma – between Maguire and Roberts."

"Uh-huh." Maguire was SDLP, the barely acceptable face of Irish nationalism. Roberts, like Henry's da, was DUP – but, as much as the DUP had a spectrum, Henry's da and he were at opposite ends of it. Roberts talked to the Catholics now and then.

"And they were talking about how a friendly match between us and them would go down well in our ward, and Maguire knows the guy who owns a place where it could be held, and the Fenians have some rising star of their own, so Henry's da says, great idea! I know just the lad for our side!"

"Who?" Will asked.

Alan stared at him as if he was the stupidest person on Earth.

"Who do you think Henry's daddy suggested? Henry!"

Will smiled as he stirred his tea. "What, just him?" He had a vision of Henry on his own facing down a charging mob of twelve Catholics in football kit.

"Of course just him! How many do you think a boxing match needs?"

The spoon Will was twirling in his tea went suddenly still. When Alan said 'match', he usually meant football match, and that was what he had assumed this kind of match was.

"So." Henry dusted his hands together and flashed his most satisfied smirk. "The Fenians think it's going to be a friendly game – and who are they going to be up against? How about the most unfriendly lad you can think of? You've seen Henry fight. It'll be a walkover."

"And where is this fight?" Alan asked slowly, though already he saw the answer approaching with the slow, deadly inevitability of a train wreck.

"That place." From the way Alan's mouth twisted, just referring to it seemed to leave a foul taste and he almost spat out the name. "McGarry's. Come on – let's get going. The fight starts at six."

McGarry's, Will thought bitterly. Of course. And who would the Catholics' rising star be? None other than. Conor had said he had a doctor's appointment. Will didn't even know how it had gone, but obviously he had been given the all clear.

The kitchen clock showed it was getting on for half past five. Conor would already be at the gym, Will thought with dull resignation. He had probably been practising all afternoon. All week, even, which was why he had never heard the phone ring. He had never been at home.

But a week was all it could have been. Was a week long enough to prepare for Henry?

There was a drawback to Conor's brilliant system, Will realised – to hear the phone ring, you had to be around.

* * *

So, this is McGarry's ...

Will stood before the old building, gazing up like that fella in the Meat Loaf song, a sinner before the gates of heaven. Will had heard the way Conor's voice changed when he mentioned this place, in a way that Conor himself probably didn't realise. Conor loved McGarry's, and anything Conor loved, Will was prepared to love too.

What made it even more special was that Conor would be in there, right now. And the knowledge that he had no way of communicating made Will sick at heart.

The brickwork glowed red in the late afternoon light. Will must have seen the place before but he had always paid it no mind. It hadn't meant anything to him then. Now, sheer association imbued every brick with a deep interest and he scanned it hungrily, drinking in every detail. It stood three stories high with a flat roof on the corner of two roads, and dominated the terraced houses around it by its sheer presence. The original entrance had been replaced with a steel and glass front porch with a painted McGarry's sign above it, in the same style as on Conor's shirt. Will couldn't help noticing it had somehow escape the attentions of the graffiti artists, which had to mean it had some kind of unspoken – or possibly very much spoken – protection.

An advantage of being tall was Will could scan across the crowd that was pressing in through the small reception area. There were faces he recognised – even some fellas from work.

There was Mr Mitchell and his wife. There was Sergeant Moore and a couple of constables – not going in, but keeping a careful eye on the crowd, nodding and smiling in a friendly sort of way but with eyes like steel that constantly scanned for trouble. The one face he so badly wanted to see wasn't visible – he was probably in the changing rooms, getting ready, or whatever a fighter did before the game. Though even if their eyes had met over a crowded gym, he wasn't sure how he would be able to communicate what he really needed to say. *This isn't a friendly and Henry's an ape who is out to paste you.*

A surge of anger hit him so hard and so suddenly that he had to clench his teeth and force himself to stare straight ahead, rather than follow his instinct of rounding on his brother and shouting.

You made me throw that fecking rock, you made me hurt him, you made it so he had to stop training ...

But even if pigs went supersonic and he did say it and Alan understood the feck what he was talking about, he would give the obvious answer:

I didn't make you do anything. You could have not *thrown that rock ...*

Will didn't want to go there.

Still, if there was one thing Conor wasn't, it was stupid. He would work it out. If Henry gave him time.

"Hey, there are the boys." Alan had clocked a knot of his friends who had already made their way in. "Get us in, right, Will?" Without waiting for an answer he was pressing forward through the crowd and into the gym. When he was challenged by a slim, dark haired fella about the same age as him, wearing a McGarry's t-shirt, he just impatiently gestured back at Will. Will wearily acknowledged with a nod, and shuffled his way the remaining paces to the busy reception desk to cough for two tickets. It was probably against Alan's principles to give money to Fenians anyway, even if it was to pay for the sight of watching one of them get beat up by a Prod hero. The desk was staffed by a pair of young women whom Will very quickly guessed were Conor's sisters.

"Here you are," the girl said cheerfully as she pressed the two slips of paper into Will's hand. "Enjoy the fight!"

He had to bite his tongue not to say, "So, are you Claire, Grace or Rose?" Christ, she even had the same crooked smile and quirk of the head as her brother. It was a look that felt genuinely friendly even if she didn't know you from Adam and it was odd to see it on the face of a complete stranger. He was feeling hurt that she didn't recognise him.

"Thanks," he mumbled, and went on through.

The boxing ring dominated the middle of the wide floor, with rows of seats set up on all four sides. For all the supposed friendliness, you could see the two sides had already gathered together into their own camps. Alan and his mates had formed their own little clique and from the way Alan gestured at him, it was pretty clear Will was expected to join them.

"That's Russell!", a horrified Alan gasped as Will took his seat. His eyes burned holes in a man on the other side of the ring, standing in the front row where the dignitaries were, hands casually thrust into his pockets as he chatted to his neighbour. "Sure he's pure IRA! Why doesn't anyone arrest the fecker?"

Because he's a Sinn Fein councillor, was Will's obvious answer. He had identified another member of the McGarry clan, a balding man in a tracksuit who was old enough to be – and almost certainly was – Conor's father. He made his way along the front row, nodding to the honoured guests, chatting with some of them, pressing the occasional hand. Will was pleased to see he and Russell simply eyed each other and exchanged barely two words.

One of the councillors, a DUP man, climbed between the ropes into the ring, trailing a cable from the microphone in his hand. A few experimental echoing taps, a howl of feedback, and his voice echoed around the warehouse, welcoming everyone, "from so many different neighbourhoods, all united in our love of a good, clean game!"

Hoots and applause came in equal measure from the audience.

"Good, clean, aye, that's right!" Alan shouted.

He was followed by the umpire, a man in a white shirt and bow tie, who took the mic and proceeded to lay down the rules.

"There will be no winners or losers tonight … The game will consist of twelve three-minute rounds, unless either player concedes before that … We will leave it up to the audience to judge for themselves who played the better game …"

Will guessed it would be an argument that would play out endlessly into the small hours in a dozen different pubs either side of the interface.

"And now, the moment you've all been waiting for – let's meet the players! In the blue corner, local lad and rising star, a big hand for … *Conor McGarry!*"

The Fenian half of the crowd raised the rafters with their cheers, loud enough that amid the desultory applause from his own side, Will could clap and cheer a little louder without standing out.

Conor came down the aisle between rows, clad in a robe tied at his waist, accompanied by his father. Will realised he was grinning with sheer delight and forced his face to go more neutral, clamping down on the tumult of pleasure and concern all mingled up together inside him. Conor didn't see him. His face was lowered a little and he gazed out at the ring from under dark brows. His face was set and determined, but he only looked like someone tackling a tough question in his homework, not facing up to a boxing match.

"And in the red corner, visitor and challenger, *Henry Wilson!*"

The Protestant side erupted in cheers and whistles and stamping feet as Henry approached from the other direction, also in a robe, accompanied by a coach Will didn't know. His progress was very different to Conor's, as he grinned and waved at the crowd like his victory was already granted.

And Will could see why he might think that. Conor and Henry had moved into the centre of the ring. Will already knew that Conor was a little shorter than him, and Henry maybe a little taller, but seeing them stand up to one another really brought the difference home – their heights, and their weights. Conor's neutral, thoughtful expression didn't waver as he looked up, while Henry smirked down at him, in his assumption of victory and inflicted pain and humiliation.

Will remembered Conor's proud definition of a middleweight. *Eleven stone exactly, not a pound over.* No fecking way was Henry a pissing eleven stone.

He tugged Alan's sleeve, interrupting his brother's cheers and claps.

"Co–… the Fenian's outclassed!" Will had to shout into his brother's ear. "Henry's way stronger and heavier!"

Alan shrugged and shouted back, not taking his eyes off the ring.

"Aye, well, we might have given the impression our lad was the same as theirs. So what are they going to do, stop the match and look stupid?"

The same thought seemed to be occurring to the umpire. Maybe it was the first time he had seen the two contestants in the same place and time. He gestured for the two coaches to come forward and a vigorous three-way conversation began, while the noise from the crowd grew to rattle the rafters of the old warehouse.

Conor settled the matter. While the adults argued, he simply tugged at his robe and let it fall to the floor, and held his gloved hands out to bump with Henry. Henry returned the gesture and the coaches bowed to the contestants' choice. McGarry Senior reluctantly retreated to Conor's corner and climbed out of the ring, taking Conor's robe with him, while Henry's man went the other way.

The fighters went face to face, Henry slowly turning from side to side to grin and smirk at his supporters, Conor simply standing and taking him in.

And Will was taking Conor in. For the first time, seeing him in boxing shorts and a singlet, he got a real appreciation of his figure, in a way he hadn't been able to back at the cottage with his very brief glimpse of Conor wearing a towel. He looked away out of instinct, when he realised he was enjoying what he saw – but then he deliberately looked back again. Since seeing Conor in a towel, they had kissed long and tenderly, he had felt Conor getting hard like him, and he no longer had a girlfriend so it wasn't even cheating. He was entitled to enjoy the view and he fecking well would.

From where Will was sitting, Conor was in a three-quarter profile, which as far as Will was concerned showed him off to the best advantage. Will had heard of a V-shaped body but never really seen one demonstrated so clearly. Conor's legs and waist were slim, and his bum-hugging shorts were drawn in at the waist, outlining a tantalising hint of what lay beneath. His torso swelled upwards from his hips into a pair of broad, powerful shoulders. He wasn't the kind to bulge with muscle – every muscle he had was defined just as much as it needed to be. Somehow Conor's figure summed up Conor's character – compact and measured, nothing wasted, everything exactly where it should be.

Henry ... well, Henry *did* bulge. There was no other word for it. He was a solid, overflowing lump of Fenian-bashing Orangeman who would be able to put Conor in hospital with one blow in the right place.

The umpire said a few final words to the two of them, and raised his hand. The noise level dropped to as close to silence as it would ever get. He chopped his hand down abruptly and stepped back; a bell rang and the fight was on.

And Henry moved much faster than Will had expected. Even while Conor was getting into his fighting stance – and he was no slouch – Henry's fist came whistling out of nowhere, and only Conor's quick reflexes stopped it being a knock-out blow. Will was on the edge of his seat, his voice adding to the shouts and yells but for a very different reason to Alan next to him. Conor pulled back and dodged just in time. If Henry had had the brains to follow through with another, while Conor was off guard, and another still, even Will could see that might have been the end of it.

But that wasn't Henry's style. In Henry's style, you hit someone hard enough to hurt them and then you stood back while they cried, or picked themselves up, or regained consciousness, and smugly received the appreciation of your friends.

What you didn't do was run the experience through a mental computer, analyse your opponent and revise your strategy. And you certainly didn't come back. Will could almost see the wheels turning as Conor's mind set itself to new parameters. *Okay, so that's how it is.*

The contestants circled, fists raised. Henry attacked again; Conor simply raised his gloves in front of his face and took the blows. *Float like a butterfly, sting like a bee …* For the first time, Will saw Conor's application of Muhammad Ali's advice.

But Henry did get through, from time to time. Whenever it happened, it was only a glancing blow – but a blow nonetheless, and it didn't take even the inexperienced Will long to see what was happening. Conor was favouring his left side, the side his wound had been. There was a weakness in his defence, and if Henry had any talents at all, finding weaknesses was one of them.

The bell rang for the end of the first round and the fighters returned to their corner. Conor's dad was immediately all over him with advice, and Will guessed it might be the same thing he had spotted, as Michael McGarry tapped the left side of his head. Conor nodded grimly, his eyes fixed dead ahead.

A short minute later, the next round was on. Conor pushed his mouth-guard back in and stood up to face the foe again.

At first it was more of the same, but now Will detected a gradual change.

First, Conor was picking up confidence, risking his left side as well as his right if he had to, able to believe that the wound wasn't going to re-open.

And second, he seemed to have the measure of Henry's technique, which was to put all his strength into a single blow, wait, withdraw arm, stand by for next blow. Henry never had anything in reserve, while Conor never put all he had into anything. It was like even his deadliest blows only used eighty percent of his strength. There was always something left, and Conor could be straight in with it when he needed to.

Will watched, transfixed. Conor had demonstrated his moves back at the cottage, but there had been a cushion in the way and Will had barely been able to see them. Now they were on full display.

Henry was not completely stupid and he was able to defend himself. He didn't have the mind for defence, though. He *had* to attack, and Conor had picked up on it. Now he was deliberately goading Henry into attacking, offering openings which abruptly closed up when Henry fell for them. Henry was using up strength while Conor still seemed fresh as a daisy.

The next minute between rounds was barely enough for Henry to get his breath back. Conor had him back down to his former level of tiredness within a minute of the third round starting, and there were still two more minutes to go. Henry was growing sluggish while Conor's movements were delicate and poetic. In Will's awestruck eyes he seemed to glide across the ring, his feet barely touching the floor. There was no other word for it – Conor was beautiful. Will realised with a sudden shock that his body was reacting again, and it would not be wise to stand up without discreetly readjusting himself.

Henry's confusion was growing. Now, whenever he aimed a punch at where Conor was, suddenly there Conor was not. At one point Will had to choke back a laugh as Connor skipped up behind Henry and gave him a hit that was more like a poke, a polite tap on the shoulder to say, "*Here I am!*" Conor was playing with him. Henry's supporters had picked up on this and their cheers were changing to growls and boos and shouts of anger.

The end came very soon in to round four. Henry threw a punch and stumbled forward under his own momentum, his guard down, and immediately Conor was in with his trademark machine gun fire that Will had only felt before, not seen. Henry seemed to wilt under the barrage, and then a final killer blow sent him down to one knee.

It wasn't a full knock-down. The umpire signalled Conor back. Henry knelt with his head hanging and his chest heaving. The umpire was asking him a question whose wording Will could guess – *D'ye want to go on, son?*

Henry raised his head and glared sheer hate at Conor, who returned the look with a neutral gaze. Then he lowered his head and shook it. The umpire crossed over to Conor, took his wrist and raised his hand above his head.

The Catholic side of the warehouse and Will jumped to their feet, cheering … and only then did Will realise Alan was looking up at him with shock and horror.

"Well, I mean …" Will shrugged. "It was a good fight …"

Alan pulled him angrily back down to his seat.

"You do *not* cheer those fuckers!"

But there were plenty of exceptions to that rule, even on the Protestant side, even if they had been cheated of eight of the promised twelve rounds. Most of everyone there that night had come to see a good fight, and they had, so honour was satisfied all round. Michael McGarry hung Conor's robe over his shoulders and he made his triumphant, modest way out of the ring. Then he disappeared as the crowd started to clamber to their feet, pulling hats and coats together, getting ready to hit the pubs and diagnose the fight until the sun came up.

Will didn't see what happened to Henry. Presumably there was only one men's changing room – were they both going to end up back there? Hmm, that could be interesting for both of them …

But all that was swept from his mind by the sudden sight of Wendy in the milling crowd.

Chapter 17: Then What?

Conor was running on the spot, on his own in the gym office, warming down to let the adrenaline drain. The dispersing crowd was still loud outside, and he could see milling bodies through the half-silvered windows. He and Da hadn't even had to consult on it – he would let Henry Wilson get well clear of the men's changing room before Conor used it himself.

The door opened, just enough for Michael McGarry to slide in.

"Shouldn't you be out there, Da?"

His father smiled.

"Cormac and the others can see to them. I want to get in with the celebration first!"

He unlocked the top drawer of his filing cabinet to produce a bottle of whisky and a pair of paper cups. Conor slowed down to a stop.

"Home distilled? Da, you shouldn't have!"

"Nothing but the best for you, son. Sláinte!"

Conor slumped into one of the chairs with the cup and returned the toast. He sighed happily, and not just at the way the hooch slammed into his taste buds. He felt … he felt bloody fucking good.

All that was missing was Will to share his triumph with. Maybe Will had been out there? He had kept trying to call throughout the week to let him know about the fight, but somehow they just hadn't connected.

"That was a set-up, wasn't it, Da?"

Da snorted.

"Son, they couldn't set up a coffee table, but aye, that's what it was meant to be. I think you set it down again very nicely." He raised his cup. "I should have guessed the second I learnt Councillor Wilson had got himself involved." He checked his watch. "Wilson must be out of the changing room by now. It should be safe for you …"

A heavy knocking interrupted him. They looked quickly towards the door, both prepared for aggression from a pissed-off Protestant. Da suddenly grinned at the shape that was trying to peer through the mirrored strips, and crossed the floor in two quick steps to pull the door open.

"Tommy! I didn't know you were in town."

"Yes, well, I was passing through …" an English voice said. "No, no, sit down, Conor, sit down!"

Conor had shot to his feet as Tommy Clifford surged into the room, his mohair coat billowing behind him. The Englishman barely acknowledged Da, both his eyes fixed firmly on the champion of the moment. He grabbed Conor's hand and pumped it as if money was already coming out of his mouth.

"That – was – *excellent!* I thought bear baiting and public executions went out of style years ago but not in Northern Ireland, apparently … Oh, thank you …"

Da had handed him a third paper cup. He drained it in a couple of swallows, forcing the last drops down with a cough and a grimace.

"*Jee … ee … sus …*" He blinked away tears and shook his head. "Well, I've seen what I came to see! Conor, that was perfection. I couldn't ask for more. I wanted to see you fight and now I have. You haven't been headbutting any more roof tiles, then?"

Conor smiled, suddenly bashful.

"Not lately, Tommy. I try but they keep dodging me."

"Well, stay away from them because as far as I'm concerned, you're coming to England. Michael, could you write your home address down for me? Thank you. Now, Conor."

Clifford swung back towards him, and suddenly his eyes were hard steel and the smile barely hovered at his lips.

"A contract is going to land on your doorstep within the next few days. It's not negotiable, it'll be my best offer and you can take it or leave it. There'll be two copies, so if you decide to take it then you sign both and post one back to me. You're over eighteen, you're allowed to sign for yourself. Understand?"

Suddenly feeling like a twelve-year-old having his fortune read by the headmaster, Conor nodded dumbly. At the back of his mind, he clocked that as far as this Englishman was concerned, an eighteen-year-old Catholic had all the rights of an eighteen-year-old Protestant, and that felt strange and wild and good and frightening; but he left the thought there at the back, to take out and examine later.

"But before you sign, read it very, *very* carefully because it is going to govern your life for the next few years. You're going to be a busy man. You're going to work hard, you're going to train hard and you get a private life when I say – though don't worry, I'm not unreasonable and I know when to let you young men off the leash, ha ha!"

Conor smiled politely.

"And after all that …" Clifford held him by the shoulders and fixed him with a final, hard stare. "You'll come out famous at the other end, or I'm a Dutchman. Gotta go, I've got a flight to catch …"

The door closed behind Tommy Clifford and left Conor and his father feeling like a whirlwind had just blown through the office and their lives.

"Shit," Conor said quietly. There was none of the elation they had felt at the end of the Englishman's first visit. Suddenly it seemed too big for that.

"Aye," Da said heavily.

"I …" Conor looked slowly around him, seeing not just the office but the gym beyond it, and beyond that, Belfast – his home. The city that held everything and everyone he had ever loved and known. "Da." His voice was very small. "I don't know if I can …"

"You stop that right now, Conor McGarry!" Da jabbed a finger right under his nose. "You can and you will!"

"But …" Conor said helplessly. "You need me at the gym …"

"We'll cope."

Conor said again, "But …", and this time he could only wave his hands in a vague sort of way that said, *everything*.

"Son." Now it was Da's turn to take his shoulders, with infinitely more compassion than Clifford but just as much resolve. "Sure we'll miss you, but you know, it's a hour flight to and from England? And there's such a thing as phones and from what I hear you don't even have to shout to be heard at that distance anymore. And no, it won't be easy having to hire someone to fill in for you when they'll go and expect a decent wage and all – but, the best thing you can do for us, for the gym, for yourself, for all of Belfast is go over to England, and use the opportunities you will never have over here in a million years, and then come back, rich and famous so no one can ignore you, and show that even a working class boy from the Falls Road area can make it."

Conor puffed out his cheeks as he felt his shoulders slump and he knew every word was true. Truth to tell, he had known it even before he said anything. But it helped to share the misery a little.

"Can I at least finish the decorating?"

"Ach." Da waved a hand to dismiss it. "Forget the decorating. This is more important …"

"No, Da!" Now it was Conor's turn to be firm. "I promised Katie! And I'm almost done. I'm just going to finish off the mural."

Da shrugged.

"Aye, well, what kind of uncle would break his word to a little girl who has no idea he promised her anything on account of not yet being able to speak English? Sure, do what you have to, son. That mural could be fiddly, though. Will you want a hand?"

Conor opened his mouth to answer, and then shut it, because it was suddenly dawning on him that with all his thoughts about the future, he had left one person right out of it.

"It's fine, Da. I'll get a friend in to help out."

* * *

Wendy was perched on the short wall outside the pub when Will finally emerged from the throng inside, two brimming pints miraculously unspilled in his hands.

"Thank you." Wendy took her glass and Will plonked his backside down next to her.

"Thank *you*," he said sincerely.

She had seen him in the gym at the same time as he saw her. Her face had not lit up with a sudden ray of hope. She had looked at him, maybe a little wistfully, and then she had began to turn away.

But then she had paused and looked back, and he had pressed his hands together in a praying gesture and mouthed one word.

"*Please?*"

Alan had seen their glances across the crowd, and even he could see it might be best to withdraw, though not without a final smirk and patting Will on the shoulder in a man-to-man way.

And here they were.

"Well."

"Well."

Will opened his mouth to speak. He had decided not to beat about the bush – just go ahead and say it. It was more honest than building up to it with polite small talk.

She surprised him by going in first.

"You never really had a go at trying to get into my knickers, and I wasn't sure if I was glad or not, but thank you. I kind of liked not being pawed at like some of my girlfriends. I might have liked a few more snogs because you're not a bad looking fella, but then what? Say you wanted to stick your lad into me. Say I let you. Then what? Say that one day I find a man who'll marry me. Say that he's had his share of girlfriends already. All I'll know is that however much he says he loves me, he couldn't be arsed to wait for me, and he'll know the same about me and him."

So ... I was never marriage material?

That was the only interpretation Will could put on what she was saying. 'Say that one day I find' implied that she hadn't already. He bounced the interpretation around in his head a few times, studying it from different angles, trying to work out what he made of it.

"So you'd only do it with a guy you think you might marry?"

She shrugged and sipped her pint.

"Who can even know that? But aye, let's just say you only do it if you think there's a good chance. You're giving him the benefit of the doubt. Then what? You have to imagine that this is the fella you'll be waking up next to every day for the rest of your life. Jesus, that's scary."

Will probed the implications carefully, like he was feeling for a broken bone beneath the skin.

"Could you imagine waking up next to me every day?"

"Honestly? No. But that's not a strike against you. I can't imagine waking up next to anyone like that. You've been a good boyfriend, though. You've always respected me and I know my life would have been a lot harder without you around. But I'll be moving down to Queen's next month … Whatever we've got, is it enough to keep going?"

The whole conversation was so rooted in the past tense that Will could only draw one conclusion. He was being dumped – and not because of what she thought had happened in the cottage. This was something she must have built up to over time.

She had given him an opening. He could just walk away now, act like the better man, be magnanimous in defeat.

He clamped down hard on the gush of relief. She deserved better than that.

Because she was right. She had brought out into the open a private fear he had had ever since she announced her plans of becoming a teacher – and maybe before that, too. They weren't going to marry. They probably never would have. Accept it.

"Whatever you heard my prick of a brother say, I was not shagging anyone at the cottage."

A look of annoyance, swiftly concealed, crossed her face.

"Will, it doesn't matter, I was just saying …"

"It does matter," he said firmly, "because I heard everything you just said, and I didn't hear anything there that said we can't stay friends. Not boyfriend and girlfriend, just friends. Right?"

She tipped her head in acknowledgement.

"Right."

"And I've got my pride too. I don't want to be your friend despite you thinking I'm the kind of guy who cheated on you behind your back."

Her eyes narrowed a little, but she nodded again.

"Fair enough. Okay. So you weren't shagging anyone at the cottage."

"And I didn't tell Alan I was, either. Everything you heard was just Alan getting hold of the wrong end of the stick."

"So what's at the right end? Whatever you were doing, it was something you couldn't just tell me about."

He drew a breath, and she pointed.

"And there it is again. There's *something* that means you have to think about your answer. Okay, so you weren't shagging. But there was someone else, at the cottage, that you don't want me to meet?"

It was the exact opening he had been hoping for. He could just come out and say it. In fact, she was probably the only person in the whole province that he could just say it to.

"There was someone I would really like you to meet, one day. I think you'll get on."

"Oh?" Her eyebrows were up. "Tell me more."

"Well …" Here it comes. "There's two things you should know about him."

He gave it just long enough to see it start to sink in – the fact that yes, he really had said *him*.

"And the other is he's Catholic."

Her pint was sagging in her hand. He had to catch it before it started to spill onto her knees.

She mouthed the one word silently.

"*Him?*"

He nodded.

"Him," she murmured. She looked quickly around to make sure they weren't being overheard. "I won't even ask how you met a …"

"No," he said sincerely, "please don't."

"*Him.*" She drew a long, thoughtful swallow from her pint. "Is he good looking?"

Will choked on a laugh. It was so unexpected – and it was so good to be able to say things like this out loud.

"He's … I think so. You tell me. You've seen him."

"Oh?"

"Just this evening. The Catholic lad in the ring. Conor McGarry." His tongue gently caressed the name as it came out.

"The one who beat Henry?" She burst out laughing. "I like him already. Aye, you're right. He'd be a catch and I'd love to meet him. But how did you –…? No, I said I wouldn't ask." She frowned and lowered her voice. "I really didn't realise you were the kind of guy who …" She waggled her head.

"Nor did I! Not until … recently."

"So, you weren't shagging in the cottage, but are you going to …?"

"I don't know!" The words burst out in frustration. "I wouldn't even know how to … you know, with another fella."

She took another sip.

"I've heard there are ways," she said mildly.

"Aye, but I … Well, everything you were saying about couples just now? It works the same here, too. We feel like this about each other … but what we do next? Then what? I have absolutely no idea!"

It was baffling and ludicrous and suddenly they were laughing and crying together.

"So, you can see why I don't want to tell my brother about this?" Will said eventually. Laughter danced in her eyes.

"There's about a bazillion people you don't want to tell but sure, let's start with him. And also …" She sighed, and looked straight ahead. "Will … you do know … two men … you know it's illegal?"

Will felt a sudden surge of anger.

"Only if you … You know." At least, that was what he assumed. What they had done in the cottage – just kiss – could that get them into trouble? "Just fancying each other … that can't be illegal … Can it?"

Was it? Christ, that was unfair, if it was!

He imagined what Conor would say if he could overhear that thought. The sardonic retort: "You think *that's* unfair, Mr Protestant?"

"Oh, Will." She rested her hand on his knee, a gesture of affection between two friends who cared for each other. "Just – be careful. There's plenty of fellas who deserve to be beaten up way more than you, and who never will be. I don't want it to come to you instead."

They sat and silently finished their pints together. She set her glass firmly down on top of the wall.

"I always wondered what our break-up talk would be like."

"Did you."

"I can't understand what's going on your heart, Will, but you've always respected me, and been good to me, and I wish you and Conor well. Just … be safe? Please?" There was only sorrow in her eyes. "You could so easily be hurt, Will, by either side, and I couldn't stand that."

"We'll be safe," Will promised, without the slightest idea of how they would go about it. Wendy slid of the wall and held her arm out.

"And perhaps you could walk me home?"

Chapter 18: Mural

Sunday 10th August

"You're taller," Conor said. He rested his head on Will's shoulder. Their arms around each other's waists, they studied the freshly painted wall together. "You can touch it up by the ceiling."

"Sure." Will let his hand slide away from Conor's hips as he turned to survey the four walls of Katie's future nursery. Conor had used a roller to paint them in facing pairs, two a soft orange and two a gentle blue. But if he had got too close to the top then he would have scuffed the immaculate white of the ceiling, so closing the gap had always been a touch-up job left until last. "You've done a fine job here."

"Aye, well. She's worth it."

They smiled at each other, and Will wondered if they should move in for another kiss. But no, Conor was always the kind to put work ahead of pleasure, and he supposed he was too.

Conor had finally got through to him that morning. They had talked about the fight and Will had owned up to being there. And then he had lowered his voice and shyly mentioned the effect that seeing Conor move had had on him, and he was pretty certain Conor was pleased about it …

And then the bombshell.

"So, you know where the gym is, then? Well, could you come round after lunch …"

It wasn't quite being invited to meet the folks but it was as personal as Will inviting him to the cottage. But then Conor had admitted there was a reason … So Will had come dressed in scruff jeans and t-shirt. Conor had directed him around to the rear of the building, and the backdoor into the extension.

They had kissed, briefly, the moment the door closed – but that was all. They both knew they were still at the stage of trying to work out where they went from here. And meanwhile – well, they had the prospect of an uninterrupted afternoon in each other's company, and that was just fine.

The nursery was the last room that needed doing. Cormac and Claire had already started moving stuff in to the room next door. Piles of boxes, a mattress perched on its edge, furniture stacked one item on top of the other. The boys got to work silently, just enjoying each other's company while the radio played in the background. Will could easily reach the ceiling and do the final touching up, while Conor got busy on the very last job – tearing up stripes of masking tape to sketch out the mural on the wall. As Will worked his way along the ceiling he was vaguely aware of Conor throwing him glances.

"What?"

"Oh." Conor was suddenly coy. "Nothing."

"*What?*"

Conor tore off another strip, and smiled up at him.

"When you lift your arm like that … your shirt rides up. You're not bad."

"That's two of us." Eye contact lingered a second longer before they went back to their jobs, smiling secret smiles.

Will finished his job first, and then he could help Conor. Conor had sketched out the basic design on a notepad and now he was copying it onto the wall with the tape. Three very simple teddy bears – a mummy bear, a daddy bear and a baby bear.

"We'll just fill them in with solid colour," he said. "Then we can do the eyes and Katie gets her mural."

Will laughed when he saw that the bears were going to be green, orange and white. They crouched next to each other, arms and knees and shoulders sometimes brushing as they worked, each contact sending another thrill into their bodies that now felt completely safe and natural. Will remembered the thought he had had when he fell asleep at the cottage with Conor's arm over him: if this was as good as it got, well, that was still pretty fecking good. Will concentrated on the white mummy bear – "It's the only colour we've got in common" – and then used the stencil Conor had made out of a sheet of cardboard to put in the eyes and nose and mouth.

"I didn't know you could do art too."

"Aye, fucking Renaissance Man, that's me."

At last it was done, and they could carefully peel away the tape. Conor scrunched it into a sticky ball and side by side they admired the friendly teddy family waving back at them.

"She's going to love this room," Will said proudly.

"Aye, she will." Conor's voice was soft and full of love for the little girl.

Will felt Conor's arm slide around his waist again, his head go back on his shoulder. He returned the gesture and instinctively twined a finger into one of Conor's belt loops. His thumb delved idly into the gap between waistband and smooth skin.

Conor suddenly jerked as if he had been stung and tore away.

"Fucker!"

Will stared in hurt surprise and Conor glared at him with something like outright hostility, an instinctive, defensive reaction. Then he sucked his cheeks in as he realised he had just made himself look foolish.

"Sorry."

"What?" Will demanded, still hurt. "What was that?"

"Oh …" Conor made a transparent effort to shrug it off. "Nothing."

He sidled back close to Will, bit by bit, almost as if he wasn't quite brave enough to get close again. Will frowned, puzzled. All he had done was brush his thumb against Conor's waist and …

Understanding dawned with a slow, big grin.

"You're not ticklish, are you?"

"No," Conor said, just a bit too quickly, taking a smart step away again.

"You are!" Will's grin spread as he moved towards Conor. "You're fecking ticklish!"

"I am not ticklish!" Conor backed away, his arms clamped to his side. "How the fuck can I be ticklish, I'm a boxer, a boxer can't be ticklish and *stay away!* I'm warning you, Billy-boy, don't make me hurt you, you know that I can …"

He had backed himself into the corner. Will lunged forward with stiff fingers probing into Conor's waist, and Conor shrieked and writhed and collapsed to his knees, laughing and howling as Will drove him mercilessly down.

"*Stop it! Stop it, you fucker, you bastard, you … HA-A-A-A-H!*"

Conor toppled over onto his back, wriggling helplessly and laughing under Will's assault.

"*Okay, okay, that's enough, that's enough …*"

Suddenly his hands flashed up and gripped Will's wrists like steel cuffs, a hold Will could never break free of.

"That's enough," Conor said softly. He kept his grip on Will's wrists as his breathing slowed down, and their eyes met.

Then he gently laid Will's hands down, flat against his stomach, and let go of his grip.

"That's enough."

Their smiles slowly faded under their locked gazes. Conor reached a hand languidly up behind his head to act as a pillow. His eyes were fixed unwavering on Will's face, a challenge, an invitation to take this any way he would. Barely able to believe this was happening, Will crouched next to him, his hands still resting on Conor's stomach just above his belt. Conor's body was warm through the fabric of his t-shirt. Will moved a hand, cautiously, gently, not wanting to trigger another tickle reflex. Beneath the shirt he felt smooth muscle and heat. The fabric rucked up a little to reveal a few square inches of smooth, taut skin, Conor's belly button, a line of dark hair leading due south to below his buckle. Will swallowed, his mouth suddenly dry, and slid his hand beneath the shirt. Conor's body heat blazed direct into his palm, skin on skin. He slid it gently up. He felt the rippled muscles of Conor's six-pack, the curves of his pecs. Downy chest hair tickled against his palm; a finger brushed against a nipple.

Conor suddenly sat up, so abruptly that their heads almost banged together. In a swift movement he pulled his t-shirt off and flung it across the room. Then he lay back, his hand back behind his head, still with his silent, appraising gaze fixed on Will. Will stared in awe at the perfection of Conor's torso.

"You're beautiful," he murmured. "I knew you'd be beautiful …"

He pushed his face down into Conor's stomach and inhaled the scent and taste. He extended his lips and gently brushed them against Conor's skin in the softest of kisses. He felt Conor take hold of the back of his head, his fingers twining into his hair, gently caressing him, guiding him as he kissed his way up Conor's ribs, his chest, his neck. The faint gleam of sweat in the crevices of his collarbone was salty on his tongue. Conor craned his head back, exposing his throat, still guiding Will to kiss him there, and up to his chin – bristles brushed against Will's lips – and then Will's mouth finally reached Conor's, where his lips and tongue lay ready for him.

He felt Conor fumbling at his waist, tugging at the hem of his top. He briefly straightened up, holding his arms out straight so that Conor could tug it over his head and throw it over to join his own. Will flushed as for the first time in his life he felt the appraising gaze of a lover run over him, knowing that they liked what they saw, that he had nothing to apologise for.

"Aye," Conor murmured. "You're a fine thing." His hand rested very gently on Will's buckle. "We're going to, aren't we?"

Will's heart pounded heavier than ever before, every beat almost enough to send cramps through his body.

"You've done it before."

"Aye. With girls."

Will leaned forward again to kiss him.

"Show me," he murmured, his breath gusting against Conor's lips. He felt Conor's mouth expand into a smile, and a harder tug at his buckle.

"Small problem with that."

Will gazed into Conor's eyes, two deep pools of love meant only for him.

"Show me anyway."

Conor gazed up at him, then suddenly, again, sat up abruptly.

"Well, whatever we do, we're not doing it on the fucking floor."

* * *

Later, they could say they had slept together, though there was no sleeping. Perhaps they had dozed. They lay entwined in a naked tangle of arms and legs on the mattress, and said very little, their hands still gently, idly, toying with the other's body, wrapped up in each other, each occasionally looking into the other's eyes and seeing only the same amazement and wonder reflected back at him.

Will rested his head on the mattress and stared at Conor's profile. Conor twisted his head to look at him.

"What?"

"I can see into your ear."

"And?"

"Daylight all the way through. I knew it."

Though in fact he had been looking at where he knew the rock had hit Conor.

One day, he was going to have to come clean about that. Now was not the moment … But Will didn't want a single secret between them, ever again.

Will snuggled up close, rested his head on Conor's chest, felt Conor's arm go around him. Conor's heart beat a powerful, thudding rhythm in his ear. He ran his hand gently down Conor's side, caressing the curves and muscle of his lover's outline. Arm to waist to thigh to knee, marvelling that he could feel smooth skin all the way.

"That just really fecked things up, didn't it?" he murmured.

"It didn't make life any easier." Something in Conor's tone made Will look up. Conor stared up at the ceiling and Will could see the signs of an inner struggle rising to the surface. "It might not matter anyway."

"Oh?" Will propped himself up on an elbow to look down with concern. That sounded a bit too final for his liking. But Conor's smile showed he didn't need to be worried.

"I'm waiting for a letter."

"What kind of letter?"

"I'll tell you when it arrives. Don't want to get your hopes up."

Will smiled.

"It's not my hopes that's getting up …"

* * *

The afternoon couldn't last forever. Will reluctantly got up and crossed the room to start sorting through their discarded clothes. Conor lay back on the mattress, hands behind his head and a complacent smile on his face.

"Enjoying the view?"

"You bet." Conor's smile was the cat who'd got the cream.

Will grinned, shyly, as he picked his clothes up and Conor still gazed at him with frank admiration and happy memories. He wondered how long it would take to get used to it.

"I'm guessing not many people see you in the nip?"

"Not many," Will agreed as he started to pull his underwear back on.

"That's good, because you'd have a hell of a time explaining how you got paint down there."

Chapter 19: Interface

Wednesday 13th August

"Why are we always fecking 'and finally'?" Alan spat at the telly.

Alan was out of his suit and into his civvies, dressed to go out with the boys and looking sometimes at his watch while he waited for his ride to turn up, but until it got here, the Johnstons were watching the BBC's *Nine O'Clock News*. Philip Johnston had always watched it, so that was what they did too. Da had believed in keeping informed about the rest of the world …

… Even if the rest of the world thought Northern Ireland was only worth the 'and finally' slot – the last report in the bulletin before the weather. Tonight, a reporter was standing in front of City Hall while a demonstration filed past behind him.

"Aye, you're not wrong," Will agreed, even though he recognised a rhetorical question. He was just glad to have something to distract Alan. In just the last forty eight hours – the time since he and Conor had made love – his thoughts had been whirling as he tried to think through his new situation, and of course the ever-vigilant Alan had already noticed something different.

"*What is it about you?*" Alan had been waving his finger in the air at breakfast, as though he physically wanted to put it on whatever was bothering him. "*You're up and down. You're all happy and …*"

"*Sad?*" Will had asked.

"*No, not sad. Just … not-happy.*"

Then their mother had put a plate of biscuits in front of them and that ended the conversation.

It hadn't ended the distracting thought processes, because Will knew he and Conor were no closer to finding any solution to the situation they had got themselves into. No *acceptable* solution, anyway. One solution was they could always separate and not do it again: *not* acceptable.

Whenever he closed his eyes he remembered the perfection of Conor's naked body entwined with his. He had never realised how deep the intimacy of sex could go, if you let it. If you gave your heart as well as everything else. They had become one in every way you could.

"Ach, turn it off," Alan spat suddenly. Will would have been happy to let the news run but he didn't want to pick a fight with his brother – he didn't want to do anything that would invite further scrutiny into his life – so he started to cross the room towards the telly.

"Wait!" Ma said suddenly. "Isn't that Deirdre Ferguson's boy? Davy?"

Will paused, his hand over the 'off' switch, and he and Alan both peered more closely at the screen.

"Oh, aye." Alan sounded pleased. "He's one of the good ones."

Davy Ferguson was one of a group of placard-wielding supporters standing as background behind a tall, middle-aged man with steel-grey hair, who was bellowing into a microphone as he addressed the demonstration. The man had the build of a concrete wall clad in a macintosh, and a mouth the size of a railway tunnel, and every gesture, every twitch, every syllable broadcast an implacable anger and suppressed violence, though Will knew the man would always claim with hand on heart to be a man of peace, and perhaps he even believed it himself. This was the Reverend Ian Paisley, the man who had founded his own church and then his own party because all the other alternatives were too liberal, and used them to become the loudest and most significant voice in Northern Ireland's religion and politics. As much as anyone could tell the two apart anyway, he was the point where one blended into the other.

And then he saw what had aroused Alan's anger. It wasn't Ian Paisley – never that! – or the placards. It was what the placards said.

SAVE ULSTER FROM SODOMY.

Will slowly returned to his chair. He vaguely knew Deirdre Ferguson's boy; he wasn't surprised that Alan considered him to be one of the good ones, and he wasn't *at all* surprised to see him cheering in the middle of Paisley's supporters.

Paisley's tirade was tuned down as the reporter explained.

"The Save Ulster from Sodomy movement was created by the Reverend Ian Paisley three years ago in response to the intentions of the Westminster government to decriminalise homosexuality equally throughout the United Kingdom. Homosexuality is already legal for relations between consenting adults aged twenty-one or more in England and Wales, and Scotland is widely expected to follow suit …"

The image changed to another talking head, a weedy looking fella in his thirties with greasy hair and glasses, explaining why Paisley was wrong. The caption said he was from the Queen's University Gay Society. Alan snorted.

"More like Queer's University."

Will frowned at the caption. The third word had caught his attention. Gay? In the context he had to assume it meant what he thought it did, but he felt it was not the most helpful way of putting it. Who thought that one up?

Paisley was back, and at full volume.

"And I tell the government in London that this kind of immoral, unnatural perversion will become legal in Ulster OVER MY DEAD BODY!"

Ma was squinting at Davy's placard.

"So–… do–… my. What's that, then?"

Alan and Will looked at each other, both biting down a smile in a moment of unexpected unity.

"It's … Will, explain to your mother."

"Get up the yard!" Will put all his malice into his smirk. "You're the man of the family."

Paisley had been replaced by a grimacing colour photo of some old fool with a moustache who according to the caption was a Conservative MP from London, and an English voice was speaking over a phone. The gist of it was that Paisley was absolutely right. The words 'filth' and 'vile' were used.

Alan drew a breath, sighed.

"Okay, Ma …"

Alan's cheeks blazed red but he gave it a manful attempt, using as few syllables as it was possible to do while Will just grinned.

He kept the grin at Alan's awkwardness, though a small voice inside began to scream and he made himself ignore it: *This is what Alan thinks of you!*

Alan was articulating what Will already knew and hadn't let himself think about. Different things that had been floating around in his head came together and he finally saw them all as pieces of a bigger picture.

Of course he hadn't exactly come home on Sunday and blurted out, "Ma, Alan, you'll never guess what I just did with a Fenian boy!" He didn't think he had done a thing that was wrong, but he wasn't stupid and he hadn't thrown an instinct for self-preservation away along with his other inhibitions.

But for the first time it occurred to him that he and Conor were now, legally speaking, homosexuals. Or to put it more bluntly, as Ian Paisley probably would, sodomites.

"You know, Ma, like Mrs Hamilton's son, remember?" Alan finished. "He went off to England all of a sudden? He got caught in the toilets by the undercover policeman." He smirked. "Fella got an *awful* beating." It did not sound like he thought it was awful.

"Oh." Ma pouted and clicked her tongue, like she had just heard Mrs Hamilton's son's infraction was on the same scale as leaving turds floating in the toilet, or swearing in church. "Sure why would any man want to do that? Or have it done to him?"

Alan stared at Will with a silent plea for help. Will just shrugged back at him, while the voice kept screaming.

"Not everyone agrees …" the reporter was saying. The camera showed a few more angles on the demo, and lingered briefly on a young round-faced man Will's own sort of age, a wee bit stocky in build, standing on his own on the edge of the demo with a placard that looked almost identical to those being waved – until you looked more closely and saw what it said. SAVE SODOMY FROM ULSTER. Will had to suck his cheeks in to stop himself laughing. Christ, that boy had to have the biggest balls of anyone on the march.

The impulse to laugh went very quickly away again, as the implications continued to sink in with a leaden finality.

Homosexuality … Sodomy …

He had not required Alan's explanation of those long words. He had known what they meant for a long time, ever since the pastor – a man of impeccable married moral pedigree – had come into Boy's Club and delivered the most euphemistic explanation Will had ever heard to a bunch of squeaky-voiced boys whose only body hair was on top of their heads, who despised girls as inferior beings and had never felt an atom of sexual desire for anyone in their lives. He still remembered the strange feeling of listening attentively, along with the other boys, and expressions changing as the penny finally dropped, at different speeds in different parts of the room, as to what the man was talking about. To tell the truth, their reaction had been very similar to his mother's just now. Men who put their *what*, *where*? *Why?*

Conor and he were those sort of men.

And as Wendy had pointed out, and as Paisley was kindly reminding the whole world: what those sort of men did was actually illegal. They were lawbreakers, too.

And as Conor had said, back in the cottage, when all they had done was kiss: their lives could become very unpleasant and very unlong. Very unslowly.

And that was just the start of what lay ahead of them.

Will looked at his mother's profile with a quick sideways glance, and a pang went into his heart. He didn't want to be keeping anything from her. He certainly didn't want to be lying to her. She and Wendy had always got on, and he would love for her and Conor to have the same easy relationship. But her remark had made him see the huge gap that lay between her understanding and his. It wasn't just a case of telling her that her baby boy was in love with another boy. To have a meaningful conversation they would have to start a long way further back than that.

On screen, the news story ended with a close up of Ian Paisley's face. *And there's the problem*, he thought with a sudden bitterness. How could he and Conor ever have a future for one second when this man, and his kind, spent every minute of every day preaching hatred against them?

A fresh surge of sheer love for Conor pulsed through him. This was what his boyfriend had put up with every day of his life, and he could still smile. Smile, and joke, and love someone on Paisley's side.

He wished someone would do to Ian Paisley what Conor had done to him. It might actually shut the man up. Briefly.

Out in the hall, the phone rang twice and stopped. Ma clicked her tongue again in irritation.

"Fecking thing's been doing that all day, and yesterday! I should talk to the Post Office about it."

* * *

Conor's feet scuffed the litter as he lurked impatiently in the shadow of the interface at the end of the alley. He was too stoked to stay still. His kitbag lay at his feet and he was in his grey trackies. The family knew he was on his way to the gym and he should have been there by now. If one of them decided to come on down, they would wonder where he was. Where was the eejit?

Will had actually heard the phone ring and called the phone box ten minutes later – but what Conor had to say was too important for that, too much to risk on the pips going off as they both ran out of coins at exactly the wrong moment. So he had directed Will to meet him here. Much riskier, yes, but worth every second of it. Will trusted him enough to take him at his word, and –…

"Conor?" the whisper came through the nearest crack in the interface. "You're there?"

"Aye." Conor crouched down and peered through. Will's eyes shone back at him with love – and a little understandable curiosity. He clocked what Conor was wearing.

"You're on your way to the gym?"

"Aye, in a moment …"

The boys reached towards each other and their fingers twined, sending a thrill like an electric shock through Conor's body.

"I wish I could kiss you," Will said. "I want to kiss you."

"Give it time, fella, give it time."

Will cocked his head.

"Oh?"

Excitement surged through Conor's guts.

"Y'know I said I was waiting for a letter? It arrived! And … it's everything. *Everything!*"

It had fallen on the doormat that morning, first class post from England, and the entire McGarry clan had gathered around to read it through. Several times. Even Nana Clodagh had commented on the nice quality of the paper. If there were any traps in it, they were very well hidden, and he was pretty sure you would have to get up very early indeed – and an Englishman, even earlier – to get one past his Da. No, it really did seem straight. God had truly delivered.

"Every what?"

Conor took a few breaths. Usually so good at saying it as it was, now it was all getting jumbled up in his head. He had always made himself keep calm, look one step ahead, avoid any traps or dangers. It was scary to suddenly be rushing into something and he mentally took a few steps back.

"Okay. The fight the other night? There was this Englishman there. I've not told you about him before, he wasn't important back then, but … This letter! It's sponsorship! It's a fucking contract! It's for me to go to fucking *England* and be paid a fucking *salary* to fucking *fight! Paid!* And there'd be help with what he calls relocation, which basically means finding a home …"

Their fingers slid apart.

"You're moving to England." Will's tone was suddenly very odd. Flat. Dead, or at least dying.

"No, no, no!" Conor insisted hastily. "*We* are! Can't you see it? You and me. *We* go! Okay, the contract's only for me, you'd have to get a job too, but cars work the same in England, don't they? Sure you'd find a job in a garage, easy! And we get a place together, and …"

He gave Will half a second to gather his thoughts and respond to his bombshell, and then ran out of patience.

"Will … it can work! Look, the first time I met this guy, his name's Tommy Clifford, he made a crack about mixed schools, and I thought he meant Catholics and Protestants, but no! He meant boys and girls! In England, *that's* a mixed school! The whole Catholic and Protestant thing – it just doesn't exist in England! And, and, and …" He leaned closer, dropped his voice even lower. "I saw this report on the telly. What we did? It's legal in England!"

"If you're twenty-one," Will said, still in the same voice. "I saw the same thing."

"Ach." Conor waved the problem away. "Like three years makes a difference, and if does then we put a knot in our mickeys until then. Anyway, Tommy already said I wouldn't have time for a private life. I'm going to be busy, but that's fine. Will, you and me, we can be together there. We'll be safe, and at the end of the day we still come home to each other, and from time to time there'll still be ... well, time."

This time he bit his tongue and made himself give Will a space to reply. He stared beseechingly down the tunnel, willing the thoughts to fall into the right order in his boyfriend's head.

Will eventually spoke, and he still didn't sound delighted.

"Maybe the law doesn't care if you're not much under twenty-one," he conceded, "but what does everyone else think? Did you see that English MP prat on the telly? Do you think people here are only against it because it's against the law, and changing the law would change anything at all?"

This time it was Conor's turn to not be given enough time to respond. Will pressed on.

"Would you still get your sponsorship if they knew you have a boyfriend?"

Instinctive fury surged inside Conor.

"They can go fuck themselves! Like it's any of their fucking business!"

"They could make it their fucking business. If I was giving someone a lot of money, that's what I would do. If I was paying the piper, I'd call the tune."

Conor forced himself to calm down. If Will needed a bit more persuasion then throwing a wobbler wouldn't help either of them.

"As far as they're concerned, we'd be two friends sharing digs," he said slowly. "So fucking what?"

He stared down the crack at Will, seeing the doubt and struggle on that face he loved so much, trying to understand it.

Will hung his head, shook it.

"Conor … you didn't see my family when we watched that thing. They … Ma wouldn't understand, and Alan and people like him … they just hate us. People like us, I mean."

"People like Alan have hated people like me all my fucking life, just for a different reason, which makes just as much sense. You get over it."

"I can't just head over to England!" Will wailed.

"Why the fuck not?" Conor could feel himself running out of patience, and his ability to care was running out shortly behind it. Maybe Will needed a few sharp words to knock the sense into him.

"I'd have to give my notice to Mitchell's, tell Ma and Alan I'm leaving …"

"Why not? Why fucking not?"

"Because they'll ask why …"

"So fucking what?"

"And I couldn't just say, oh, I've decided to up it to England …"

"*Why fucking not?*"

"*I'm not leaving fucking Belfast!*"

A pause as they stared at each other down the crack in angry horror. But Conor wasn't letting him get away with it that easily.

"Why not? Don't tell me you couldn't just walk away if you wanted."

"I ..."

The idea flew out of the night and into Conor's head. Something to hit Will with. Something to hurt and make him see sense. And it might just possibly be true.

"Is it too unknown for you?"

"Huh?"

"Is it because over there you might have to fucking work for something?"

Will stared.

"*Huh?*"

There was no holding it back now. Conor moved in for the machine gun move, with words instead of fists.

"You know? Instead of just sitting back and living the life of Reilly because you were born on the right side of the interface? Having to stop not trying? Is that all going to be too much?"

Will looked on the edge of tears.

"Conor, they would hate us!"

"I don't care what they would fucking think!" Conor shouted. "And why would you? You didn't care back when we were tearing the clothes off each other. We both knew exactly what we were doing and don't say you didn't."

"I knew it, I knew all the shite we were heading for …" Will was almost begging. "I thought we could do this together …"

"Aye, we can! *But not in fucking Belfast!*"

There! Conor crowed in inward triumph. He must have made his point. Will's face was shifting. The doubt was fading, reason was settling in …

No. Will's face had settled down to cold but it wasn't changing any further. Turned out Conor wasn't the only one who could reach for a verbal club to hurt the other.

"Bonfire Night."

Conor drew his head back, frowned.

"What about it?"

"That rock that hit you …"

"Aye, what about it?"

Will said it simply, a statement of fact, no emotion.

"I threw it."

Silence, for who knew how long.

"What?" Conor asked quietly.

"I threw it."

More silence, until …

"Why?" Conor breathed. "Why would you throw a fucking rock at me?"

Will's jaw wobbled slightly, his Adam's apple bobbed up and down. His voice was the same. Cold. Distant. Alien.

"To … to show the Fenians who's boss."

"*Really.*" Conor looked along at Will and felt nothing but baffled contempt. He stood slowly up, hands reflexly brushing his knees and thighs as if he was dusting away the ashes of their love. "Well … fuck you, Will Johnston. Fuck you and your whole cosy Protestant world."

And he walked away into the dark while tears he was too proud to cry pricked at the back of his eyes.

* * *

Streetlights blurred through watering eyes into slowly turning stars as Will stumbled by. If anyone was curious about the big young man's public distress they kept it to themselves, though he felt gazes settle on him as people turned to look safely back after he had passed. But feck them.

They were wise to keep their thoughts to themselves, because he had never wanted to smash someone's face in more than he did then. Starting with his own, the face of the biggest eejit in the world.

An eejit for falling in love with another boy.

An eejit for falling in love with another boy who also happened to be Catholic.

An eejit for managing it anyway, and creating something that was utterly beautiful and wonderful, and then banjaxing the thing they had made together with the barest minimum of words. He had reached for something, anything, that would push Conor away, for his own sake, to keep them both safe, and he had found it. Oh, he had found it.

So, now what?

Will stopped at a lamppost, leaned against it, thinking. He dragged his wrist across his nose to wipe the snot away, and blinked back the tears as he put it all together.

He was a homosexual sodomite in Protestant North Belfast. Shit.

Conor had accused him of not trying. Of not having to try. And he was right. The fact remained, he *was* a *Protestant* in Protestant North Belfast. As long as he accepted a certain kind of life, he didn't *need* to try. Good things came to him, because of who he was.

No, fuck that! he ordered himself. He fucking well *could* try. Mr Mitchell might not employ him if he was a Catholic, but he also wouldn't employ him if he wasn't good at his job. He had certificates framed on his wall at home which showed that anyone could leave their car in his hands with confidence, and he had worked long and hard to get them.

And – as Wendy would say – then what?

He leaned his head against the cold metal and moaned. Wendy. Wendy had been his gateway into a normal future, back when neither of them had known the truth about who and what he was. Everyone – the two of them included – had assumed they would marry, have kids. And maybe they would have got round to it, eventually, losing their virginities together on their wedding night and never having anyone else while they lived out their lives, maybe not blazingly happy, but not terrible either.

If he hadn't thrown that rock.

But she knew, now. She would not go through with a farce, which is what it would be if he even tried to go crawling back.

Well, he could do something about all of this, and he would start tomorrow, at work. His work would no longer just be good. It would be *excellent*. He would dazzle Mr Mitchell, he would get promotion, he would pull in a decent salary, he would get to the point he could offer any girl who wanted it a home of her own. Owned and paid for. Somewhere to have kids and be a proper family together.

And he could do something about the other thing, too. It had been that one time with Conor, and never again. From now on, Will Johnston shagged only girls. He had to cross Wendy off the list of possibilities and start all over again. Find a girl who didn't know what he was, get to the point where they could marry … and carry on as planned.

Laughter and music drifted from the pub across the road to disturb his mood, and he lifted his head to glare. But then he looked at it more thoughtfully.

He could start now, and why the fuck not? He knew the place, had been in there a few times with Wendy, but not much because it wasn't really the kind steady couples went to. Well, that suited him just fine. He wasn't going to meet the future

Mrs Johnston in there, but he was going to deal with something far more fundamental. He no longer had a girlfriend or a boyfriend, so he wasn't cheating on anyone. He was an eighteen-year-old red blooded male virgin and he had a lot of catching up to do.

He set off across the road, and the tall, handsome fella who entered the pub was nothing like the weeping eejit of a few moments earlier. Maybe still a wee bit red-eyed, but apart from that he was calm, confident, self-possessed and on the pull.

It didn't take long. Will was deliberately sweeping the room with his eyes even as he placed his order at the bar. All the time and effort he put into his appearance was paying off – he could even split up with his lover and still look good. Whenever he had been out with Wendy, he had always been aware of other girls' eyes on him too, and it had amused both of them because she had known he had no interest in anyone else.

And there was a pack of them, as he had guessed there would be, over in the corner, herded together for mutual protection and support. He let his gaze linger on the finest looking one for a second longer, and he saw her faint smile and nod.

"And whatever she had last," he told the barman, cocking a finger like a pistol in her direction.

She came sashaying over to the bar to get it. The drink.

"What's the craic?"

"I was just thinking you've got amazing eyes."

The amazing eyes rolled, a little. Okay, it wasn't the best line. Will made a mental note. He shouldn't let his inexperience show. Just make it clear he had everything she was expecting.

They chatted a little bit more, drank their drinks together. It wasn't long before he ordered another round. And then another. His head was starting to buzz pleasantly and he had already forgotten her name.

He also realised, suddenly, he was forgetting what he was here for. He was too used to being Mr Nice Guy with Wendy, and not taking it any further because he didn't want to. He still had to deal with being a hom–… hos–… homsomexual dosomite.

He burped, and had still had enough social grace to let it fill the back of his mouth before letting it silently out through his nose.

"Do you want to go somewhere?"

She smiled.

"My place or yours?"

He puffed his cheeks out while he thought it through. His place, out of the question. Hers, he didn't know a thing about it and shit, he didn't want this to turn into anything.

"How about somewhere nearer outside?"

"Jesus, you don't hang around, do you? Okay, but you're buying me another after. I know where we can go."

It was starting to drizzle so the beer garden was empty, but there was shelter and a dark corner leading into an even darker alleyway. She led him by the hand and Will followed meekly until they were out of sight of the pub's back door. She turned towards him and started to kiss him, and he had to remember to put his arms around her. *Come on, you've done this much with Wendy at least!*

What else did Wendy like him doing?

He dredged the memory up and tentatively started to kiss her neck, her throat, getting towards her breasts. The appreciative noises said he must be doing something right, though he was aware of getting dangerously near the edge of his experience.

Looked like it was going to be a knee trembler, which he had on good authority was not a lot of fun. How exactly did they do that? he wondered muzzily. Were both people standing? She would have to open her legs up, which would mean taking her feet off the floor, and girls didn't just hover. She must need some kind of support.

But she was backing away, propping her arse up on a low wall, lifting her legs to wrap around his waist. Question answered. He pushed his body forward to hold her there, and again that seemed to be the right thing to do.

Sooner or later he would have to have to get his lad out – well, he could do *that* – and find the right place to put it. Hopefully she would guide him. And then, how difficult could it be? You stuck it in and you moved it in and out until you finished. Job done, and you were no longer a sodomexual homosite.

He wondered what girls did about the mess if you weren't wearing a johnnie. Maybe it just sort of got absorbed.

She was fumbling at his zip. He let her while he kept on kissing her – lips, neck, face. Everyone should do what they were best at, and she would know what do do. The zip came down and she slid her hand inside.

"Oh …"

"Oh what?" he mumbled into her neck.

"Nothing. You nervous? Give me a moment …"

Her hand was still inside his trousers and she started to work at what she found there, kneading it like a lump of dough, which was about as hard and erotic as an uncooked Belfast bap.

And suddenly all he could think of was the last time he had been touched down there – the gentle caresses and strokes, the love and wonder shining in the eyes of the owner of the hand, the intimate pleasure it gave to both of them.

He threw his head back and howled a long, tragic moan which she was in no danger of mistaking as a compliment to her skill.

"You're just too plastered, ain't ya? Tell you what, lay off it and stop wasting my time. Maybe come back tomorrow." She pushed him off her without difficulty and headed back inside, her dignity intact.

A PETROL BOMB OF LOVE

Chapter 20: Pick-up

Will went through two more pubs, staggering out of each one after the landlord refused to serve him any more. He swore at a lamppost that bumped into him, but then since it was there anyway, he put out one arm to brace himself steady and think.

He hadn't tried any more getting off, because there was no chance of being anymore successful than the first attempt. However much he drank, the more and more pissed he got, one thought shone true and straight, beaming through the alcoholic fog in his head like sunlight through a crack in the cloud cover. The one straight line that let him navigate.

He was going to lose Conor – and he didn't want to.

Well, fuck that. He went where Conor went – if Conor would still have him. Shit, even if his choices were being safe and miserable stuck in Northern Ireland on his own, or stuck with Conor across the water and not having the faintest idea what was coming, just being with Conor would do as a first step.

He wasn't going to plead or beg. He had said things that couldn't be unsaid. But Conor now knew everything about him, every dirty thing, his worst unspoken secret. There would be no more landmines to tiptoe around. Maybe he had destroyed their love, but had he destroyed their friendship? They had got on okay before they became lovers. Maybe they could withdraw to where they had been and go forward again, more carefully, more knowledgeably?

Maybe they would never be lovers again. Maybe that was too broken. Maybe one or both of them would end up doing what Will had been thinking – marry girls and all that. But their future lives would be built on a foundation of having each other.

Even if that meant going to England.

If Conor was okay with it.

Only one way to find out.

Will straightened up and set his face to point down the road. Gas welled up inside and he let out a long, puke-flavoured burp. Suddenly his stomach heaved and he leaned over double, propping himself again with one hand on the lamppost – but no, false alarm, apart from a bit of bile that trickled up into the back of his mouth and back down his throat again. He was keeping it down for the moment.

He straightened up, focused his eyes on the way down the pavement, and set off again. Stopped, when he realised he had no idea how to do this. How to get in touch with Conor?

Go home, phone twice? He bumped his head against the metal post again because staying upright under his own strength was too distracting. He wasn't sure he could face staying conscious and coherent enough to get home, and remember the number to call, and then go out again to the phone box and wait.

He would much rather do this face to face. He owed Conor that much. But no way could he get over the interface like this, and even if he did and managed more than three steps into the Fenian side before being torn limb from limb, he had no idea how to get to Cavendish Street, or which house Conor lived in.

So, phone it was …

For the third time, he set off – and then he remembered.

Conor had been in his trackies.

He was going to the gym.

Perfect!

It only took a slight revision to his course and mumbling at one passer-by for directions, and he was stumbling towards McGarry's.

Cars were sliding past on the street and he didn't pay much attention when powerful halogen headlights blazed from behind him. He had more important things on his mind as a Ford Capri pulled up ahead with the throbbing of a powerful exhaust. And when the back doors opened and two dark-clad men climbed out, he was just irritated that they were in his way.

He lifted his head a little as one of them stood in front of him, and then his eyes one at a time went round with recognition, and he managed to say, "Hey!" before they grabbed his shoulders and pushed him down and onto the back seat. The doors slammed and the car pulled away.

The car smelled of warm leather and stale fag smoke. Will was squeezed between two shapes on the back seat, and one by one he recognised everyone who was with him, starting with the fella in the passenger seat.

"I'm not going home," he mumbled.

"Good." Alan twisted around and grinned back at him. "Neither are we."

Now, he recognised the car, too. The driver – Robbie – had paid Mr Mitchell through the nose to get a Ford Capri like the one Lewis Collins drove in *The Professionals*.

"Alan said we couldn't let you walk in that state," said the shape next to him, whom he realised was Henry. Henry smiled in a way that bared his teeth but didn't show any friendliness at all.

"Thank you," Will said automatically. Now he didn't have to concentrate on walking, he could feel his eyes growing heavy and his head drooping, as his body shut down to cope with all the stuff he had put into it. But he didn't want to rest his head on Henry's shoulder. He shot a glance at the boy on his other side, Alfie, and just got a blank, unfriendly stare in return. No, probably shouldn't rest his head there, either.

Something was puzzling him. It all whirled around a bit before he could put his finger on him.

"But you don't know where I *am* going."

"You're going where we take you, Will. You're all right, it'll be a treat. We can drop you off wherever after." Alan squinted back at him, considering. "Maybe you'd best stay in the car. We'll have to move quick when it kicks off."

"When what kicks off?"

"You'll see."

Will guessed he'd better stay awake, then. He swallowed and gazed with blurring eyes at the street passing by on either side. The route looked kind of reminiscent. That was lucky. Looked like they were all going the same way anyways. Alan had saved him a walk.

Sure enough, a few minutes later, McGarry's loomed ahead of them. Robbie slowed down as they went past and all heads turned to follow it. Just the sight of it put a happy smile on Will's face – the knowledge of what it was, the closeness to who was in there – until he remembered he was sitting next to Henry, who might not appreciate someone regarding it fondly.

The doors and windows were grilled up but there were still lights on inside. He didn't know how late the gym stayed open, but surely by now the regular customers must have gone home. So the light meant …

"Someone's in," Robbie muttered, which made Will smile more widely. Alan's own smile was like a predator's.

"Fuck them, then."

Robbie chuckled and shifted down a gear. The Capri speeded up and McGarry's slid away behind them.

Will frowned, trying to piece this together. They weren't just sight-seeing the locations of Henry's least finest hours, were they?

"So, what …"

The car swerved suddenly as Robbie turned hard into a side street. They surged down the middle of the road between cars parked on either side, halogens blazing the way, and turned again. Even Will's fuddled sense of direction could tell they were now heading back the way they had come. McGarry's stood on the corner of the main road and a side road, and they were about to come out onto the side road.

Which they did, a minute later. The car pulled over into the dark space between street lights and stopped.

Something shifted in the air. A low growl of anticipation, body language tensing up. Faint tendrils of alarm prickled at the back of Will's mind.

"What?"

Alfie who wasn't Henry was passing around black somethings. Will watched fuzzily as they each took one and pulled it over their heads. Black balaclavas.

"Hey, Alan, we've got a spare." Alfie waved it in his hand and Alan gave Will an appraising stare, up and down, before answering.

"Okay. Get it on him."

"Hey?" Henry protested. "He'll just hold us up."

"He deserves this chance. Do it."

Before Will could protest, Alfie had pulled the spare balaclava over his own head. It smelt of stale sweat and old wool.

The crew piled out of the car, Will being half pulled out into the fresh air, though with the balaclava on there was no way of appreciating it. Robbie lifted the lid of the boot and Alan delved into it. Something clinked, and then Alan was handing out milk bottles stuffed with rags at the end and full of gold-yellow liquid that reflected the street lights with orange sparkles. The air was suddenly thick with petrol fumes and Will's stomach heaved as he realised what was happening.

"Oh, Christ, Alan, no …"

Alan went up, masked face to masked face with him.

"You were there on the fight night," he hissed. "You saw those IRA murderers hobnobbing like Lord and Lady Muck. Even *you* were cheering the fucking Fenians! This place is dangerous. It's a menace. It's a honey trap, so the lads and I have decided we need to burn it out."

He grabbed Will's hand, turned it palm upwards, slapped a petrol bomb into it.

"Alan …" Will moaned, but his stomach churned again and he retched before he could speak.

"Jesus, at least get your mouth clear if you're going to puke," Alan muttered. "Just keep your face hid." He took hold of Will's arm in a grip Will had no chance of breaking and marched him along the street. Will had to walk fast to stop being dragged over.

"He'll just hold us up!" Henry protested again, behind them.

"Then we'll fecking leave him behind! But he's going to see this. He's going to know which side he's on. It's what our Da would have wanted."

Will recognised the low wall ahead. It was the back yard of the gym. Inside it was the extension he had helped Conor paint, where he and Conor had seen and enjoyed each other's naked bodies, and been as close and intimate as it was possible to be.

"You can't do this," Will whispered. "You can't do this, you can't do this …"

"Shut the feck up. Stop here, lads. We need to get these up onto the roof if it's going to make any difference."

Henry slapped both hands on top of the wall and heaved himself up to peer over.

"There's something out here, too," he reported. "One storey, flat roof."

"Grand. You do that one, we'll do the rest …"

"You can't do this!" Will shouted. Thick wool clogged his mouth and he fumbled at the balaclava. He had to tug hard to free it and pull it clear of his head. "*You can't do–…*"

"Jesus, shut him up!" Henry hissed and Alan's fist pounded into his stomach. Not hard, just a friendly tap compared to what Henry could have done, but he doubled over and fell hard to his knees as the air whooped out of his lungs.

"*Shut up!*"

Will struggled to breathe, struggled to get up, and then both of those were secondary problems as his stomach finally gave up and heaved, and he spewed long and hard out onto the pavement.

"Jesus!" Alan leapt aside just in time. "Fuckit, leave him …"

Another wave of puke came, and Will had no strength for anything else. Dimly he heard the sound of a cigarette lighter striking, heard the soft *whoof* of petrol-soaked cloth catching. Orange light flickered for a moment through his closed eyelids, and far off there was the tinkling smash of glass.

A third and final surge of puke came as Alan grabbed him under the arm and marched him back to the car. Most of it went down Will's front.

"You said you were leaving him!" Robbie protested.

"Aye, I did, but he's my brother."

"He's not spewing in my car!"

"He works at Mitchell's, you eejit. He'll clean it up for you, gratin. Now, get us out of here."

Will was thrown without ceremony into the back. Bodies piled in on either side and the Capri started moving even before doors slammed.

Whoops of exultation rang fuzzily in Will's ears and he burst into tears.

"D'ye think it'll burn?" someone asked.

"The extension had an asphalt roof," Henry reported with satisfaction. "It was burning nicely. Maybe the rest does too."

"Aye, then, it'll burn!" Henry punched the driver on the shoulder, turned to beam at the others. It only faltered a little as his gaze passed over his sozzled, sobbing brother. "Jesus. Okay, get us round the block and drive up slowly from the other direction. We're going to turn up all like innocent bystanders and watch."

Chapter 21: Roadworks Smell

"I'm leaving now!"

Dumb … fuck … dumb … fuck …

Conor barely heard Cormac as he pounded the bag through a teary mist, instinct telling him where it was with each swing because he certainly couldn't see it.

A Cormac-shaped blur was standing next to him.

"You'll turn off and lock up the front …?"

Conor grunted and waved a gloved hand, which anyone could tell meant 'Yes, sure.'

"Okay …"

The blur was gone, and Conor was vaguely aware of being alone in the gym.

There had been other customers in, when he turned up, the usual weekday evening crowd. None of them had bothered him when they saw the look on his face. Even Cormac, who was most entitled to ask what was wrong, had left him alone. But this would no doubt be reported back to the family. There was a time for keeping quiet and a time for speaking out, and they all had too much at stake in Conor's welfare. So, it would be Cormac's duty to report to Da that something was bothering Conor, and he would have to give an explanation when he got home, so he might as well make the most of the time he had now to pound it out of his system.

Dumb … fuck …

Whether the dumb fuck was Will or himself – well, who could say?

He had tried to imagine the bag was Will's face, but he couldn't do it. He had never borne that much animosity towards any one person, and he certainly couldn't start with Will now. So each blow was his own personal assault on all the injustices he had felt in his own life.

For every ten, twenty, thirty blows he allowed himself to think a thought, hold it, think a new one, put them together one by one. It took time – he lost track of how long exactly – but a picture slowly emerged in his head.

Conor was certain he had stayed alive as long as he had by trusting only his own people. It was a habit that had served him well for over eighteen years. So why the *fuck* had he been so stupid as to go and break it? And for why? Because Will – a complete stranger, one dark night – had kissed him! How much sense did that make?

Maybe he had thought that it would work precisely *because* Will had kissed him, and he had kissed Will back. They were different. They were two fellas who fancied each other, and that was a *so* different it had to beat all the other things between them, all the other strikes against them. Didn't it? Well, it had seemed like that.

But Jesus he had opened himself up to Will he had given him his heart not just his body he had given him everything he had been as vulnerable as you could ever be he had thought he was safe ...

"*Fucker!*" he howled, with a final punch at the bag that would have knocked a human onto his back. He reached out with both hands and caught the bag on the rebound, stopping it in mid-swing. Breathing heavily and eyes still blurred, he rested his forehead against the cool leather, drawing in its unique scent. It was an old and familiar friend and it calmed him down, helped his mind return to its usual analytical state.

There was another scent too – somewhere, something foul and acrid was burning. Maybe they were doing roadworks outside, laying down tarmac.

Okay. Time to get a grip.

Trusting only the right people was just one way he had stayed alive. Another was to be always in control. To know exactly what he was doing, and why, and to whom. He had never allowed himself the luxury of self-pity, not for his mistakes (well, he should have known better, shouldn't he?) and not for the things that he couldn't help (so what are you going to do about it?).

So here was how it was.

The fragile thing he had made with Will over the last few weeks – it was just too precious not to be worth salvaging, even if all he got back from it was the fragile remains of a tentative friendship. However unlikely it was, the fact was that *they had found each other*. It could not just be thrown away.

So, Will wasn't coming to England. If Conor wanted Will to respect and understand his reasons then he had to respect and understand Will's. That was only right and fair. It was probably too late at night now, but the next day – well, he would try the two phone rings thing again. And keep on trying it, until Will answered and he could tell Will that if they were parting, they were doing it as friends. Still.

He glowered at the punchbag.

"Aye, and what the fuck do you know anyway?" he muttered. He sagged against it, all his strength suddenly gone. He was too tired and drained to go on so he might as well go home. But while he was here, he would hit the showers. He was hot and sweaty and the water at home would be cold by now.

Sometimes you got people banging on the front doors even when it was obviously after closing time, so he crossed over to the main wall panel and cut the lights for Reception and the big gym lights. The interior was plunged into gloom but enough street light came through the main windows to see his way by, as if he didn't already know the place like the back of his hand.

The roadworks smell really was strong. They must be mixing a powerful load of tarmac outside. He turned slowly on the spot and ran an eye over all the windows, to see if one was cracked open and letting the fumes in. He should shut it up before he went.

No, they all seemed fine. He cocked an eye up at the skylights …

"*Jesus!*"

All each skylight showed was flickering, orange fire.

He didn't hang around. His feet were already ahead of him before his brain caught up, fleeing towards the door through to Reception and the way out.

The frame of the skylight above the door gave way and flaming debris tumbled down into the gym in front of him.

"*Fuck!*"

Conor skidded to a halt, arms waving for balance. Acrid smoke tore at the back of his throat and the fire burnt hot on his face. He turned and headed for the only other way out – the back door through to the extension.

He started to detour around the boxing ring in the centre, and another skylight collapsed just in front of him. He ran back the other way around the ring, stumbling as press benches slammed into his shins. Calm down, calm down, take it easy … but he could feel the place filling up with smoke, his eyes were starting to water and his brain was fizzing. He stumbled across to the far side of the gym, slammed into the wall, he thought. The centre of the room was dangerous, so he would make his way along the wall sideways to stay as far away as he could from the skylights and anything else that might fall through. But it took much longer. The smoke was black and thick and alien. Some firemen had come to his school once to teach the kids about fire safety. What had they said? How many hundred people was it who died each year because they stayed in a burning building? Couldn't remember but yeah, definitely hundreds.

Conor pulled his shirt up, held it over his mouth and nose with one hand, felt his way with the other, eyes squeezed shut against the stinging of the smoke. Now he couldn't see, his mind was full of nightmare fantasies of sidling straight into burning flame, and he had to tell himself, no, the fire is over *there* and anyway you'd feel it before you walked into it ...

At last – his shoulders slid into the recess of the back exit and his groping fingers closed around the warm metal of the handle. He turned towards the door, twisted the handle ... and the door stayed shut.

He howled.

... *lock up the front* ...

That was what Cormac had said. The implication being, he had already locked up the back. Self-control forgotten for a moment, Conor thumped angrily on the warm wood.

... Why was the wood warm?

He pressed his face to the frosted, wired glass window set at face height into the door. Orange light flickered back at him. He touched the glass cautiously, and snatched his hand away as he felt the heat.

How the fuck did the fire get that side of ...

Whoompf.

The orange light flared suddenly white, the door shook, and heat pulsed through so hard that Conor took an involuntary step back

"*Fucker!*" he bellowed. Never mind that his escape was cut off. In his mind's eye he could see the ruination of all his lovingly rendered work in there.

But he also had time to realise that not being able to get through that door at the first try had probably saved his life. The fire must have reached the stash of paint materials. He cocked an eye at the ceiling and silently addressed the God he half believed in.

Get me out of this and I'll dial it up to at least three quarters ...

Smoke burrowed into his eyes and he squeezed them shut again, tears streaming now for a whole new reason. Only thing for it was try to make it round the side of the gym again to get to the front door. Maybe the wreckage that had come down had burnt itself out now? Because there was no other way out, and he had no choice. Even through the fabric of his shirt, breathing now was like inhaling burning glass down his airways and it took every atom of self control not to start coughing. He risked a final, deep lungful of the foul air and this time he held it there. It had to do until he had fresh air to breath again.

Conor kept on his way, sidling around the edge of the gym. His shoulder bumped into the junction between walls so he knew exactly how far he had to go, and oh Jesus, he wasn't going to make it, was he? His lungs were bursting. He started to breathe out, through his nose, very slowly, pushing carbon dioxide out of his body, fooling it into thinking it was breathing again.

Suddenly there was nothing behind his back and he tumbled arse over head into the ladies' changing room.

Perfect!

He slammed the door shut. The air in here was already full of smoke but perhaps it could stay breathable a little longer. The windows in both changing rooms were slits in the wall at head height, designed to open only a hands' width. He stood on a bench and whooped the foul air out of his lungs, and breathed in deep on what little fresh air came through from outside.

Which was a mistake, because it was still smoke-laden and it was enough to tip the balance into a coughing fit that ended with him lying on the floor in an oxygen-purged daze. It was the cleaner air down there that revived him enough for a few final, coherent thoughts.

There was no way out of this burning building. All he could do was delay dying until the fire brigade got here, which surely had to happen soon.

The gents' and ladies' changing rooms were mirror images of each other, with the showers either side of the central wall. He grabbed a hanging towel and stumbled into the tiled shower area, shambling around the side, feeling his way and turning on each shower as he came to it. Blind, he heard the hiss of water on tiles, felt it rain coolly down onto him. Maybe the water would wash the smoke out of the atmosphere? Da hated people leaving the showers on, wasting water, *Jesus, don't they know who much it costs ...* The memory forced a weeping, sobbing laugh out of him. *Bill me, Da!*

He slumped into the corner of the room. The water soaked into his shorts, cold and cleansing against his skin. Would wet cloth be a suitable filter? He had no idea and his thoughts were fading. He held the towel under the nearest stream of water until it was truly sodden, then wrapped it around his head.

The towel was so soaked that breathing through his nose was almost like drowning, but the wet smell was slightly nicer than the smoke and maybe the air that got into him now was slightly cleaner.

But it couldn't last.

Faces floated through the haze around him. People he hadn't even thought were dead. Ma, Da, all his sisters, Cormac ... and Will, for some reason holding Katie as they came smiling towards him. He was glad the people he loved most in this world had finally got to meet.

So it's true, he thought sleepily. *You see your loved ones. That's okay, then.*

Darkness grew around him and Conor McGarry settled in to die.

Chapter 22: No Hard Feelings

"I'd expected more flames …" Robbie said casually. His head was over to one side as he drew on his fag, an artist surveying a work that hadn't quite come out as expected. The rest of the gang lounged casually back against the wall and surveyed the scene. Will sprawled on the pavement at Alan's feet, still sobbing, all hope wiped out of him.

The first fire engines and police Land Rovers had arrived. Blue light pulsed over the brick walls, flashing through the dark columns of smoke pouring out of the gym's windows, while the fire crews unravelled hoses and sought out the nearest hydrants. The flames from the petrol bombs had burned themselves out but they had done their job.

"They'll all be inside," Alan proclaimed with confidence. He breathed out the smoke of his own fag. Will's nose was too snotted up to tell the difference between clean tobacco smoke and the choking smell of burning building that hung over the whole area. "What d'ye think makes all the smoke in the first place?"

Shouts came from the fire crews, orders flying back and forth. The men took an extra grip on their hoses and they opened up with a gushing roar. Hot brick hissed as powerful jets played over the front of the gym and through the smoking voids of the windows.

Another drag, and Alan grinned down at Will. "Isn't that right, Will? Now, if I take my foot away, are you going to behave?"

Will turned his tear-blotched face up and glared hate. "Fuck. Off."

They had had to wrestle Will screaming to the ground. Alan had grown tired of thumping his little brother in the guts, so as Will had put both his hands down flat on the ground to push himself up again, his boot had come down on Will's outstretched fingers. Not hard enough to break anything – yet – but enough to make him scream. There was no way Will could free himself without snapping bones or at least scraping the skin off his fingers, and he had been forced to subside and just watch.

Which he had made himself do. He owed that much to Conor. If he couldn't prevent his lover's passing, he could mark it and mourn it. Conor had to be dead by now, didn't he? To his surprise he was all sobbed out. All he felt was cold emptiness, and sheer loathing. He would kill Alan for this. One day.

Alan shrugged, ground his foot down just a little harder.

"Fair enough." He frowned down at Will. "Jesus, this has really got you. What's this place to you?"

"Oh, shit," Alfie murmured, at the same time as a breezy, "Evening, boys!" reached their ears.

Alan gave another, slightly harder, warning jab with his foot and straightened up.

"Good evening, Ian."

Sergeant Moore strolled over, his usually affable features set into a frown.

"It's Sergeant Moore when I'm policing a crime scene, I'll thank you." Moore puffed his cheeks out as he watched the activity, hands behind his back. "It's a crying shame," he said quietly. "A place like this could do us all a lot of good. I need to talk to witnesses. Did you lads see anything?"

"It was burning when we got here–…" Henry began.

"And what happened to young William here?"

"Too much to drink." Alan paused, then casually took away his boot half a second before Sergeant Moore's gaze swept down to the pavement. "Blithering about there being someone in there."

"Oh, I doubt that," Moore said casually. "The crew manager said they're working on the assumption it was empty at this time of night, and you never know with these things. It could be a set-up to lure us in, so we'll just have to let it burn…"

Will howled, "There *is* someone in there!", and he lunged up and barged his way past Moore, running towards the gym. Moore stuck two fingers into his mouth and whistled hard. A couple of the constables turned around and saw Will shambling towards them. They moved to intercept him – too slowly.

At the last second and on pure instinct, Will swerved to avoid them, like he was carrying a ball five yards from the try line. He left them stumbling in his wake and kept on towards the gym, still babbling the same words over and over. Four more officers formed a solid line in front of him and the long-dormant rugby-playing part of his brain kicked in again, working out how to get through them. But he was out of practice and he faltered, just long enough for one of the two behind to throw himself at his waist and bring him down to the tarmac in a sobbing heap.

"There *is* someone in there, there *is* someone …"

"Too late if there is, son," a constable said with rough sympathy.

Moore was coming up to them at a steady trot, with Alan and the others a safe distance behind him. Alan's eyes blazed warning which Will could no longer give a fuck about.

"There was someone inside." Will looked Moore in the eye and spoke with slow, cold clarity, concentrating on every syllable to get it past his swollen tongue. "The owner's son. Conor McGarry."

Moore's eyebrows went up.

"What, that lad that gave our Henry here the drubbing? Well, that would be a sad loss. What makes you so sure he's in there?"

Will was aware of everyone's undivided attention but he didn't care.

"He was wearing his trackies," he said. "He said he was coming here."

Alan's eyes started to go wide, but with Moore present there was nothing he could do or say.

"And he often practises late after everyone's gone home," Will went on.

Moore jerked his head at one of his men.

"Tell that to the fire boys. Our man McGarry's on his way here and I want to be able to look him in the eye."

The man nodded and hurried away. Moore gazed after him, then reached out a hand to help Will up.

"I won't lie, son, young McGarry's chances aren't good … How are you knowing all that, anyways?"

"He's … my friend." Will thrust his jaw defiantly out as he climbed to stand on his own two feet. "I saw him this evening."

"*You*–…?" Alan exclaimed. Moore cocked an eyebrow back at him.

"It's not against the law to have a Catholic friend, Alan," he said mildly.

"He doesn't have any Catholic friends! And why would he cry like that for just a friend? You'd think they–…"

Will could see the exact moment the realisation hit his brother. He forced himself to meet his brother's stare as Alan's jaw dropped and his face slowly went white.

"What the fuck does it matter?" Henry demanded, distracting Moore's attention from whatever might be going on between the brothers. "So there's a dead Fenian in there! So fucking what?"

Moore's tone was still mild but it had grown a cutting edge.

"That would be the Fenian who had you down on the mat as I recall, Henry Wilson? Now, here's the thing you boys don't seem to grasp. Sure we're all loyal Protestants, God bless Her Majesty and all that, and I will hunt down and destroy any and every enemy of our union. Any man calls me a Taig lover and I'll step out the back with him right now. But like it or not we live in a community, and it's the community I serve. I heard what went down the other night, your finest hour, and I saw Protestants and Catholics having a wild old time together and loving it. I spend my days out on the streets in this part of town, I have a sense for the atmosphere, I can tell when we're getting along famously or when things are about to kick off, just like you can smell the rain in the morning before it comes – and I can tell you that seeing you get beat up has put a spring into everyone's step. The more occasions we get like that, the less there will be petrol bombs and kneecapping and riots, and that means I'm doing my job properly." He raised a finger.

"And anyone – *anyone* – who disturbs that sacred task of mine, I will come down on *hard*. And now, here's me thinking …"

He stepped back and surveyed the group like a parent making sure his kids were dressed suitably for an outing.

"Young Will here, reeking so much of booze he can barely stand and has puked down his front recently and seems powerful upset about something. Him, I am discounting from my enquiries because if he was capable of setting fire to anything tonight, I'm a Dutchman. But you four lads, all dressed alike …" Alfie and Henry looked self-consciously down at their black tops and dark jeans. Robbie and Alan just blandly returned Moore's gaze.

"… And all apparently just happening to be here to lollygag, when we all know you're more likely to be sat in a pub or at the lodge rather than taking in the night air. And …" He sniffed delicately. "Is that the faintest aroma of two-star hanging around? You see, the funny thing about petrol bombers is they're like smokers – they'll put their hand on their heart and swear to God they don't reek of their disgusting habit because they honestly can't tell. Now tell me again, and think very carefully before you say a word – did you see anything tonight that could help me with my enquiries?"

All the good humour and friendliness of a few minutes before had evaporated into the night air. No one answered, but four heads distinctly shook from side to side.

Moore turned abruptly to Will.

"And you, Will?"

"We didn't see anything," Henry said, shifting impatiently.

"You weren't called Will when I first lifted you, and you're not called Will now. Will?"

Will's eyes narrowed as he looked past Moore, straight into Alan's face. His brother, already pale from what he had just guessed, slowly seemed to wilt.

"I can't say," Will muttered, and everyone present knew he had as good as pointed a finger straight at Alan.

But they also all knew there was nothing Moore could do about it.

"I see ..." Moore's gaze swung to Robbie like a tank turret tracking its target. "Robbie Andrews. Do you still drive that jazzed up cruiser of yours?"

The little victory already seemed to be giving the lads confidence, and Robbie's mouth moved into a very slight smile.

"I do."

Moore jerked his head down the road to where the Capri sat by the roadside.

"Is that it parked over there? I wouldn't find anything interesting if I had a look around it, would I?"

"Why would you want to look around it, Sergeant?"

Their gazes locked, and then Moore gave a little wiggle of his shoulders, a shrug that seemed to dismiss the whole matter.

"Well, why indeed? Okay, lads, no hard feelings, you all understand I had to do my job." He held out a hand to Alan; Alan paused, then graciously reached out with his own. Before he could react, Moore had grabbed it and sniffed his fingers. Alan snatched his hand away but Moore had already backed off and now his hand rested casually on the grip of the gun in his belt holster.

"Will, you'd better get yourself home. Someone's going to have to break this to your good mother. *Constable!*" A man came running over. Moore pointed. "The Ford that looks like a big willy with the add-on headlights. Impound it now – no one gets to touch it without my say-so. And Robbie, I'll take the keys now, thank you …?" He held his hand out, palm up.

"You can't …"

"I won't …"

"Why …"

They could gabble in frustrated rage, but everyone knew there was no point in running for the simple fact that Moore knew where each of them lived.

Will backed away slowly, no longer willing to endure the condemnation in Alan's gaze.

"Will," Moore said with forced patience, "I said, get yourself …"

"I'm going to see them take Conor out." His voice only trembled slightly as he spoke.

Voices were raised among the firemen. They were running together, consulting. Two of them in breathing gear pulled a folding stretcher from the back of the ambulance and ran into the smoke pouring from the front doors. Moore raised an eyebrow.

"Looks like you won't have to wait long, then."

Chapter 23: Aftermath

Thursday 14th August

Will quietly set the two tea cups down between his mother and the visitor, and pulled back to a safe distance.

"Thank you, Will." Sergeant Moore made no move to pick his cup up, and neither did she. In the time it had taken for the kettle to boil, Moore had already told Ma pretty much all there was to say, and that was pretty much what Will had told her when he staggered home the previous night.

The newspaper lay folded in half and face down on the table top next to them. Will had put it like that because he couldn't bear to see the photo that took up the top half of the front page. McGarry's, still standing, but minus a roof, with scorch marks burnt into the brickwork above the windows, and a dark haze hanging over the whole site.

An eighteen-year-old man is believed to have been recovered from the wreckage by fire crews. He has not been formally named ...

No mention of whether Conor was alive or dead, and the uncertainty was gnawing at his guts.

"Why not sit down yerself, Will?" Moore asked, in a way that was almost an order, in his own kitchen. Will slipped into a chair, sitting bolt upright with his hands folded together in front on the Formica top.

The phone rang in the hallway. No one moved to answer it.

"What will happen now?" Ma asked, her voice barely more than a whisper. Moore wiggled his head.

"Alan stays with us as our guest until he comes up before the magistrates. I'm sure we can turn it all around very quickly. But there will be a court date, Alice, I have to warn you of that now. Don't go getting your hopes up now."

She nodded wearily.

"I feel in some way responsible myself, Alice," Moore went on, sadly. "I thought the code by which I run this patch was evident to all. Clearly I failed in young Alan's case."

She laid a gentle hand on his; an automatic response, which Will thought had probably been the idea.

"Oh, you shouldn't blame yourself, Ian."

Will thought: *Hmm*.

He thought back to the blue Nissan that he had innocently cleaned of all forensic evidence. At the time, he had felt pissed off about being played, but that was all. He hadn't felt bad about helping a Loyalist shooter get off the hook, which was apparently what he had done. Not when he heard who it was who the man had shot.

And he was absolutely certain there was no discrepancy at all in Moore's mind about now and then choosing to apply a law of his own devising rather than the law of the land. You were just meant to *know* what was right and what was wrong.

Mostly, it worked, but he could see how the Alans of this world might get confused.

Moore's attention swung suddenly over to him, like a gun coming to bear.

"Now, Will …" A notebook and pencil were in his hand – Will hadn't seen them come out. His heart pounded and he forced himself not to grip the sides of the table. "I do need a statement from you. I'll not ask what you saw or who did what. There was enough evidence in the car to convict all of them straight off, and anything you might say to try and clear them – well, son, it would just insult my intelligence, to be quite frank. And nor do I want to give you the chance to settle any scores you might have with your brother. He will return to this house, eventually, and I don't want it awkward between you."

Will swallowed, and nodded, suddenly very grateful after all for Moore's flexible approach to law enforcement.

"Besides, any fool could see the state you were in, you couldn't strike a match, let alone burn down a building. But I do have to ask how you came to be on the scene."

Will swallowed again, and tried not to show his relief that he could tell the plain truth.

"I'd had to much to drink," he stated. "I was going to see a friend. They saw me and they pulled over to give me a lift."

It was a very short explanation, and what Moore scribbled down was even shorter, but he nodded in satisfaction.

"As a good brother would, of course."

Will could stand it no longer.

"Is he alive?" Moore and Ma both looked at him, and he felt the floor open beneath him as he remembered she had no idea Conor even existed. "Conor McGarry. Ah ... that's the fella they took from the gym, Ma."

"Oh."

Moore pushed his chair back, reared up onto his feet.

"I only know he was unconscious at the last report, Will, but you're right, I should check in. Well, I'll see myself out ..."

"I'll show you to the door," Will said automatically. They left Ma sitting at the table with her ever colder cup of tea and he followed Moore out into the hallway. Moore jumped as the phone suddenly rang, right next to him, its harsh bell echoing in the small space.

"You should get yourself one of those clever machines like they have in America," he suggested. "You know, like Jim Rockford on the telly – do you watch that?" Will nodded dumbly while Moore took his uniform cap down from the hook and set it straight on his head. Then he moved his head closer to Will's and lowered his voice. "I didn't want to say it to the poor woman, because she has enough on her mind, but you have to know, if you haven't worked it out – whether young McGarry lives or dies? That will make all the difference between whether your brother and his friends are charged with simple arson, or murder."

"They broke the eleventh, didn't they?" Will surprised himself by saying it out loud, and so bluntly. Moore's hand hovered on the latch and he glanced back in surprise. His habitual friendly expression hardened, a layer of frost just discernible beneath the affable surface.

"Not perhaps how I would have put it, Will." An abrupt nod. "I'll be in touch."

He let himself out. Will watched his shape recede through the frost glass, and then he headed back to the kitchen.

"Ma, you've not touched your tea. Will I make you some more?"

It was very unusual for one of the Johnston boys to be waiting on her instead of the other way around when it wasn't Christmas, or her birthday, or Mother's Day, but today it seemed right.

A very slight shake of the head.

"You're all right, Will."

She summoned enough strength to pull her mug towards her. She gazed down at it nestled between her hands without seeing it.

Will had already phoned up work and claimed a stomach bug, and now he just wanted to head upstairs and curl up in his room. But he couldn't just leave her quite like this, so he pulled out the chair where Moore had been and sat down next to her.

"Show me the paper again," she said quietly, and after a pause he silently held it out to her. When she didn't take it, he unfolded it for her and laid it out, moving her plate to make space for it. He forced himself to look again at what was taking up most of page 1, and tears pricked at his eyes.

Was Conor alive?

There were two very simple things he could do to find out.

He could call the hospital and ask.

Or he could call the McGarrys. He had their number.

And how well would they take that? Whether Conor was alive or dead, Will didn't feel he had the right to be the one to break the news of his existence to them. That right belonged to Conor alone, and if Conor was no longer able to tell them …

The pang of sorrow struck straight to his heart, and he squeezed his eyes closed against a sudden gush of tears, and bit on a sob.

If Conor was no longer able to tell them then they would never know. No one would ever know. He would take it to his grave.

She didn't notice anything going on with him. Her eyes were fixed on the page, moving slightly from side to side as she scanned the report.

And then they narrowed, and her lips tightened, which was the most reaction she had shown ever since he broke the news to her last night. Her jaw moved from side to side, her mouth moved. Will found himself holding his breath.

"The bloody eejit!"

Will blinked. The last time he heard her say anything stronger than 'fecker' was … he couldn't remember.

"The stupid, stupid *eejit!* What the *hell* did he think he was doing? What would his father think? I tell you, Will, Philip would have thrown him out of the house, so he would. Arson! Fucking *arson!* When I think … I think …" She gripped his hand, stared suddenly into his face. "Am I a bad mother, son?"

"Eh?" Will recoiled in surprise. It was not a question he had ever considered. She was just … his mother. Good or bad didn't come into it. "No, Ma, no!"

"Hmm." She side-eyed him sceptically. "You say. No, son, I've not been good to either of you since your da died. You know he took care of everything, all our money, paying the bills and the mortgage and it was all so much when he went, I was happy to leave it to your brother …"

"Well, he is a clerk …" Will was in the unusual position of justifying his brother.

She snorted.

"He was a seventeen-year-old tyke back then but I still gave him that responsibility. I tell you, son, it went to his head, so it did. Wearing your da's clothes, sitting in his fecking chair, even …"

Will was even glad the 'fecking' was back.

"Oh, I spoiled him! But never again. *Never again*, son. You've been a saint to tolerate his crap, so you have, but now it's …"

She paused. Will pricked up his ears.

The phone was ringing yet again.

Twice, then it stopped. Just like – it came bubbling up out of Will's memory – it had all the other times it had rung that morning.

"Oh, fer feck's *sake!*" she exclaimed.

* * *

Will's feet pounded on the pavement as he navigated through slow-moving pedestrians like the *Millennium Falcon* through an asteroid field.

"Sorry, 'scuse me, sorry, out of the way …"

Swerve the lady with her pushchair, dodge the man reading a paper, come up slap bang behind three old grannies with their trolleys who had thrown a very slowly moving roadblock across the pavement, dart out into the road to get around them, leap back as a car braked sharply with an angry blast on its horn …

The telephone box was ahead, and not getting any closer. It was like trying to catch up with Conor running ahead of him on Black Mountain. And – in the corners of his eyes – one, two, three people, half of fecking Northern Ireland were converging on it to use it before him.

Will let out a mighty bellow and forced his feet to go that bit faster. In the last second the crowd of potential users shrank down to one middle aged man who glared at him with disgust as he barged in front and hauled on the door.

Phone box doors weren't designed to be hauled open. It seemed to take about half an hour to crack open just wide enough for him to slip in, but he didn't bother apologising to the man or offering an explanation or responding to the muttered 'fucker'.

With one hand Will lifted the receiver and jammed his finger into the dial, with the other fumbled for change. How long since the phone at home had rung? Ten minutes yet? He hadn't been able just to bolt from the house, he had still had to make it look natural … *I'll just pop out, Ma … No, it's fine, I'll just …*

Time was doing its strange thing again. With each number, the dial rotated slightly more slowly than the average hour hand to get back to zero before he could dial the next.

Pip-pip-pip-pip-pip …

Will jammed the coin in.

"Hello? Conor? Conor, is that yourself?"

"*No.*"

The strange male voice at the other end made Will recoil, almost drop the receiver. Ashen faced, he dared to put it back to his ear, holding it cautiously like the phone might develop teeth and bite.

"H-hello?"

"*You'll be Will?*" It was a man's voice, and Will's heart began to beat more steadily as he picked up the tone. It was calm, cautiously friendly, and did not sound like someone who had bad news to deliver. "*My name's Cormac and I'm married to Conor's sister ... Aye, he's fine. He's in the Royal Victoria and he wants to see you.*"

* * *

The bus took about a year to crawl the mile from Agnes Street to the hospital, and eventually Will leapt out at the next stop and ran the rest of the way. And then he had to hop from foot to foot like a little boy badly needing a slash while the receptionist looked up Conor's name, and then ...

"Are you family? A brother?"

"Ah ... no ..."

"I'm very sorry, but the doctors are still checking him and they need to approve visitors who aren't immediate relatives."

Will fought the urge to scream. To calm himself down, he had to dig deep into his memory, to the time he had been bollocked by a customer at Mitchell's who had managed to drive his car into an oncoming van after picking it up from the garage, and was blaming the mechanic responsible – Will – for sabotaging the steering.

There was no point taking anything out on the wrong person.

"How long will that take?" he asked, enunciating each word very carefully. A sympathetic shrug was the best reply.

"An hour, two hours …? We have a waiting room and there's a very nice tea shop …" Will packed the room anxiously with butterflies franticly flapping in his stomach as he nervously awaited news from the nurse.

In fact it was closer to three hours than two, with Will checking in every thirty minutes, and he lost count of the numbers of cups of tea, or the times he could have just walked home and back. But then came the time she smiled as she saw him approach the desk, and he already knew the good news, and she laughed at his delight as she told him, and then he had to walk very patiently up to the ward because if he even looked like he was going to break out into a run, disapproving faces turned on him and told him to keep it steady.

But then he was through the double swinging doors into the ward. He had vaguely pictured a big room the size of a football field and lined with beds down either side, but it turned out to be divided into smaller rooms with five or six beds in each, and he was told which one Conor was in and then feck patience, he began to run, getting faster and faster and then having to slither to a halt on the polished floor, arms waving to hold himself upright.

And there was Conor, in the bed by the door, wearing a hospital gown and with a plastic tube taped to his upper lip beneath his nose, sitting up in bed with plumped-up pillows to support him. Most of the other beds were empty apart from the one directly opposite which held an old man, fast asleep with his mouth open.

Conor hadn't seen him out in the passage, and a sudden uncertainty gripped Will's heart and rooted him to the spot. He had wondered how this would go. They had not parted well … but Conor had asked to see him, so didn't that give him permission to be here?

He squared his shoulders, stepped into the room, stood at the end of the bed. Conor glanced up and turned his head slowly towards Will. His smile was weary, like he had emerged battered but triumphant from a full-on twelve rounds; his voice was weak, exhausted.

"It's yerself."

Will felt his face crumpling, his eyes beginning to leak.

"Ah, shit, he's going to cry …" And suddenly the biggest smile Will had ever seen flashed onto his face and he held out his arms, "Come here; you eejit," and Will ran forward, and flung himself onto the edge of the bed and wrapped his arms around his lover and sobbed into his neck while Conor gently stroked his hair.

"Will … *Will* …" Will stopped sobbing long enough to blink up. Conor indicated with his eyes. "If you come around this side of the bed by the wall, no one can see you through the door …"

Will's heart pounded as he realised what Conor meant. He scuttled around to the other side of the bed, and perched there – sure enough, he couldn't see out of the door from this angle – and Conor scooted himself over and they snuggled together and their lips brushed, for half a second, before Conor's oxygen tube grated against Will's mouth and he pulled back in surprise.

"Work around it," Conor suggested, and they did, slowly, passionately, savouring the life in each other while Will caressed Conor gently, tracing the line of his jaw, his neck, the muscled outlines beneath the gown.

"Will, there's no easy way to say this …" Conor's voice was even quieter and Will had to move his head close to hear him. "There's a plastic tube up my cock and it's not very comfortable when it gets hard, so could you not …?"

"Shit, sorry!" Will quickly snatched his hand away. Then he moved his head back close to murmur into Conor's ear. "It is a very fine cock."

"From a total cock like you, that's a compliment." He leaned back into Will's cradling arms, leaned his head against Will's chest. "I hear you're the one who told them I was in there?"

"Who told you that?"

"Some RUC sergeant was in here just now. He seemed to know you. You missed him by ten minutes."

Will shuddered. Moore had said he would visit – but of course he would have faced the same visitors rule as Will. Maybe he could flash his braid about, but only a little. He would have had to wait too; just a couple of minutes either way and they would have bumped into each other. What he would have made of this hospital visit from Will – who knew?

But that wasn't his problem now. He had Conor back, and intended to keep him.

"I was an arse," he said bluntly. "I'm sorry. I … I'll come to England, if you'll have me." Conor just looked at him. Will pressed on, wondering what he was standing on – solid ground or the thinnest of ice. But he had to get it out. "I mean, if you don't want … me … you know … like … we were …" He swallowed. Conor wasn't throwing him any bones. "Even if we never …" Another swallow, a wiggle of his head. "… again, I want to be your friend because …" He gazed hopelessly into Conor's face, and lowered his voice again. "Because there's no one else like you."

There was the faintest twinkle in Conor's eye as he leaned his head in close.

"I will for sure have you in England."

Hope surged inside Will, and then the double meaning sank in as Conor shook in his arms with silent laughter.

"Ah, feck off!"

The laughter slowed down and Conor's face showed that now he was being serious.

"If you're sure?" he asked.

"I'm sure–…" Will began. Conor gently rested a finger against his lips.

"You came up with some pretty convincing arguments, and you weren't wrong. People like us – aye, we'll be legal, in three years time, but there's still a lot of people still won't like it. I've no idea what Tommy Clifford will make of it and I'm not going to announce it with trumpets. As far as everyone is concerned, you'll just be my friend from home."

"I know. I know."

"And then …" Conor sucked his cheeks in and shook his head. "Like yer favourite bard poet said, 'Love is not love which alters it when alteration finds'. We're going to alter, Will."

Will frowned.

"We are?"

"Sure we will." Conor leaned complacently back into his pillows. "Sure you've fallen for this handsome face and hard stomach and fine head of hair, and what sane man wouldn't, but we're going to get older, Will. The hair for one will all be gone by the time I'm thirty, if I follow my Da's lead."

"I don't care," Will vowed furiously. "It's not your hair I love, for feck's sake–…"

"Aye, but he's not wrong about it," a voice said behind them.

Will spun around in horror, poised to leap up from the bed, held down only by Conor's tight grip on his arms.

Michael McGarry was leaning against the door jamb. Conor's father ran a hand over his hairless head.

"I gave up combing it over when I was twenty-nine. I thought I'd surrender with dignity."

"Da ..." Conor bumped Will gently with his head. "This is my friend Will and he's coming to England with me."

"I didn't come up the lough in a bubble, son, and I have ears."

Michael looked exactly like Will would expect of a man whose livelihood has just burnt down and who had nearly lost a son. His face was drawn and his eyes were exhausted, though they lingered on Will and sucked in every scrap of information.

"And what did your ears tell you?" Conor asked quietly. Michael shook his head, in exactly the same way that Conor just had, and Will saw where the mannerism came from.

"Son, I have just discovered a whole new level of the very worst thing that can happen, and frankly I have difficulty getting worried about anything else. I swore I'd always trust your judgement, and I can see this boy's been sobbing his eyes out for you, so – you get the benefit of the doubt, Will."

"Thank you," Will tried to say. His throat was dry and only a hoarse whisper came out.

"Da, you going to let us in?" someone said behind Michael. He stood aside, and about a thousand more McGarrys trailed in after him.

In fact, Will saw through his panic, it was only seven of them, and a baby. An older woman who had to be Conor's mother, and the sisters, and the men who must be their husbands, one of them jiggling a baby in his arms.

They must have expected a happy reunion with all of them crowding around the invalid in the bed. They all stopped short when they saw the Protestant stranger, apart from the young man with the baby who grinned and nodded.

"So you're Will, then?"

Which broke the logjam, and now the McGarrys were swarming all over both Conor and his friend who had been the one to save his life.

"So, Will …" It was Penny McGarry who finally asked the awkward question, her head on one side. "How do you know our Conor?"

Conor got in there first, by not answering.

"Will's coming to England with me, Ma."

"Ah, well." That seemed to satisfy her and she beamed. "It'll be good to have a friend in a strange new place, isn't that so, Michael?"

"Aye." Michael McGarry nodded slowly. "We'll be trusting Conor into Will's hands."

Conor groaned and fell back into his pillows.

"Ah, shit (sorry, Ma), I'm dead then."

* * *

It was only fair to leave Conor to his family. Will left the hospital with a spring in his step. The sun was shining more brightly, the air was sweeter, the very pull of gravity on his feet was so light he thought he might as well walk back to Agnes Street rather than take the bus.

He let himself in at home, turned straight left into the living room.

"I'm …"

The cheery greeting died on his lips as Alan rose slowly from his chair.

The brothers looked at each other. The last time they had seen each other, Will had told himself he would never be browbeaten by Alan again.

So he smiled down at their mother, who was still seated, and staring at him, her face grey as if she had just read his obituary.

"Look, Ma, Alan broke out of jail already."

"Police bail," Alan said, "on ma's recognisance."

Will remembered Sergeant Moore's words.

"They'll still be charging you, though?"

"Oh, you'd like that, wouldn't you?"

Will looked him in the eye.

"To tell the truth, aye, I would."

"Will …" Ma whispered from the chair, like all the strength had left her and she couldn't speak any louder. "What Alan's said about you. Is it true?"

Will looked up, saw the triumphant glint in Alan's eye. Whatever brief victory he might have scored by not being an arsonist had just evaporated and he had no ground at all to stand on.

So he made what he could of it, while it lasted.

"What? True that I told them Conor was in the gym?"

"No." Still whispering. "Not that."

Will spoke to her but kept his eyes on his brother's face.

"True that I was begging Alan not to do it, so hard he had to slug me in the gut to shut me up?"

Alan's face flushed, and twisted.

"You know exactly what Ma means, Will."

Will shrugged.

"Aye, well, here's the hard facts. You're an arsonist, I'm not, you're going to jail, I'm not, and unless you're going to try and hit me again …"

Alan smiled, much more than he ought to, and that was the first signal something was wrong. And then there was the way the air shifted, and Will could just sense there was someone else in the house. Someone large, standing behind him.

"I don't want to hurt you, Will." Alan cocked his head. "But does Henry …? Tchk, that's a hard one."

Chapter 24: Reflections

<u>Thursday 14th August</u>

Cars driving down Agnes Street made the wooden frames in Will's window rattle. He was so used to the phenomenon that before today he had barely ever paid it his attention. Now, lying on his bed, hands behind his head, it was all he had to occupy him. That, and watching the patterns of sunlight that reflected off their windows skip across his ceiling.

He was in that position when he heard the doorbell ring. Will immediately perked up. A visitor on a weekday morning, when everyone would usually be at work, was unusual – and this whole situation was already unusual, so the two unusual things were probably connected.

He jumped up and craned his head out of the window to get a glimpse of whoever it was, but at the same time he heard the muffled thud that you could hear throughout the house of the front door opening and closing. The visitor was already inside. Men's voices, muffled, then footsteps on the stairs, and then the voices again outside his room. He recognised them both, and let himself relax, a little.

Will wondered how to greet his visitor. Stand in the middle of the room? Pull the door open the moment the key turned?

Too desperate, too concerned. So he lay back on his bed, hands back behind his head.

The key scraped in the lock, the door opened, his visitor stepped in without asking. He was a portly, middle aged man with thinning hair and a friendly smile, and Will smiled back with genuine warmth and affection.

"Good morning, Doctor Robinson."

"Good morning, Will." Robinson came into the room, carrying his medical bag. "How are you?"

"Oh, I'm grand, thank you, just grand. I mean, I'm being kept under house arrest by my brother, but apart from that …"

* * *

The gleam in Henry's eye had practically begged for violence. Will had made himself return it calmly, without blinking. His conscience was clear. They had all broken the law of the land – him and Alan and Henry – so legally speaking there were three criminals in the room, but there was no comparison in what they had done. He and Conor had not hurt anyone; Henry, Alan and their friends could have killed someone. He, Will Johnston, was better than any of them.

"So, what happens now?"

"You're going to your room."

Will had bit back a laugh and almost said, *"What, for being naughty?"*

But Henry's gleam was still there, and so he said nothing. He didn't think even Alan would actually allow violence against him in the same house as their mother ... but there was no getting around that gleam, and so he had meekly gone up the stairs, Henry one step behind him all the way, Alan trailing a few paces after that, a master keeping a watchful eye on his pet gorilla.

Will had wondered if Henry was going to stand guard outside, but Alan had a simpler idea. Will heard the metallic scrape and click of the key in the lock, and that was when he began to worry for the first time.

That had been yesterday afternoon.

He had gone straight to the window and looked out. Could he get out that way? He had never realised just how high up he was, until for the first time in his life he had pictured jumping. It had to be fifteen or twenty feet off the ground. He could break a leg. Even if he hung his full length from the windowsill to reduce the distance between his feet and the ground as much as he could – without anyone noticing through the living room window, directly below – he would be jumping on to hard concrete, and chances were good his face would scrape against the rough brickwork on the way down. Now he would be the one in hospital.

Which might be one answer to his problem – but while he was injured, he would be at Alan's mercy, and he didn't want to face up to his brother with anything less than his full physical capacity.

And so, he had been here ever since.

He had no idea what Alan was planning. Maybe Alan didn't either. Maybe he just knew Will had to be isolated somehow from society until … whatever. Until he thought of something. Alan wouldn't want to broadcast what he knew about his brother and his Fenian lover – the shame would just be too great – but if there came a point when he felt the advantages of hurting Conor outweighed the disadvantages of the scandal, Will was certain he would go public. Just because he was keeping silent did not mean that either Will or Conor was safe.

Will could have hammered on the door, shouted loudly, demanded his release. If he used all his strength, he could probably shoulder it open. And what would Ma make of that? Would she snap out of her stupor, get furious like she had when she heard about Alan's arrest? Would she demand that Will be set free? Alan probably couldn't stop her then.

Or, would she turn that fury on Will himself? Was he the worse offender, in her eyes?

So Will had kept quiet. He had to emerge from this the better man. He had to keep his dignity. Sooner or later, someone would decide something that let him get the other side of the door. And then – well, maybe he still had some tricks up his sleeve.

At least Alan wasn't going to starve him – or maybe that was Ma's unseen hand at work. Either way, Will's brother brought him sandwiches for dinner that evening, and some toast for breakfast. After that he had just lain on the bed and waited. At first he had the radio for company, until he got tired of Buzzcocks asking if he had ever fallen in love with someone he shouldn't have fallen in love with, and he turned it off to enjoy the silence instead.

The front door opened and closed, and he peered out of the window. Ma was heading out, no doubt for tea and biscuits with her group of friends. She would discuss Alan's case with them. Probably not mention him.

He went back to lying on the bed and looking at the patterns on the ceiling.

An hour later, the doorbell rang.

* * *

Doctor Robinson nodded, still smiling, earnestly projecting the picture of what Will knew he indeed was – a fair-minded, conscientious family doctor who only wanted what was best for Will.

The doctor, Will realised, must have been sent to 'cure' him.

"That might be for your own good, Will, at least until we get to the bottom of all this. May I sit down?"

Will silently extended an arm towards the one chair in the room. Doctor Robinson lifted it over to sit himself down beside the bed and gaze benevolently down at his patient.

"Get to the bottom of what?" Will asked innocently. The doctor gave him a sideways, 'you know perfectly well what I mean' sort of look.

"Your brother has made some … some very serious allegations about you, Will."

"You mean, that I have a Catholic friend?"

Robinson smiled patiently.

"He might indeed call me for that reason, but unlike your brother, I don't actually regard having Catholic friends as high treason. I have some very good Catholic friends and they hardly ever try to overthrow Her Majesty's lawful government or install the throne of the anti-Christ in City Hall. But what your brother alleges goes much further than mere friendship, Will. Please don't insult me by pretending you don't know what Alan is alleging. Do you deny it?" The smile lingered but his eyes turned harder as he leaned forward and lowered his voice. "Have you and this boy sinned carnally? Have you been unclean?"

"With the hugest respect, Doctor Robinson – I'm going to say that since my friendships are none of my brother's business, they're certainly none of yours."

The doctor nodded wisely, face and tone back to normal.

"That is fair enough and I respect your position. But, Will, what your brother alleges is not just friendship. It's a crime, and it's a sin. It offends against the laws of both God and man and that makes it a police matter – but we don't have to bring in the police, do we? I can have a friendly word with your minister, who I know will be only too happy to counsel you. With repentance, this can all be put behind us and no one ever need speak of it again. But if you continue on this path – well, then, the police will have to be involved. Now, you can decline to answer my questions, which are made informally by a friend of the family who has known you all your life, here in your room, but would you still keep quiet if you were being asked under caution at the police station? Because as God is my witness, it would break my heart to see one of Philip Johnston's boys in such a position. So you see, Will, coming clean about it now is probably the best thing you can do. It would certainly stand in your favour, if only for your father's sake."

"And Conor?"

The smile grew flatter.

"Is that his – your friend's – this Catholic boy's – name? Well, I can't speak for him, but your father was very highly regarded in our community."

"Conor's father is very highly regarded in his."

A sad, gentle shake of the head.

"I don't think that would make a difference. Anyway, let them clean up their own mess. We can look after ourselves."

Will looked up at the doctor – the man who had given him inoculations as a baby, and set his broken bones, and always been ready with a friendly, helpful word – and felt that he was gazing across a great gulf that could never be bridged. They were already too far apart. The last thought he might have entertained of having anything to keep him here in Northern Ireland evaporated at that point.

"You talk about breaking the law? I'm pretty certain that keeping me locked up here is illegal too but you seem happy enough to go along with it. If Alan's willing to do something about that then maybe we can talk about other things, but until then – I'm very sorry, Doctor Robinson, I've nothing to say to you."

"I see." A pause, and then he stood. "I'm very sorry to hear it, Will."

The doctor headed for the door without looking back. It hadn't been locked again after he came in – Alan must have been lurking outside.

Will called him as his hand reached the door knob.

"Doctor …" The doctor looked back, a sad smile without hope on his face. "There is one thing you could do, if think it will help."

* * *

It took another couple of hours, but Will had expected that. She would have been at work and couldn't just head off because the doctor called her. She would have had to arrange for someone to cover her.

But eventually there was the sound of the doorbell, and the front door, and the footsteps outside, and the voices on the landing.

Wendy: "Do you want me to use my wiles to cure him?"

Alan: "Yer wiles, yer tits, just fix him."

The door opened and Wendy came in, her eyes sad, her face without expression. Alan remained in the doorway, scowling with suspicion, and they both just stared at him until he went away again.

It didn't take long for whatever hopes Alan had had to be dashed. He left them alone upstairs, retreating back to the ground floor in the vague hope that miracles do happen and if they did actually end up shagging then he didn't want to hear it. But instead all he heard was voices raising, getting louder and louder, Will starting to shout, Wendy pleading and sobbing and finally screaming back at him.

He waited at the foot of the stairs until Wendy emerged, dabbing her eyes with a hanky. She came down, holding herself proud and erect, and for all that she was half Taig, Alan almost admired her for her dignity.

She shook her head as she reached the bottom.

"I'm sorry, Alan, I tried." She whispered, her voice almost shaking, just about holding steady. "His mind is made up."

"Thank you, Wendy," Alan forced himself to say. He pulled the front door open. "I'm sorry too. You deserve better."

She inclined her head to acknowledge the compliment, and then she was out of his life for good as he closed the door behind her. He scowled up the stairs at Will's open door, and quickly headed up in case his brother had any ideas about regaining his liberty.

Will still lay on his bed, his face expressionless as he met the scorn in Alan's gaze.

"You – stupid – fucker," Alan said simply. Will just shrugged as he closed and locked the door again.

Alan headed down to the kitchen to make himself a cup of tea, and took it to drink at the table. He was not used to feeling uncertain. It gave him a headache and a bad taste in the mouth.

Will was just *too* calm. It was impossible, for someone in his position. He *had* to know what the future would be like for him … Didn't he? He should be quaking, climbing the walls, down on his knees begging Alan not to let his secret get out. Christ knew, that was what Alan would be doing in his position.

The only alternative was that Will had something up his sleeve, some plan he could still fall back on, though Alan's mind only drew blanks as he tried to picture what it could be.

And he had asked to see Wendy … Alan had seen absolutely no good reason why he shouldn't. Surely if anyone could help him fancy girls again, it would be his ex-girlfriend? Or had that been part of whatever this plan was too?

He had been suspicious and vigilant during Wendy's visit, ears peeled for the slightest sound of an attempted escape, eyes fixed on the front window where Will would have to appear if he got out that way.

Nothing.

So, with Will at least still contained in one place, Alan could think his way ahead.

So far, only Henry knew what Alan knew. Alfie and Robbie might suspect it, but they had had other things on their mind when Alan worked it out. Henry could be trusted to keep quiet and he, Alan, certainly wasn't going to broadcast the glad news to one and all that his brother was a bender *and* a Taig-fucker. (Did it count as fucking if you were with another boy? Whatever it was, it wasn't good.)

Maybe Doctor Robinson would have an idea, now he had met the patient? Even bringing him in to the secret had been a risk, but Alan was at his wits' end and, well, surely it was an illness and doctors made people better, didn't they?

There were only two ways out of this that Alan could see. Either Will got better (and the little shit was too stupid to do that on his own) or …

Alan scowled down at his tea.

… Or, Will just disappeared out of his life.

"Feck …" he whispered. He couldn't picture killing Will. His little brother. But he couldn't let him go and live with the Catholics, could he? Their Da would turn in his grave and it would be terrible for Ma.

The phone rang. He cocked an ear, waiting to see if it was another of those phantom two-ring calls.

But no, it kept ringing. He went curiously out into the hall and picked it up.

"Hello?"

"*Alan?*" It took a moment to place the voice. She was tearful, desperate. "*You've got to come round. Will's gone mad.*"

"Wendy?" He frowned at the receiver, then scowled up the stairs at Will's shut door. "What do you mean?"

"*He jumped out of his window and he's here … He's limping, I think he hurt his foot, but he's shouting and ranting … Alan, I think he might hurt someone.*"

"Wendy." Alan spoke firmly. "I don't know what bullshit this is, but Will's in his room …"

"*He isn't, I tell you! He's here! Outside our house! You know where we live, don't you? He jumped out of his window and he's here ...*"

"Wait there."

At the other end of the line, Wendy heard the *clunk* of the phone being put down on the hall table. Footsteps receding as they ran up the stairs. A distant, echoey, "*Feck!*", and footsteps getting louder as they ran back down. The scrape and fumble of the phone being picked up again.

"I'm coming. I'll be there in five minutes."

Alan slammed the phone down; half a minute later, the house shook as the front door banged shut behind him.

There was silence in the house in Agnes Street, for as long as it took someone to count one-Mississippi, two-Mississippi, all the way up to thirty.

Then the ceiling hatch into the attic shifted and a pair of feet appeared. Then the legs, then the rest of Will as he dropped vertically down to the landing, just missing the bannister he had had to stand on to get up there.

He headed swiftly into his room where the window stood open and grabbed the bag he had already packed from behind the door, where Alan would not have seen it. Alan had also been too distracted to see that the frames which had held Will's certificates now hung empty on the walls, and if he had seen the sheet of paper in the bin that Will had torn out of one of his old school books – thin enough to slide under the door and catch the key on the other side as it fell from the lock – he wouldn't have understood what it meant.

Will trotted downstairs, grabbed his coat, and headed out into the rest of his life.

Chapter 25: Lots of Love, Will

Wednesday 27th August

Will wrote carefully at the bottom of the sheet of paper: *Lots of love, Will xxx.*

He had barely written anything other than his signature and the occasional cheque since he left school, and his fingers were tingling, so he flexed them open and shut a couple of times. Then he stretched himself back in his desk chair so that his hands brushed one wall of the tiny B&B room and his feet pressed against the other.

He picked up the letter and read it from the start. It was the third and final draft.

The first draft had been fine until he had shown it to Conor. "Jesus, he's illiterate …"

Conor had rewritten it, mostly with Will's original words, adding items like punctuation which Will had never really got the hang of. Then Will had copied it out again. His mother deserved a letter in his own writing.

Dear Mum,

First, everything Alan told you about me is true. Maybe he used some words I wouldn't agree with but yes, I am in love with a Catholic boy, and because that makes it impossible to live in Northern Ireland, I'm going with him to England. Though to be honest I would go with him anywhere. I'm sorry I won't be there to keep you company when Alan gets sentenced but if I stayed then I'd have to give up Conor and that just won't happen.

I know how much a surprise this must be to you. I know it because it's a surprise to Conor and me too! There's nothing you could have done that would make us any different.

Mum, you asked me if you'd been a bad mother and the answer is <u>NO!!</u> Maybe Alan and me ...

Conor had changed this to 'Alan and I'; Will had changed it back because it just sounded more like him.

... could have been better sons but you and Da together were the best parents. When Da lost his job, when you were ill that time, I saw how you stood by each other and it really showed me what it means when one person loves another. Above all I've seen the <u>massive</u> hole he left in your life when he went. That's how it's going to be for us. I'm going to put into practice everything you've taught me.

> *I'll send you my new address in England once I know what it is. I'll keep writing ...*

His eyes misted and a lump rose in his throat at the next bit, but he had to be realistic.

> *... and I hope you'll write back once in a while.*
>
> *Lots of love,*
> *Will xxx*

Then he sat back and read it once again, but halfway through he determinedly folded it up into the envelope, and slid the envelope into his inside pocket. Then he stood up and grabbed his bag from the bed, picked up another envelope with the landlady's name written on the front and the balance of his rent inside, and left the room for the last time.

Will had moved into the B&B the day he left home. After that, he had set about dismantling his life in Northern Ireland, which proved surprisingly easy.

He had parted with Mr Mitchell on good terms. If the garage owner had heard rumours about him, he was keeping quiet. Mr Mitchell's ear was close enough to the ground for him to detect some kind of falling out between the brothers, but all he knew for sure was he was losing one of his best and most promising workers, so last night there had been an after-hours piss-up and he had been presented with a card and a cheque for £50.

Conor had been around to his room a few times, and each time had been great, though they still hadn't completely repeated what they had done that memorable day in the flat at the back of the gym. The tiny room wasn't really big enough for the two of them, and Conor had other things on his mind – training, and getting ready for England, and doing what he could to help while his Da negotiated with insurers and the Council, who had resolved to help rebuild McGarry's afresh with only a handful of dissenting votes.

Councilman Wilson had been very noisy about what a good thing it would be to have McGarry's back, so it would.

Will had met Conor's family again, different members at different times, though he and Conor had kept their hands to themselves because everyone was just going along with the notion that the two of them were friends going to England to keep each other company. It left a slightly sour taste, having to pretend even to loved ones, but neither of them could see any point in rubbing their noses in it.

The best night of the last fortnight had been going out for fish and chips with Conor and Wendy. They had had a grand old time getting drunk together after and he had been proved right – Wendy and Conor got along famously.

Will trotted down the stairs with bag in hand. He left the rent envelope on the hall table and pulled the front door open.

And there was Conor, his finger just reaching out to the bell. Will's heart still leapt every time he saw his lover.

"Hi!"

"Hi …" It was too public to kiss out on the pavement, but Conor silently pouted his lips, and smiled, and stepped back with his hands in pockets to let Will get out of the building.

Will looked expectantly up and down the street, then in surprise at Conor.

"Where's the taxi? … Or your bags?"

Conor's smile grew wider.

"I took the bus. I've a couple of surprises for you …" He peered down the road behind Will, and his face froze. "But this isn't one of them," he muttered.

Will turned around, somehow already guessing what the issue might be.

Alan was walking towards them.

Will abstractly noticed the similarities between his brother and his boyfriend. They both walked like they were cruising for a fight, fists clenched, arms swinging slightly out from their body. In the corner of his eye he sensed Conor come to stand beside him. They were a couple, united against the threat.

Will put out a hand and gently pushed him back, then took a step forward to meet Alan.

His brother's eyes darted over Conor with blank disgust, then came to rest on Will. He sneered.

"You're not going to hide behind your boyfriend?"

"I would if you'd brought Henry," Will conceded, "but you, I can take on my own."

Alan's eyes were in motion again. They settled on the bag.

"You're off, then?"

Will shook his head in admiration.

"Nothing gets past you, Alan."

There had always been the possibility – the teeniest, tiniest, remotest chance – at the back of Will's mind that Alan might make his peace. Accept Will for who and what he was, even if he didn't like it. That blood would be thicker, whatever.

The sheer, curdled loathing when he looked into Alan's eyes finally extinguished the spark.

"Don't come back to Northern Ireland, Will. Not if you know what's good for you."

Another contemptuous glance at Conor, and Alan turned on his heel and marched away. Somehow he left Will with the memory of having spat at his feet, even though – Will looked down at his toes to double check, the memory was so strong – it hadn't happened.

Conor rested his hand gently on his shoulder.

"You okay?"

"Aye." Will swallowed, and realised there might just be a tiny blurring in his vision. "Aye, I'm grand. I thought I might give him the letter to deliver – but nah, I'll post it."

"That's good, because here's the first surprise.

Conor nodded down the road and a scruffy Chrysler Sunbeam pulled up with Cormac at the wheel.

"What's the craic?" Cormac asked cheerfully as he got up and pushed the driver's door shut, chucking the keys to Conor. Conor answered the question Will was asking with his face,

"It's my new car," he said with a proud smile.

It was, to be frank, the crappiest new car Will had seen; he could immediately think of a few things he would do to it if he could, but you don't insult other people's babies, or loved ones, or cars.

"I didn't think you can drive."

"I can't …" Conor chucked him the keys in turn and Will snatched them automatically out of the air. "… But my friend can! You're on the insurance, third party only. Come on, we should shift."

* * *

"Isn't that yer girl?" Conor asked suddenly.

Cool sea air and diesel fumes blew in Will's face. You got a panoramic view of the city and the very same docks that the grand titanic had set sail from. As they stood on the boat deck

Will had to pull his eyes away to follow where Conor was pointing.

And yes, down there on the quayside was Wendy. Will whistled – no idea if she heard him over the sounds of the ship's ventilators and the seagulls and the city's traffic rumble – and waved both hands above his head, until finally he saw her eyes fix on him and her face light up and she waved back.

"Aye, it is …"

There were at least a dozen other families down there, waving to other passengers, including the entire McGarry clan, who were all waving at the boys, apart from Katie who was waving at a seagull that had caught her eye.

"Hey, they should meet each other!"

With shouts and gestures, Will and Conor guided the two parties towards each other. Just as they saw Conor's parents turning towards the young woman on her own, the quay began to slide past below them.

The cityscape of Belfast, with the iconic Samson and Goliath beyond, moved slowly away as the ferry backed out into the lough. The ship began to turn, blocking the shore from view with its own bulk as it spun around in its own length to head out into the wild Irish sea.

Conor darted suddenly away from the rail, hurrying across the deck to fix his eyes again on his receding family from the other side. Of course, Will thought, Conor was saying goodbye to far more than he was. He studied his lover's profile. Conor's jaw was set, his face expressionless, which Will was learning to understand meant there were a whole lot of expressions he would have liked to let out, hiding just below the surface.

He gently slid an arm across Conor's shoulders.

"Do you get the feeling of being chased away?" Conor murmured quietly.

Yes, Will thought. He tightened his arm.

"You'd be doing this even if you hadn't met me. Going to England. This is what you need to do."

"Aye … but would I need to leave home for another country in the first place if my home wasn't Northern fucking Ireland?"

They stood at the stern rail, their arms around each other's waists, and for the first time in their lives watched the land of their birth fall back towards the horizon, the foam-flecked steel-grey water magically expanding between to fill the gap them.

Chased away. As usual, Will thought, Conor had come up with exactly the right words. And they weren't even sailing away into a happy ending. Neither of them had any idea of what the future held for them, or even whether they would still be together this time next month, let alone after a lifetime.

But for the moment they had each other, and they could feel safe. That was enough for today, and tomorrow could look after itself.

"Think we'll be back?" Will asked quietly.

"Fuck, yeah." Conor was brash and confident, no room for doubt.

Will remembered something. The Sunbeam was down on the car deck with the other traffic, but …

"What was the other surprise? You said there were a couple."

"The other? Ah, yes." Conor butted Will's shoulder gently and wiggled his eyebrows. "I got us a cabin. Want to try it out?"

A smile spread slowly over Will's face and he felt the sudden fire in his loins, burning at the very thought.

"Oh, aye. I do indeed. Only …" He looked back at the receding coastline. "It's so beautiful. Shall we watch it a little longer?"

"If we like." Conor snuggled complacently close to him. "It's eight hours to Liverpool."

"All the time in the world," Will agreed.

Printed in Great Britain
by Amazon